THE MYSTERY PRINCESS

THE FOUR KINGDOMS AND BEYOND

THE FOUR KINGDOMS

The Princess Companion: A Retelling of The Princess and the Pea (Book One)

The Princess Fugitive: A Reimagining of Little Red Riding Hood (Book Two)

The Coronation Ball: A Four Kingdoms Cinderella Novelette

Happily Every Afters: A Reimagining of Snow White and Rose Red (Novella)

The Princess Pact: A Twist on Rumpelstiltskin (Book Three)

A Midwinter's Wedding: A Retelling of The Frog Prince (Novella)

The Princess Game: A Reimagining of Sleeping Beauty (Book Four)

The Princess Search: A Retelling of The Ugly Duckling (Book Five)

BEYOND THE FOUR KINGDOMS

A Dance of Silver and Shadow: A Retelling of The Twelve Dancing Princesses (Book One)

A Tale of Beauty and Beast: A Retelling of Beauty and the Beast (Book Two)

A Crown of Snow and Ice: A Retelling of The Snow Queen (Book Three)

A Dream of Ebony and White: A Retelling of Snow White (Book Four)

A Captive of Wing and Feather: A Retelling of Swan Lake (Book Five)

A Princess of Wind and Wave: A Retelling of The Little Mermaid (Book Six)

THE MYSTERY PRINCESS

A RETELLING OF CINDERELLA

MELANIE CELLIER

LUMINANT PUBLICATIONS

For Alexandra,
my newest sister,
who shines inside and out

ROYAL FAMILY TREES

THE FOUR KINGDOMS

KINGDOM OF ARCADIA

King Henry—Queen Eleanor

Parents of

Prince Maximilian (Max)—Alyssa of Arcadia
  Parents of
  Prince Henry (Harry)
  Princess Rose

Princess Lily—Prince Jon of Marin
  Parents of
  Prince Owen
  Princess Hope

Princess Sophie—King Dominic of Palinar
  Parents of
  Prince Arthur
  Princess Grace

(Deceased: Princess Mina, younger sister of King Henry, married to Prince Friedrich of Rangmere, *parents of* Prince Damon)

KINGDOM OF RANGMERE

King Josef (deceased)—Queen Charlotte (deceased)

Parents of

Prince Konrad (deceased)—Princess Clarisse of Lanover

Queen Ava—King Hans
Parents of
Princess Ellery

(Missing: Prince Friedrich, older brother of King Josef, married to Princess Mina of Arcadia, *parents of* Prince Damon)

KINGDOM OF NORTHHELM

King Richard—Queen Louise

Parents of

Prince William—Princess Celeste of Lanover
Parents of
Princess Danielle

Princess Marie—Prince Raphael of Lanover
Parents of
Prince Benjamin
Prince Emmett

KINGDOM OF LANOVER

King Leonardo—Queen Viktoria

Parents of

Prince Frederic—Evangeline (Evie) of Lanover
Parents of

Prince Leo
Princess Beatrice

Princess Clarisse—Charles of Rangmere
Parents of
Princess Isabella
Prince Danton

Prince Cassian—Tillara (Tillie) of the Nomadic Desert Traders
Parents of
Prince Luca
Princess Iris
Princess Violet

Prince Raphael—Princess Marie of Northhelm
Parents of
Prince Benjamin
Prince Emmett

Princess Celeste—Prince William of Northhelm
Parents of
Princess Danielle

Princess Cordelia—Ferdinand of Northhelm
Parents of
Princess Arabella
Prince Andrew

Princess Celine—Prince Oliver of Eldon

BEYOND THE FOUR KINGDOMS

DUCHY OF MARIN

Duke Philip—Duchess Aurelia

Parents of

Prince Jonathan—Princess Lily of Arcadia
  Parents of
  Prince Owen
  Princess Hope

Princess Lilac

Princess Hazel

Princess Marigold

KINGDOM OF TRIONE

King Edward—Queen Juliette

Parents of

Prince Theodore (Teddy)—Princess Isla of Merrita

Princess Millicent (Millie)—Nereus of Merrita

Princess Margaret (Daisy)

KINGDOM OF PALINAR

King Dominic—Queen Sophie
  Parents of
  Prince Arthur
  Princess Grace

KINGDOM OF TALINOS

King Clarence—Queen Sapphira

Parents of

Prince Gabriel (Gabe)—Princess Adelaide of Palinar

Prince Percival (Percy)

Princess Pearl

Princess Opal

KINGDOM OF ELDON

King Leopold—Queen Camille

Parents of

Prince Oliver—Princess Celine

Princess Emmeline

Princess Giselle

KINGDOM OF ELIAM

King George (deceased)—Queen Alida (deceased)

Father of

Queen Blanche (Snow)—King Alexander

KINGDOM OF MERRITA

King Morgan—Queen Nerida (deceased)

Parents of

Princess Oceana—Lyon of Merrita
    Parents of
    Prince Edmund
    Princess Eloise

Princess Coral

Princess Marine

Princess Avalon

Princess Waverly

Princess Isla—Prince Teddy of Trione

(General Nerissa and Captain Nereus—brother and sister of Queen Nerida)

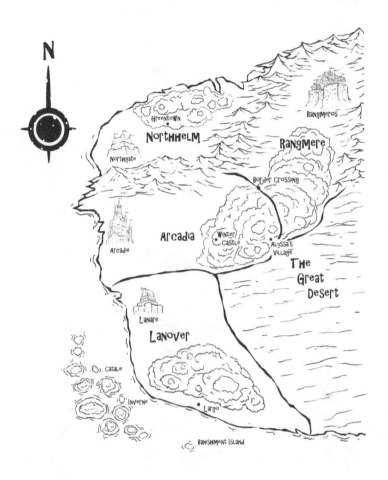

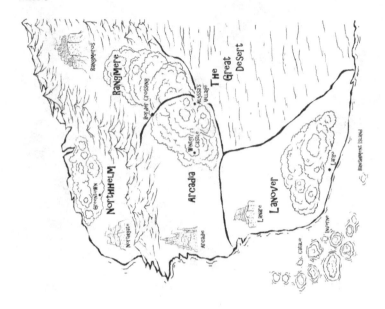

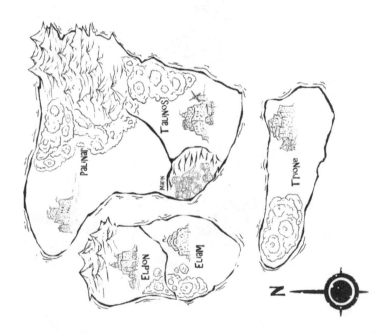

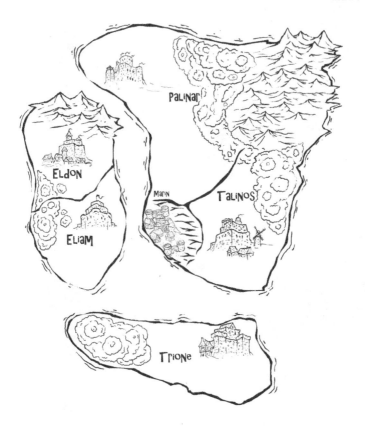

PART I
THE TRAVELING MERCHANTS

PROLOGUE

I watched our damaged ship limp away southward before looking around at the remote beach and then down at the solid ground beneath my feet. Why could I still feel the movement of the waves?

Surreptitiously, I observed the others with me. The longboat had conveyed four delegation members, two maids, and a collection of guards ashore from our leaking vessel. Many of the guards moved awkwardly, and even Princess Giselle of Eldon—now the head of our motley delegation—walked with an unusual gait.

I wouldn't mention the matter to her, then. I didn't like to bother her when so many things had already gone wrong. This unheralded arrival was hardly the auspicious beginning we had hoped for on our tour of the Four Kingdoms.

I bit my lip. What would Snow think? Or Queen Blanche as I should refer to her in this foreign place. When the Eldonians had assembled a royal group to visit the distant Four Kingdoms, Snow had asked me to represent our kingdom of Eliam. But since she had failed to give me any specific objectives for the trip,

I could only conclude her true purpose was to give me an escape from her court—a place where I had never fit in.

"Daria!" Cassie called, gesturing for me to join the others as Princess Giselle and the guards marshaled us all to begin walking toward the Arcadian capital—our intended destination before the accident to the ship. Even Arvin, Giselle's beautiful but strange horse, fell into line without restraint. He was a magnificent creature, and the princess treated him almost as if he were a human. I agreed with the guards, who clearly thought him odd, but it wasn't my place to question Giselle.

As we walked, I tried to focus on the bright sun and the pleasant sound of birds, instead of the strange tricks of my mind that wanted me to believe I was still on the ocean. We were following the road through ordered fields being readied for planting, and the day was perfect for walking.

Eventually the strange sensation faded, and I looked around for Princess Daisy. At least I had been able to make myself useful on the trip by keeping an eye on the energetic thirteen-year-old. In her usual style, she had been more than delighted when our ship sprung a leak and forced this unexpected adventure on us. But in the course of the walk, she had abandoned me, put off by my abstraction, perhaps, and was instead chattering at full speed to Cassie.

Cassie appeared to only be half-listening, but we'd spent enough time together on the sea voyage that I knew her distraction wouldn't cause a problem. She could easily follow a conversation using only half her mental energies.

With Daisy occupied, my eyes again examined the scene around us. Many generations ago, the people who founded my own set of kingdoms had left the Four Kingdoms in search of new lands. But since impassable storms had separated us for so long our two peoples had virtually forgotten each other, I had expected to find Arcadia less familiar. But it seemed spring planting here was much like planting at home in Eliam, or in any of our kingdoms.

Although news of the rediscovery of the Four Kingdoms had swept our lands years ago, I had never dreamed of visiting them myself. Snow's suggestion that I join the Eldonian delegation had taken me entirely by surprise.

I would have liked to refuse, since an orphan without family hardly belonged in a delegation of princesses, but I couldn't say no to a royal request. And Snow had been quick to point out that I wouldn't be the only non-royal, since Cassie also lacked position or title.

A copse of trees appeared in the distance, the road disappearing under the branches. An even stronger surge of familiarity seized me. I had spent many years living in a forest, and I never liked to be too far away from trees.

The reminder of my childhood made me look for Daisy again. I had spent a lifetime caring for children of varying temperaments, and I knew youngsters as full of energy and independence as Daisy were wont to get themselves into mischief. Giselle didn't treat me any differently from the royals in the delegation, but even if she hid her awareness, I was conscious of my different status, and I wanted to be as helpful as possible. I could see the relief in her eyes whenever she saw I was keeping a watchful eye on Daisy.

We had barely stepped under the canopy of the trees when Daisy lost interest in Cassandra, her attention instead caught by something in the woods. She slowed and drifted to the side of the path, stepping among the trees. I frowned and turned toward her but pulled back when Giselle swung around and hurried in Daisy's direction.

I was still watching them from the corner of my eye, however, and I caught a flash of movement in the trees behind Daisy. I turned my head, my mouth opening, but the scream that reverberated across the road didn't come from me.

"Daisy!" Giselle shrieked the younger princess's name as something jerked her out of sight among the trees.

At the same time, a guard at the head of our small procession gave a shout and chaos erupted on all sides. A guard behind me screamed, and I spun around to find him lying on the ground, blood pooling around him. My eyes flew to the guard who stood over him, drawn sword in hand.

I gasped and stumbled backward as the man looked up, his gaze latching on to me. I had time for no more than a squeak before he lunged at me.

Instinctively my body responded, my arms raising in self-defense. But the basic moves I had been taught would do me little good against a sword in the hands of a trained guard.

A blur flashed past me as Cassandra appeared from one side, her foot lashing out to connect with the guard's stomach. He dropped his weapon, doubling over and gasping for breath.

I whirled around, but on every side, our guards grappled with each other. A small hand grasped my arm and tugged, dragging me off the road and into the trees on the opposite side to Giselle. I stumbled after Cassie, trying to find my balance. When she paused, just inside the trees, I pulled myself free, standing upright and sucking in shuddering breaths.

My eyes sought for Giselle through the chaos of the road that lay between us. I found her just in time to see her gesturing to Cassie, clearly telling us to flee into the trees. I hesitated, not wanting to leave her, but Cassie hissed beside me.

Her eyes were focused on the road, where the fighting seemed to be slowing. With a sick feeling in my gut, I saw the guard who had unleashed the conflict calling orders and directing those who remained. If the fight was ending, it was because those who had turned traitor against us were winning.

"We need to run!" Cassie said, and I nodded my agreement.

She tried to reach for me again, but I shook my head. "We'll move faster separately."

Cassie didn't stop to argue, dashing into the trees with me close on her heels.

"Where can we go?" I gasped out between breaths.

"Away." Cassie sounded grim, and I didn't waste any more breath on questions.

The Eldonian girl was intelligent and resourceful, and my best hope was to stick close to her. She might not have any ideas right now, but she would think of something.

Someone crashed through the trees behind us, shouting loudly. My feet sped up, although I had already thought I was running at full pace. I swerved around a tree and then another, moving too fast now for safety within the wood.

A large bush loomed in front of us, and I swerved left, realizing too late that Cassie's momentum was carrying her right. For a brief second I pulled back, ready to change direction, but as I glanced at her, the uniform of a guard appeared through the trees behind us. I shook my head and increased my pace again, staying on the path I had committed to. I would rejoin Cassie on the other side of the bush.

But the impassable undergrowth expanded, driving me further to the left. When I finally followed the curve of it back toward my right, the tinkling sound of a stream caught my ears. I sucked in a worried breath just as the water burst into view. It came from deeper in the woods and disappeared into the undergrowth. The water must go underground somewhere in the middle of the bushes I had just skirted because I was now cut off from the other side—cut off from Cassie.

For a brief second, I hesitated, wondering if I could safely leap across it, but footsteps sounded behind me again. I groaned. I didn't have time to waste fording the stream.

Instead I took off running again, heading deeper into the trees.

My breath rasped heavily through my throat, my steps lagging slightly as I began to tire. How long could I outrun the guards?

A mental image of being struck down here in this unknown place filled my mind. Determination swelled inside me, enabling a new spurt of speed. I refused to die alone in a foreign wood.

A moment later I realized I was moving more quickly because the trees were thinning. New fear filled me. It had only been a small wood, and I must be about to reach the other side. So far I had managed to elude my pursuers only because of the terrain which hid me from view until they were almost upon me. How could I avoid them in the open?

I glanced from side to side as I ran, looking for somewhere to conceal myself—or even a tree with branches that would allow for climbing—but nothing caught my eye. The trees thinned further, and a road appeared, angling briefly to touch this edge of the trees.

I was gasping now, my lungs screaming for air, and my legs burning from the length of my unaccustomed sprint. I burst from the trees, looking back over my shoulder for signs of pursuers.

My feet stumbled slightly as I hit the edge of the road while still looking back, and I nearly fell. I pulled myself up just in time, drawing back as a horse appeared around the bend, whinnying a protest at my presence in the road. Its rider expertly calmed the beast, slowing almost to a standstill.

I met the girl's eyes, and I could see in her face that she read the fear in mine. Her eyes flashed over my head to the wood behind me.

"Quick." She leaned down from her horse's back. "Come with me."

My eyes latched on to the brown hand held out to save me. I didn't hesitate as I reached forward to grasp it.

CHAPTER 1

tried to calm my breathing as I walked into the town beside the older woman and younger girl. I had been hiding at their camp, cowering in their wagon as much as possible for over a day now. I had to come out and try to discover what had happened to my companions and how I could safely rejoin them.

The woman, Lilah, kept casting me concerned looks. I knew she had a warm heart because she had accepted me without question when her daughter brought me to their wagon and said I needed shelter. Their wagon caravan had been about to set out, and the feeling of moving away from the site of the attack had helped calm my nerves. But now we had made camp outside a town and would be remaining for two days as the traveling merchants bought and sold goods.

"The market here is a good one, Dee, despite the size of the town," the girl, Tallulah, said, clearly trying to cheer me up.

I managed a smile, although it felt tremulous.

"You'll be safe with us," Lilah said, a determined note to her voice, as if she could will her words to be true.

"Thank you," I whispered, my gratitude forcing me to speak.

We stepped into the center square of the town. Most of the other merchants had beaten us here, setting up their temporary stalls among the smattering of more permanent set ups that must belong to local shopkeepers.

Lilah led the way to one of the stalls which was already mostly covered with various items of apparel.

"We don't yet have enough wares to warrant our own stall," she said with a faint trace of embarrassment. "But my creations sell well on this one."

"Aida!" Tallulah waved to another girl around her age, before dashing off to join her behind the stall without stopping to ask her mother's permission.

Lilah tensed slightly before sighing and following at a more sedate pace. When she unpacked the large parcel she carried and began to lay out various pieces of intricate jewelry, I gasped.

"They're beautiful!" I reached out to run my fingers along one before snatching my hand back as I tried to remember when I had last washed my hands.

"Lilah has a good eye for jewelry," the man behind the stall said with a decisive nod. "Her items are popular with those who cannot afford more expensive adornment."

"I don't work in gold," Lilah explained as she positioned the items carefully among the other displayed wares. "Or with large gemstones, but the stones I do use are real."

I nodded. I could see that for myself, although I didn't recognize the dark metal she used in the elaborate designs.

"When do you find time to make them?" I asked.

She sighed. "In the mornings or evenings of travel days, or on rest days. If I had more opportunity, I would be doing better, but..."

She stepped toward the far end of the stall to place the final pieces, and the other merchant spoke in lowered tones.

"Most of us are traders, not craftspeople, but setting up shop in a large city would take more capital than she has available. She inherited the wagon from her husband and does well enough selling from town to town."

I nodded, unsure what to say. The merchants seemed to think I was a relative of Lilah's, and I didn't want to disabuse them of the notion until I had a better idea of exactly what had happened the day before.

An hour passed and then another, and I began to relax. No one paid me the least attention, the locals focused on the merchants' wares and the merchants busy wangling the maximum amount of coin from their sales. My own gown had ripped during my headlong flight, so I wore a dress borrowed from Tallulah. Although a little snug, it fit well enough not to attract notice, and as long as I kept my mouth closed, nothing marked me as a foreigner. Only the lilting accent of the merchants connected them as a group, their appearance and skin tones as varied as the towns they traveled through.

When not actively engaged in a sale, the merchants enthusiastically gossiped with the locals—both passing on news from their last stop and hearing what the townsfolk had to share. I listened keenly, keeping my mouth closed and my ears opened, but it seemed news of the attack hadn't reached this far yet. Another load of tension lifted from my shoulders, and I turned my mind to the future.

The merchants had carried me away from Arcadia's capital, but maybe I could find a way there from this town. Surely the other girls would also congregate in Arcadie.

My biggest problem was my lack of funds. I didn't relish a journey on foot, traveling alone without food or shelter.

I was still pondering the issue when Lilah gave me a coin and sent me to buy us all some sticks of meat from a nearby vendor. The succulent smell of the sizzling meat had attracted many people, both locals and merchants, and I ended up at the end of a long line.

When my progress stalled while we waited for a new batch of

meat to finish cooking, I drifted over to huddle in the shade of a nearby building. A small alley divided it from the next, and a small huddle of others also sheltered there.

It took several moments for their conversation to attract my attention enough for me to take in the details of their appearance. I stiffened, intending to edge away again when I realized they were a rough looking group, two of them with worn looking swords strapped at their waists and knives in their boots and belts.

But their words caught my ears, making me freeze.

"We'll pay well for news of any newcomers to the town in the last day—young girls especially." The man had an accent unlike either the merchants or the townsfolk. A foreigner.

One of those without a sword snorted, although his expression looked disappointed.

"You picked the wrong day to ask about newcomers." He gestured out toward the market square. "The traveling merchants are in town, so we're awash with newcomers of all descriptions."

I slowly swiveled, turning my face away from them and sinking back into a convenient alcove, trying to disappear from sight as my ears strained to hear the rest of the conversation.

The second foreigner, the only one I could still see from the corner of my eye, grimaced. "Well there's still gold to be had. We'll leave a coin for you both if you'll accept a commission."

"What do you want?" The second local sounded suspicious.

"Nothing too difficult. Just keep your eyes out for such a girl —or two girls together. And if you see either of them—we've a message for you to pass on."

One of the locals grunted. "A message we can do. What is it?"

A slow smile spread across the face of the second foreigner. "Let her know we're on the lookout for her. We'll be waiting in the capital. And watching all the roads."

I gulped, stiff with fear as he stroked the hilt of his sword.

"Ha! A pretty message," one of the locals chuckled. "Although we might be the wrong messengers if you're hoping it will send her running back into your arms."

The foreigner grinned again. "Far from it. If she's any sense at all, she'll start running in the other direction, and she won't look back. Not now, not ever."

They all chuckled at that, and the clink of coins reached my ears. A small group of merchants brushed past, and I slipped away from the wall in their wake, using their passage to hide my movement.

My heart hammered so hard I could barely hear the sounds of the market as I fled back to Lilah's stall. She took one look at my face and hurried forward to join me.

"What's the matter?" she asked, her voice sharp. "Did something happen?"

I shook my head. "No. I..." I looked down at my hands and realized they were empty. "The line was too long, and they needed to cook a fresh batch."

Tallulah gave a groan. "I was looking forward to those."

"Never mind that," Lilah said. "I've sold all I'm likely to in a town this size. We can head back to camp and cook there."

I looked at her hopefully, torn. "Are you sure? I don't want to—"

"Of course we'll go back now," she said briskly. "I can spend the afternoon working on a piece I've nearly finished. One of the ladies of the town expressed an interest in seeing it tomorrow. Tallie." She gestured for her daughter to join us, and the girl did so with another groan.

I said nothing further, walking close beside them and keeping my eyes trained on the ground, terrified we might run into the men who were clearly still searching for Cassie and me. My ears tuned out Tallulah's complaints as my mind ran over and over the conversation in the alley.

Why had our own guards attacked us? And who were these strange men now searching for me? If I had thought the journey to the Arcadian capital difficult before, it now loomed before me fraught with untold danger. And what would I find when I got there? If those men were to be believed, I would find them rather than safety.

We reached the camp, and Lilah directed the still complaining Tallulah to fetch water from the stream that ran beside the wagons.

"Let me do that," I said quickly, taking the bucket before the younger girl reached for it.

Tallulah smiled and took her opportunity to escape into the wagon. Lilah let her go with a sigh, turning toward the fire which needed to be built up again.

As soon as I lugged the full bucket back to the camp, I took the log she was holding from her hands.

"Here, let me deal with the fire. I can cook the food, too. You work on that necklace."

She hesitated for only a moment. "Would you, Dee? That's so kind. It would be a help, I'll admit."

I shooed her away while I set to work, the familiar activities soothing my fraught nerves. Lilah came out of the wagon with her supplies and sat nearby in a shaft of sunlight, working on the necklace. She made occasional conversation, twice stopping to appreciatively sniff the air for the smell of my cooking.

As I dished out the meal onto three plates, a thought formed in my mind. I had no idea why I was a target, but I could no longer doubt I was. If I tried to make my way back to Arcadie now, I would be in unknown danger. But the men looking for me were looking for a girl or girls traveling alone—newcomers in any village or town they reached.

And yet I had seen today that some newcomers passed through without attracting question. Traveling merchants were newcomers everywhere, but ones who were expected and welcomed. If I stayed with them, eventually their travels would take them to Arcadie or Lanare, Lanover's capital where I could seek help. And in the meantime, I'd be safe.

Tallulah emerged, led by her nose, and we all gathered around the fire to eat. Several times I tried to broach the topic of my staying with them, but I didn't know quite how to word the request. Finally it was Lilah who spoke, her voice gentle.

"I'm sorry you found the town so stressful, Dee." She used the nickname I had given them on my arrival. "I didn't mean to push you into something that makes you uncomfortable."

I shook my head. "No, it's fine. I was just..." My voice trailed off when I could think of no way to finish the sentence.

Lilah exchanged a look with her daughter before gesturing at the fire and her bowl of food.

"Thank you for your assistance. I think I'll have that piece finished by mid-afternoon, thanks to you."

I smiled at her eagerly. "I'm happy to help."

Lilah chuckled. "Hopefully that attitude rubs off on Tallie." Her tone turned more serious. "Where are your parents, Dee? I didn't like to question you yesterday when you had clearly been through some sort of ordeal, but they must be concerned about you."

I shook my head. "I don't have parents. Not for many years."

She sucked in a breath, a look of pain coming over her face. "You're all alone?"

I hesitated, considering her question. I remembered my parents from when I was a young girl. They had loved me, but they had been too broken to overcome their own problems to provide me the care I needed. Even before their deaths, I had been on my own, or close enough.

I had found friends since then, but none of them were here now. Snow had sent me away from her court, a place where I was no use to anyone, and I had no true goal in the Four Kingdoms either. My companions were scattered and potentially as much in need as me.

"I have no one I can turn to," I said at last. "I came to these kingdoms thinking to find new opportunities, but I just ran into trouble instead. Thank you so much for helping me yesterday." I took a deep breath. "I don't suppose you'd consider letting me stay with you? I could be helpful—just like today—and give you more time to work on your creations. I wouldn't be any trouble—"

Lilah held up a hand to cut me off, and I stopped the flow of words abruptly, biting my lip.

"If you have no home and no family, then of course you're welcome to stay with us." She looked at Tallulah. "I can only imagine how I would feel if my daughter ever found herself in such a situation."

The younger girl looked between her mother and me, her face more serious than usual, as if shaken by the idea. Lilah pursed her lips.

"I think it would be best if we claim you as my stepdaughter. The other merchants know I have an older daughter who is with family, so they'll accept it readily enough. We can say you were with settled family but were left alone when they died and only just managed to track us down yesterday."

She nodded decisively, not waiting for me to respond. "Yes, that will be best. Then no one can question your right to be here. I'll talk to Isambard this evening about getting you a merchant token." She touched the lump under her gown where her own token lay hidden, hanging from her neck by a leather cord.

I swallowed, overwhelmed by emotion.

"I don't know what to say. Thank you."

"Yes!" Tallulah punched the air. "I always wanted a sister." A stricken look overtook her as she slapped a hand over her mouth and looked at her mother as if she'd said something wrong.

But Lilah just smiled at her.

"Yes, indeed. This is just how everything should be."

CHAPTER 2

TWO YEARS LATER

J lifted the heavy jug of water with a weary sigh. It had been a long day. Turning my feet away from the stream, I trudged back toward our wagon. As I neared it, Tallie floated in my direction, her eyes lighting on the jug.

"Oh, thank you, Dee." She grinned at me impishly. "I knew I rescued you for something."

"Hush!" The word came out more sharply than I intended, so I drew a deep breath before continuing, giving Tallie a chance to interrupt.

"Don't worry so," she said. "No one is attending to us."

I frowned, glancing around the busy campsite of Caravan Bryant. It was true that no one appeared to be paying us any heed, but that didn't excuse Tallie's carelessness.

"Sound can travel strangely in the forest, you know that." I set the jug down inside the back of our wagon. "And you know how your mother will react if she hears you speaking like that." I glanced in the direction Tallulah had come from, muttering further words under my breath. "The same way she'll react if she knows you were off wandering around instead of fetching water like she asked."

Tallie rolled her eyes. "Which is precisely why I had to slip away just for the chance to stretch my legs. You know Mother always worries about absolutely everything. It's insupportable." She flashed me a bright, artless smile. "And I knew she wouldn't find out since you would get the water for me."

I sighed but didn't deny her claim. How could I? I always did the chores Tallie left undone. After all, she had saved my life that day two years ago—risking her own in the process for the sake of a total stranger. And she and her mother had continued to shelter me ever since. A bit of work was the least I owed them.

I bit my lip as Lilah came around the wagon.

"Ah, there you girls are." Relief colored her voice.

I didn't mind doing Tallie's chores, but I didn't like being an unwilling party to her deception. Even if I could sympathize with her desire for the occasional moment of freedom from her mother's zealous care.

I suppressed another sigh. I could never bring myself to report Tallie's escapes. The girl was nearly sixteen, after all, and well past the age of being cosseted and watched like her mother insisted on doing.

"Here's the water, as you asked," Tallie said brightly, pointing at the jug inside the wagon. Lilah barely glanced at it.

"I was starting to worry about you two when you didn't come to help with the horses."

"I'm sorry," I said quickly, and Lilah acknowledged my words with a gracious nod.

Tallie rolled her eyes again, her whole head moving along with them. She gestured around the small but bustling campsite where the wagons of Caravan Bryant had been maneuvered into a protective circle.

"What could possibly happen to us here, Mother? It's not as if we left the campsite."

I glanced at her sharply, trying to read in her tone whether or not she had ventured that far in my absence. But I could think of no reason why she would want to go wandering off among the trees. We had been on the road for days, stopping only to make evening camp, and there was nothing of interest in our vicinity.

Lilah's brows rose. "Don't tell me you haven't heard?" She swung around to look at me, but I shrugged in confusion, exchanging a glance with Tallie.

"Heard what?" the younger girl asked, a note of excitement entering her voice. "Don't tell me something exciting has happened? Has there been a sighting of brigands?"

"Brigands!" Lilah cried in a shocked voice. "No, of course not. You're an unnatural girl to sound so pleased at the prospect."

Tallie looked unrepentant. "Anything would be more interesting than our usual boring travels."

Lilah frowned at her. "We're traveling merchants. Traveling is what we do. And we should be grateful for our place here in Caravan Bryant. In fact, I heard today that we might be moved up a place soon."

I smiled back at her at this welcome piece of news. I knew how much store she placed in our position within the caravan and how she longed to move up from our spot, two wagons from the back. Before I arrived, they had been right at the back, so we had already made progress. But with only the three of us, it was hard to contribute the amount of business to the caravan that was required to advance further within its internal system.

Tallie didn't share her mother's simple ambitions. "Never mind that," she said with impatience. "What haven't we heard?"

"Caravan Hargrove is camped only a short way further up the road. They've been traveling east from Arcadie and passed through the border crossing to Rangmere only hours ahead of us."

"Hargrove?" Tallie lifted onto her toes and spun in exuberance. "They're a much bigger caravan. Please tell me they're going to host a dance."

Joining for a night of dancing and socializing was common practice when two caravans met on the road. But I wasn't as sanguine as Tallie about Lilah's current mood.

I glanced at the woman I claimed as my stepmother, and sure enough, her lined face had deepened into a frown. "I hope they will not, but if they do, you girls shall certainly not be attending."

"What?" Tallie screeched, turning on her mother in horror. "You can't possibly mean us to sit at home by the fire while the rest of the caravan goes off to a party."

I frowned, trying to suppress my own disappointment. It had been a long time since we had met another caravan, and a night of entertainment would be welcome.

"What is your concern?" I asked Lilah.

She paused briefly before hurrying into speech. "Tallie didn't wait for the rest of my news. There are foreigners traveling with Caravan Hargrove."

She said the word with as much horror as she had used earlier when referencing brigands. I stiffened but said nothing. I knew the older woman didn't mean me any insult by her tone—quite the opposite. I sometimes wondered if she had forgotten I wasn't her daughter in truth. She certainly didn't think of me as a foreigner.

"All the better," Tallie said defiantly. "So long as they're good dancers, of course."

She flashed a cheeky but winsome smile at us both, but her mother appeared unmoved. I looked at Lilah with concern.

"Ariana is the most respected caravan leader in the Four Kingdoms. Surely you cannot suspect her of harboring the fugitive Prince Damon and his followers?"

In the matter of Prince Damon, at least, I shared Lilah's fears. The son of the exiled Prince Friedrich of Rangmere and

Princess Mina of Arcadia, he had appeared in the Four King-doms two years ago and attempted to insert himself as the crown prince of Arcadia. But from the stories we heard on our travels, spoken with breathless excitement from one ear to another, Rangmere was the crown he truly thought of as his own.

He had been chased out of Arcadia after unsuccessfully attempting to murder two small children standing between him and his desired title and was believed to be hiding in the more remote regions of Rangmere.

Since these reports were always accompanied by the news that he had been responsible for the attack on Princess Giselle and her delegation, I also knew him for my own enemy. I still didn't understand what interest he could have in me, but while he remained free in the kingdoms, I deemed it more prudent to keep my identity secret. Especially since the Eldonian members of that delegation had long since returned to our own lands. My friends had gone, and only my enemy remained.

Lilah softened a little at my mention of Ariana. "No, I'm sure she would never harbor the Traitor Prince. But all the same, these are not safe times to be consorting with strangers."

"We can only suppose these travelers are not strangers to Ariana," I said lightly.

"But they are to us," Lilah said with decision, directing a quelling look at her daughter. "And so we will not be accepting any invitations to visit Caravan Hargrove. In fact, I don't want you girls leaving the camp other than to perform necessary chores." She directed a stern look first at Tallie and then at me. "Am I understood?"

I nodded and murmured my assent. There had been a time when I had been too scared to leave the protective confines of the camp, and Lilah had sheltered me without hesitation. I wouldn't defy her now.

Tallie's agreement was less swift in coming, eventually delivered in a sullen murmur. I eyed her with misgiving. Somehow I didn't think we'd heard the last of the issue.

Lilah, however, seemed to consider the matter closed. She turned to me.

"Dee, I'm going to have a short lie down before we eat. I'm exhausted from driving the horses all day. Do you think you could prepare the meal?" She glanced at her daughter. "Tallie can help you."

I tried to erase the lines of exhaustion from my face and body. "Of course. I'll start now." I grabbed the various items I needed from the back of the wagon and moved toward the communal fires that had already been started in the center of camp. But when I glanced back after a few steps, Tallie hadn't moved.

"Well? Are you coming?" I asked the younger girl.

For a moment she looked like she meant to refuse, but she finally heaved an enormous sigh and fell into step beside me.

"Can you believe her?" she asked. "She seems to have forgotten you did half the driving today."

"Not as much as half," I said quickly. "And she was the one to care for the horses after we arrived."

"Yes, while you fetched the water and did everything else to set up our camp," Tallie countered.

I eyed her discontented face. Where had this sudden consideration for my workload come from?

"And now she says we can't go to the dance! And for the stupidest reason!" The impassioned words burst out of her, answering my silent query. Tallie was in the mood to find fault with her only parent.

"Perhaps there won't even be a dance," I said in conciliatory tones.

But Tallie threw herself onto the ground, leaning against a log that had been dragged up next to the fire. "Of course there will be. Because I'm destined to miss out on *everything* enjoyable in life."

I raised an eyebrow but decided it was best not to engage. I was tired after a long day of travel, and I didn't have the energy for Tallie's nonsense as well.

"Somehow I'm guessing preparing this food doesn't fall into your definition of enjoyable." I let a note of irony creep into my voice, but it appeared to be lost on Tallie.

"No, of course not. So thank goodness you're here." She let out a loud sigh and clunked her head back on the log. "I'm going to die having done nothing but traipse around forests."

"We also sometimes traipse through fields, mountain passes, and jungles," I said with a straight face.

"Dee!" She drew out my name in exasperation. "Anyone would think you liked doing nothing but drudgery all day long."

I refrained from pointing out that I would have less drudgery to do if she actually completed her fair share of the work. I couldn't forget she was Lilah's true daughter. She didn't have to earn her place here in the caravan. They had taken me in out of kindness and had no obligation to allow me to stay.

When I had first asked about staying with them, I hadn't imagined I'd still be here two years later. But back then I hadn't realized Caravan Bryant was a smaller caravan, still earning status among the traveling merchants—which meant completing the routes less favored by the more established caravans. In my two years with Lilah and Tallie, we had never been to a capital city.

In one of the coastal capitals, I might have had a chance of booking a berth on a ship heading back to my own kingdoms. In the small towns we visited, there was no hope of such a thing. I had no idea if Damon still had his followers monitoring the roads, so I dared not set out alone for one of the capitals—especially since I had no idea how difficult it would be to find a ship once I got there.

I had sent a letter, however. Not knowing if Damon might somehow be monitoring that too, I hadn't included my location.

But I had assured Snow I had found shelter and was safe and well.

My friend would be worrying if she thought me alone and in danger, but she had no actual need of me. In truth—assuming my letter had made it to her to set her mind at rest—I could do more good here with Lilah and Tallie than I had ever managed at Snow's court.

None of the merchants had ever questioned my status as Lilah's stepdaughter. And even Tallie—who had found me fleeing the attack—had never considered I might be one of the missing girls from Princess Giselle's delegation. We were still mentioned occasionally, but the impression among the general population seemed to be that all three missing girls were princesses. I never corrected the false assumption, of course, and none of the merchants made the connection since they were never in danger of mistaking me for a princess.

I had grown up fending for myself, and from a young age had lived in a remote house in the deep forest. The elderly lady who had taken me in hadn't lived long, and her first foster child, Ben, and I had ended up giving shelter to five more children over the subsequent years. Since all those children were younger—one a mere baby—I had become proficient in every possible practical chore. Or at least those chores relating to living in the wilderness and raising children—hardly the skill set of a princess.

My mind wandered to the children, thinking of them as they must be now. They would be so big! After Snow found us and accidentally destroyed the safety of our forest refuge, she had found an adoptive family for the five younger children. Captain Tarver and his wife, Willow, would have gladly included Ben and me in their household as well, but we were too used to independence at that point.

At thirteen, Ben was the perfect age to take up an apprenticeship, and the captain had found him a good one with a local carpenter. I had stayed on with the captain and Willow for a while, to ease the children's transition, but eventually I had accepted Snow's invitation to join her in the capital. The children had needed me at first, but once they became accustomed to their new home, I could serve them better by leaving and allowing them to bond with their adoptive parents.

I often visited, of course, and the youngest—Poppy—had seemed enormous at nine years old when I said goodbye before leaving for the Four Kingdoms. She would be eleven by now, while Anthony would be seventeen. Had he already followed in the footsteps of his adoptive father and joined the Duke of Lestern's guards, as he had been planning since the age of thirteen?

Bored with my abstraction, Tallie leaped to her feet. "I'm going to see what the others are saying. Maybe one of them can convince Mother to let us go to the dance."

"If there is a dance," I said at her retreating back, throwing off my reminiscent mood. But Tallie gave no sign of having heard me, and I turned back to the pot with a sigh. It seemed one way or another, our quiet life was going to be upended for the next few days.

As I stirred the food, I admitted to myself that I hoped Tallie might be successful for once. Just because I didn't want to show ingratitude to Lilah by openly siding with Tallie, didn't mean I agreed with her. Surely these foreigners could be no threat if they had been approved by Ariana. The woman was experienced and canny. And I found my longing to attend a dance increasing.

A sudden thought made my hand still. As traveling merchants we moved through all the kingdoms. If Lilah referred to these additions as foreigners, then they must come from one of the kingdoms of my own lands. How had I not thought of this immediately? I shook my head as I resumed stirring. Lilah wasn't the only one who lost sight of our true situation sometimes.

New excitement gripped me. What if these newcomers were from Eliam? If they had spent a lot of time at court, they might even recognize me. And if they did so, I could return with them and see Snow and the children again.

Lilah wouldn't like it, of course. If she feared for my safety on a visit to Caravan Hargrove, she would never want me to leave the safety of the caravans altogether. Thought of the merchant woman drained my previous excitement. Could I really abandon her just to return to people who no longer needed me?

My gaze drifted to the other fires, trying to pick out Tallie's slim form. What news was she gathering? All my earlier irritation with her had fled, and I now wished her full success on her information-gathering mission. My usual patience had disappeared, and I longed to abandon the meal and go after her. I restrained myself, however. Someone had to finish preparing the meal, or we'd all go hungry tonight.

CHAPTER 3

*T*allie did not return until the food was ready, appearing only moments before Lilah joined us. Her mother's presence didn't stop her from pouring forth her discoveries, but the confirmation of a dance the next evening so monopolized her focus, I had to ask the question burning in my own mind.

"Where are they from?" I tried to keep my voice casual as I finished off my bowl of stew.

Tallie stared at me with confusion.

"The foreigners," I clarified. "Do you know what kingdom they're from?"

Comprehension shot across Tallie's face, and Lilah started violently, turning a wide-eyed, nervous gaze on me before focusing again on her daughter. Lilah didn't like reminders of my true origin.

"They're from Talinos, apparently," Tallie said, and I deflated.

Talinos wasn't a direct neighbor of Eliam, and they had sent their own delegation not long before ours, so there hadn't even been any Talinosians on our ship. None of them would recognize me.

Tallie continued to chatter on, but I no longer heard her

words, consumed by my disappointment. At least Lilah looked pleased. It warmed me to know that she disliked the thought of my leaving. At least I was of use here.

But as my initial disappointment faded, and I began to listen to the conversation again, a new disappointment took its place. Tallie was making no headway on convincing her mother to let us attend the dance. And now the idea had taken root in my mind, I found myself desperate to at least talk with someone from my own set of kingdoms again.

Abandoning caution, I added my voice to Tallie's.

"Surely it couldn't do any harm for us to walk down to Caravan Hargrove. Not when so many from our own caravan will be going. It might even be safer than remaining here with only a few others," I added, struck by sudden inspiration.

But Lilah frowned at me as if disappointed at my joining forces with Tallie. "You cannot imagine Isambard would fail to leave sufficient guards on duty around our wagons. No, we will be safer here. And that is the last I want to hear about it."

It was not, of course, the last Tallie had to say about it, however. She pleaded with her mother all evening, and when she failed to make any headway, spent the entire next morning complaining to me.

Lilah eventually lost patience.

"Since you are both so desperate for activity, you can occupy yourselves refilling our wood supplies. They are getting concerningly low, and this is the perfect opportunity since this foolish dance has kept us chained to this location for another day."

"I thought you were worried about our safety," Tallie snapped back. "And yet you want us to go wandering around the forest on our own, looking for suitable wood?"

Lilah raised an eyebrow. "You must have told me ten times that every single other person will be at Caravan Hargrove for the dance. So you can consider yourself perfectly safe in the woods. And if you both get to work straight after lunch, you should easily be finished before it gets dark."

I considered protesting but decided against it. What was the use? It would be less than gracious to remind Lilah only Tallie had been complaining, and I doubted it would do any good anyway. She wouldn't want to assign the younger girl a chore outside the wagon circle on her own.

As it was, however, I was delayed starting due to cleaning up after our midday meal. By the time I completed that task, Tallie had already disappeared into the forest. I shrugged and started after her. We would eventually cross paths bringing our loads back to the large container we kept strapped to the back of the wagon, and we could remain together after that.

Venturing among the trees, I tried to ignore the bustle I left behind me. But even the beautiful spring day wasn't enough to console me for being excluded from the air of excitement. Everyone else was enjoying the impromptu rest day as they prepared for the evening's dance.

My thoughts kept me occupied for the first two loads, and it was only on the third that suspicion began to overtake my mind. Not only had I seen no sign of Tallie, but the only pieces of wood in the container were the ones dumped there by me on my previous loads. I groaned. She had snuck away, leaving me to gather enough wood on my own. Of course she had. I should have seen it coming.

I plodded back into the surrounding forest yet again. Lilah had been right about our supplies getting low, and it would take me hours to find enough wood to fill the large container on my own. No doubt she hoped the effort would leave us too exhausted to long for the dance, and it certainly was likely to be successful on me, at least.

When I dumped my fourth load of fallen branches and twigs behind the wagon, I poked my head inside. I could see no sign of either Tallie or Lilah. I bit my lip. Should I go searching for Lilah to report Tallie's absence?

After a moment I shook my head and returned to the trees again. I couldn't bring myself to create yet more conflict between mother and daughter. If Tallie was determined to go off in a sulk, then I was likely better without her, anyway.

By the time the light began to fade, however, I was feeling less kindly toward the other girl. I still hadn't completed the task, and I now had to venture further from the caravan to find anything worth collecting. But if I stopped before filling the container, Lilah would want to know why, and I would have to confess not only to Tallie's absence, but that I hadn't reported it earlier.

I sighed and returned to the trees. Few people remained in Caravan Bryant now, and distant strains of music drew me in the direction of Caravan Hargrove. The dance was already under-way. I glanced down at my dirt streaked gown of dark blue. Even if Lilah was convinced at the last minute to allow us to attend, I couldn't get ready in time.

I blinked back tears. It was foolish to care so much about one night of merriment. I let my steps carry me closer to the other campsite. I didn't have to miss out entirely. I wouldn't venture in, of course, but there was no harm in gathering my wood within reach of the music.

I was humming along to the lively tune when the sound of a twig snapping underfoot made me freeze. I glanced around. When had night fully fallen?

With the moon at full brightness, I hadn't realized how late it had become. But clouds lay across its face now, obscuring its light.

Sudden terror gripped me, all Lilah's fears crowding into my mind in an unwelcome flood. Who was out here in the dark with me? Why would anyone want to leave the dance?

I told myself it might be a courting couple, slipped away for a moonlight stroll, but my pulse didn't slow. Dropping all the wood

I was carrying except for a single, stout branch, I raised it like a club. Willing myself courage, I listened intently for any further movement.

"Is anyone there?" I called loudly, unable to take the suspense of waiting.

A dark figure stepped out from behind a tree, rustling noises behind him telling me he wasn't alone. I screamed and swung my makeshift cudgel at the man, legs tensed and ready to run as soon as I made contact, just as I had been trained.

The man gave an answering shout, although it sounded more surprised than aggressive. He dodged to one side, evading my first blow, and I lifted my arms to swing again.

Before I could do so, however, the man lifted both hands up in a placating gesture of surrender. The clouds temporarily obscuring the moon sailed past, lighting the area around us enough for me to get a proper look at my adversary.

Like his shout, his expression carried no hint of danger, merely surprise. I hesitated, lowering my arms rather than resuming my attack.

For a moment we stood warily regarding each other, and then an easy smile broke over his face.

"Allow me to make my apologies," he said. "It seems I startled you."

I relaxed further at his accent and examined his face with curiosity. Here was surely one of the visiting Talinosians rather than a local of these kingdoms. I had long ago adopted the lilt of the merchants, and the sound of his voice brought a rush of nostalgia that took me off guard. With a bit of effort, I could almost imagine him originating from Eliam.

My silence must have alarmed him because he stepped forward, his face creasing in concern.

"I can assure you I mean you no harm."

I shook myself. "Are you one of the Talinosians traveling with Ariana's people?"

He nodded, and my eyes narrowed.

"What are you doing out here? Shouldn't you be dancing with everyone else?" I pointed toward the sound of the music.

He followed the gesture with a grimace. "I should be, certainly. But I have been out for the day and am returning later than I hoped."

I raised an eyebrow. "Out for the day?" I looked skeptically around at the empty forest.

He stiffened at my tone, assuming a haughty expression. "Certainly, although it is no business of yours. Perhaps I should be asking who you are and why you're wandering around out here at night."

"I was gathering wood." I gestured with the stick in my hand back toward the pile I had dropped. "I'm from Caravan Bryant."

He regarded me with new suspicion. "Gathering wood when there's a dance underway?"

I sighed. "My stepmother didn't think it was a good idea for me or my stepsister to attend." His suspicion disappeared as quickly as it had arrived, leaving a look of sympathy in its place, but my thoughts were distracted as I examined his features.

He was handsome—even in the moonlight I could see that— with olive toned skin and brown hair and eyes. His coloring matched that of many Talinosians, but a stirring of greater familiarity had sparked inside me at his momentary adoption of a lordly air. And it wasn't just the ease with which he had assumed an air of authority that alerted me.

His features themselves were familiar, although I had only met the Talinosian crown prince a couple of times while visiting in Snow's court. Even so, a sense of certainty swept over me. This wasn't just any Talinosian. It was Prince Percival of Talinos, the younger prince who was reported to look almost identical to the older brother I had met.

I stared at him in shock. He had been part of the delegation that reached Arcadia before my own. I clearly remembered the other girls teasing Princess Giselle about her parents' hopes that she might make a marriage alliance with him. What was he still doing here two years later?

Before I could forget myself and blurt out the question, the rustling behind him sounded again. My hand tightened on my branch as I peered into the shadows cast by the moonlight.

Percival, who hadn't responded to the noise, turned at my reaction, glancing behind him.

"What are you doing skulking back there?" he called. "Come out. Unless you're scared of a girl armed with a branch." There was a laugh in his voice.

Another rustle sounded before a golden horse appeared between the trees, stepping elegantly over the underbrush with an impossibly haughty tilt to his head.

I do not skulk. And I am never afraid.

Somehow, impossibly, I heard his whicker at the same time as I heard actual words. I couldn't work out if I heard them with my ears or inside my head, but I had no doubt they had come from the horse.

My mouth dropped open as I stared at his strangely familiar form. "But you're—"

Magnificent. I know. You need feel no shame—humans can't help being awed in my presence. The horse actually preened, if horses were capable of such a thing.

"—a talking horse, yes," Percival finished at the same moment before he cut himself off to look at the horse. He burst into laughter before turning back to me. "Sorry about him, he has a rather high opinion of himself."

The horse turned a poisonous gaze on the prince.

I am merely trying to set this poor girl at her ease. Naturally I do not think of myself *so highly.* He paused. *And you may tell that godmother so, if she comes asking.*

Percival assumed a serious expression. "I shall be sure to give her an exact report of your exemplary behavior."

The horse turned a suspicious look on him before pointedly turning back to me.

Their interaction had given me a much-needed moment of recovery. The prince had been no more correct than the horse in anticipating the end of my sentence. In my shock, I had been about to say that I recognized him. I searched my memory for the name of the mount Princess Giselle had brought from Eldon.

Arvin. That had been it.

I shook my head. He had always been a strange beast, more difficult pet than actual mount, and I had wondered at Giselle bringing him across the ocean with her when no one else had brought horses. But now I understood both his strange behavior and their seeming connection. She must have been able to under-stand him the whole time.

The prince smiled at me, his teeth flashing in the moonlight, and his eyes glinting. While I had seen him assume a royal manner earlier, right now he was all friendly charm and ease. And in the privacy of my mind, I had to admit his good looks set me off balance, making it hard for my erratic pulse to calm after the various alarms of the night. I wasn't used to standing in the moonlight talking with handsome, charming men, let alone princes.

"It's actually an honor you can hear him," Percival said with a hint of curiosity and interest that hadn't been there before. "Arvin decides who can understand him, and most of the time he only speaks to me."

My eyes flashed to the horse, a feeling of alarm coursing through me. Why would he be talking to me? Did he recognize me the same way I did him? My breathing hitched. Was there someone among these foreigners who would recognize me after all?

Back in the early days of my time with the caravan, there had been talk of Prince Percival. Most of the rumors said he was determined to track down Damon, but some said he was searching for the missing princesses. If I announced my identity, would he see me safely back to Eliam?

"What did you say your name was?" Percival asked.

"I don't think I did say," I replied, trying to give myself time to think. Did I upend my whole life and throw myself on the mercy of this stranger? Of all people, he would be the least likely to have ties to Damon, surely.

Another sound in the forest behind him made me jerk and gasp, still on edge. Had it been an animal, or was there someone else out here?

"Dee," I gasped out. "My name is Dee."

The prince, who had also turned to frown into the trees in the direction of the sound, turned back to me.

"It's a pleasure to meet you, Dee. I'm Percy." His smile was genuine, but something about his manner seemed on edge. "Perhaps if I help you finish gathering your wood, your stepmother might still allow you to attend the end of the dance?"

I started, having forgotten all about both my original task and the dance. I shook my head, touched at the kind thought. "The chore isn't the reason for my lack of attendance. In fact, it was supposed to be completed before it got dark." My mouth twisted. "It was more in the way of a punishment for wanting to go to the dance so badly."

His expression of sympathy deepened, and I bit my tongue. Why had I said that? I was usually more reserved.

Loyalty to my adopted family prompted me to continue speaking. "Not that my stepmother is cruel or anything. She just wants us to be safe."

"She has a funny way of showing it," Percy said with a wry note in his voice as he glanced around the dark forest.

I bit my lip, looking back toward my own caravan, wondering how long it had been since the sun set. "I shouldn't be out here. You're right, she'll be worried now that it's dark."

He gave me a gallant bow. "Allow me to see you back to your

wagon, then. Perhaps my presence will ease her mind as to your safety."

I regarded him doubtfully, but I wasn't sure how to voice my certainty that she would feel just the opposite. It seemed impolite to announce that his presence with Caravan Hargrove was the cause of most of her current worries. Especially since he had for some reason chosen not to tell me his title.

"That's not necessary," I said quickly. "You, at least, still have a chance to catch the end of the dance."

"I'm just as content with a lovely walking partner as a dancing one, I assure you." He smiled just as broadly as before, but somehow it didn't seem to reach his eyes this time.

I flushed. I didn't like false compliments or insincere sentiments. It was one of the reasons I had never been comfortable during my visits to Snow's court. I wasn't a princess or a courtier, and those sorts of games of words didn't suit me.

"Don't bother yourself," I said, more harshly than I had intended. "I know the way back."

His look of surprise made me flush again, this time with embarrassment. That had been poorly done. Nothing in his words or actions had justified rudeness from me.

"I'm sorry," I said quickly. "But I don't wish to inconvenience you." I hesitated. "Or alarm my stepmother by returning in the company of a strange man."

Understanding filled his eyes. "How about I walk you back to Caravan Bryant but don't actually come into the campsite?" He hesitated, his eyes flashing back to the trees. "Your stepmother is wise to be concerned for you. And it might be best if you kept out of the trees at night."

I gulped, taking an instinctive step back and slightly raising my branch. But although my eyes flashed around in every direction, I could see no sign of movement.

Percy must have seen my reaction, but he politely ignored it, gesturing instead for me to walk beside him. I willed my racing heart to slow and fell into step with the prince, Arvin following close behind.

The horse hadn't said anything for some time. Was he still offended from his interaction with the prince? I cast him a surreptitious glance backward, but his focus seemed to be on the forest behind us.

My muscles tensed again. What did the prince and horse know that I did not?

CHAPTER 4

$\mathcal{I}$ stopped beside the circle of wagons, just outside the reach of the firelight. True to his word, Percy stopped as well, giving me an elegant bow.

"Thank you, my lady, for a lovely walk." His smile robbed his words of any potential mockery.

I curtsied with a flourish. "Thank you for your company, brave sir." I pretended to insert the stick I still grasped into an imaginary scabbard at my side. "It seems our enemies have been frightened off by our combined forces, and we must leave vanquishing them for another day."

He chuckled and passed me the other sticks I had gathered and that he had insisted on collecting from where I had abandoned them on the ground.

"I only hope we may vanquish them—and sooner rather than later."

I dropped the playacting, examining his face. "Is it Prince Damon you're concerned about, then? I heard he was hiding in the mountain ranges north and east of Rangmeros."

Percy grimaced. "I believe he was last year. But he has been on the move for some time now." He glanced at me and then back at

Arvin before seeming to come to a swift decision. "I haven't been able to track his current campsite, but Damon is certainly in these woods—and with a sizable force of followers."

I gasped, nearly dropping my pile of sticks in my shock. "Here? Damon is here?" I looked around wildly before chiding myself. It was an enormous forest covering a large part of both Arcadia and Rangmere. Percy didn't mean Damon was literally right here.

"I don't mean to alarm you," Percy said quickly. "But neither do I want you to put yourself at risk by wandering around alone in the dark." He hesitated. "I would appreciate if you wouldn't mention the matter to anyone else. Naturally the caravan leaders know, but I don't want to be responsible for a panic."

"Of course," I said quietly. "You can trust me."

He gave me that curious look again. "I believe I can. Arvin doesn't talk to just anyone, Dee of Caravan Bryant."

I looked away from the question in his eyes, wondering again if I should say something about my true identity. But he had said Damon was here in this forest. If I told him who I was, he would be sure to tell the caravan leaders and then who knew how far the news might spread? As far as this camp of rebels?

No, it was better if I kept my identity to myself. At least for now. Which also meant I needed to keep my awareness of his true rank hidden.

"Thank you for your concern, Percy," I said. "Perhaps we shall meet again if you continue to travel with Caravan Hargrove."

"I hope we do."

I tried not to let myself be flattered by the sincerity in his tone as he bowed a second time and turned to walk back toward the other campsite. I watched him go, wondering what he had been doing all day out in the forest. Were his activities the real reason Caravan Hargrove had spent a whole day camped here, with the dance merely a cover?

I was so absorbed in watching Percy's back, it took me a

moment to realize Arvin wasn't following him. I noticed the stationary horse at the same moment as Percy stopped and looked back in our direction.

"Are you coming?" he called, sounding bemused.

Arvin ignored him, one large eye trained on me.

Have you saved any kingdoms lately?

"I beg your pardon?" I stared at him blankly.

He huffed, the sound somehow managing to convey impatience. *It is a simple enough question. Have you saved any kingdoms? Or perhaps completed some heroic deed?*

"Um…no? Should I have?"

He narrowed his eye in a gesture that wasn't at all equine. *You've found true love, though, I'm sure.*

I shook my head, unable to help a chuckle at the bizarre conversation. "I'm afraid not. Although I'm quite open to the possibility."

Arvin shook his mane, pawing at the ground in what appeared remarkably like disgust.

Not this again, he neighed. *I refuse. Last time I played along. But were my sacrifices and efforts appreciated? Not in the least. After I saved everyone, that* woman *had nothing to say but the most slanderous insults. I assure you it was not to be borne.*

I blinked. "That woman?"

He snorted. *I believe you humans call them godmothers.*

"Godmothers?" Now it was my turn to chuckle, although I still didn't understand what he was talking about. "Then you needn't worry. I certainly don't have one of those. They're reserved for princesses."

And deserving maidens. And woodcutters' sons. Those sorts of things. He sounded disgusted at these worthy sounding individuals. *The meddling of the so-called godmothers knows no bounds, I assure you. Thinking they know what's best for everyone.*

"But don't they serve the High King?" I asked. "From everything I've heard, they truly are working for the good of all. We've seen the proof of it since they returned to the kingdoms. When true love reigns over a kingdom, the whole kingdom prospers."

Yes, yes, that's all very well, Arvin whuffed, brushing aside my words. *But what does true love have to do with me? The whole thing is outrageous.*

"I don't suppose it has anything to do with you," I said, taken aback. "Just like it has nothing to do with me."

Ha! Don't fool yourself, he whinnied.

I looked at the horse in some concern before glancing help-lessly to where Percy still waited just out of earshot, a look of confusion on his face.

"I can assure you I don't have a godmother," I repeated.

He lifted his nose in the air. *Don't attempt to fool me, young human. I am a being from the Palace of Light. Or do you think I am an ordinary horse who will have forgotten you because a mere two years has passed?* A rippling shudder passed over his large body. *The godmothers have plans for you, and I refuse to get pulled in a second time. Fat lot of good it did me last time.*

He glared at me balefully as if I had somehow been respon-sible for these unknown events of the past. I stared back at him in fresh shock.

"You recognize me?" I whispered.

He leaned closer, his large eye bearing down on me suspi-ciously. *Haven't I just been saying that? Is there something wrong with you? Did you fall and bump your head in your escape, perhaps? Obvi-ously I would not expect you to rival my own great intellect, but I would have thought a godmother-chosen would have a little more... perspicacity. They must be losing their touch.* He tossed his head. *I knew it!*

"You're a talking horse," I said in a wry voice. "Who I didn't know could talk last time we met. And you're the first one in two years to recognize me. I'm allowed a bit of confusion."

He snorted and spoke in a formal tone. *Naturally my only concern was for your well-being. If you had fallen, you might be in need of medical attention. Whatever those women might think, I have great concern for humans.*

I raised an eyebrow but refrained from commenting on this assertion. "As far as I know, I am not in need of any medical assistance. And I can assure you, there's been no godmother here helping me. There was no godmother to help me when my parents abandoned me either. Or when the woman who took me in died. Or when I was sent to a new land only to be pursued by threatening men with unknown purposes on my first day."

You can't always see them, he whinnied, a dark note in his voice. *But maybe you should ask yourself how you come to be here, safe and undiscovered for two whole years. If you like,* he added, brightening a little, *I could put in a complaint on your behalf next time I see one. Two years is a long time to be kept waiting. And what better way to show them that I have nothing but concern and care for humans in my heart?*

"Please don't complain to any godmothers on my behalf," I said, alarmed. "I would never presume so."

So you're the deserving variety. He gave me another close look before turning away. *Well don't say I didn't warn you.*

He began to trot toward the waiting prince before suddenly whipping his head around to glare at me. *And don't expect me to intervene with the princeling on your behalf. I told you, I refuse to get involved this time. I want nothing to do with the godmothers' schemes. I will assist in finding and defeating Damon—as is proper—and then they will have to let me back into the Palace of Light.*

"Let you back in…" My words trailed off as he trotted away without another glance in my direction.

I stood there a moment longer. The conversation with Percy had been unsettling enough without Arvin throwing everything into greater confusion. Godmothers? Saving kingdoms? I shook my head.

I was just an orphan girl far from home. Godmothers were for princesses like Snow and Giselle—people whose actions affected kingdoms. What possible use could they have for me?

"Dee! There you are! Where have you been?" The furious voice emerged from between two wagons, returning me to my normal life.

I hurried forward into the campsite. "I'm sorry, Lilah. The moon is so bright, I lost track of the time and ended up out in the forest after it got dark."

I hurried for the back of our wagon to dump my last load of wood. When I had unburdened myself, I surveyed the container with grim satisfaction. After many hours of work, it now looked decently full.

"When you didn't turn up for the evening meal, I was worried sick!" She stood over me, hands on her hips.

"I'm sorry," I said again, and she relaxed enough to look around us.

"Wait, where is your sister? I assumed she was with you."

"What?" I froze. "She's not with you?"

"What do you mean with me?" Lilah's voice became breathless. "She was collecting wood with you!"

I shook my head. "No, I haven't seen her all afternoon."

"All afternoon? Where is she then?" Lilah's hand flew to her mouth. "Something has happened to her! She might be lying out there hurt, right now."

I frowned, a reluctant certainty overtaking me. "Before you start to worry, why don't we check her drawer in the wagon?"

"Her drawer?" Lilah stared at me for a moment before comprehension dawned.

With gathering wrath on her face, she climbed into the wagon and pulled open the drawer that stored Tallie's clothing. It didn't take her long to turn back to me.

"Her dancing dress is missing."

I nodded. "She's gone to the dance. I should have guessed it when I didn't see her."

"You should never have let her go!" Lilah seemed to swell in her anger. "I expressly forbade it!"

"I didn't *let* her go," I snapped back, the overwhelming events of the night catching up with me. "She didn't exactly tell me what she was planning. I was busy the whole afternoon with the chore *you* assigned me."

"The chore you were supposed to do together." Lilah glared at me. "And now she's gone off with who knows who, and no one even knowing to keep an eye on her."

I deflated, recognizing the fear that fueled her anger. It might be overblown and at least partly irrational, but it was still real. She didn't mean to take it out on me, and it wasn't entirely her fault she didn't know how often Tallie left the chores to me.

"She must have walked over with the others from Caravan Bryant. I'm sure they'll take care of her. Not that she's likely to run into any trouble at the dance."

But a slight uneasiness coursed through me. When I first heard Percy in the trees, I had wondered if the sounds might come from a couple on a courting walk. Tallie might be young, but I wouldn't put it past her to consider it romantic to go for a stroll in the moonlight.

Lilah picked up on my slight emotion, despite the reassuring nature of my words.

"We have to go and find her at once."

"Is that a good idea?" I looked warily toward the darkness outside our circle. With the bright firelight washing over us, the rest of the forest looked black. "Wouldn't she be safer waiting and coming back with the whole group?"

Lilah hesitated, clearly torn.

"We'll walk over to the dance together," she finally announced, "and find Tallie. Then we can wait and all walk back with the rest of Caravan Bryant."

I couldn't help a quickening inside at this unexpected chance to attend part of the dance.

"Very well. I'll just clean myself up and change my dress."

But Lilah was already shaking her head. "There's no time for that."

"But look at me!" I gestured at the dirt streaked across my gown. "I can't go to a dance like this."

"How can you be so unfeeling as to worry about such a trifle?" Lilah glowered at me. "Anything could be happening to her right now!"

"You mean like dancing. Or eating." But I kept my rebellious words to a mutter. There was no point arguing with Lilah when she was in such a state.

"It's not as if we're going to be there for the dance, anyway," she added. "We'll be there to find your sister and keep her safe. It doesn't matter what we look like."

Which was easier to say when you didn't look a mess. But I fell into step beside her without further protest. I would just have to avoid Prince Percy. I hadn't been self-conscious in the dim light of the forest, but for some reason I hated the thought of him seeing me looking so disheveled by the bright light of the dance bonfires.

CHAPTER 5

*L*ilah and I walked in silence, but it was concern and not anger I felt emanating from her taut bearing. I glanced at her surreptitiously. Her skin, darker brown than mine, was set in familiar worry lines that aged her beyond her moderate years. She never talked about the early years of her marriage, or Tallie's babyhood, although she sometimes referred to the difficult years after her husband's death. Was it his passing that had caused her to become consumed with worry? Or had she always been like this? Tallie claimed she couldn't remember her mother ever being different.

Tallie herself seemed to react to her mother's attitude by taking the opposite path—as evidenced by her impulsive rescue of me when we encountered each other two years ago. But Tallie's recklessness only increased her mother's fear, and I often marveled at Lilah's acceptance of me when I arrived at the wagon on the back of Tallie's horse, disheveled and afraid. When she frustrated me most, I remembered that one all-important fact. It demonstrated that underneath she had a caring heart.

The night had sufficiently advanced that we passed two small groups of people returning along the road toward Caravan

Bryant. We called a quiet greeting to our fellow caravan members, their replies delivered with knowing looks that made me squirm. No doubt they could all guess our purpose. You couldn't travel in such close quarters without learning each other's temperaments and foibles.

The moon shone even more brightly on the road without intermittent foliage to block its rays, and we moved at a good pace. Before long we could hear the strains of music, growing louder as we moved closer to the larger camp of Caravan Hargrove.

The first wagons came into view, set off the road in a large clearing used by many groups of travelers passing along the road between the Rangmeran and Arcadian capital cities. I admired the order of their campsite, the wagons forming a neat circle despite the much larger size of their caravan. I had met enough caravans in the last two years to be able to see at a glance that these were experienced merchants under effective leadership. Isambard, the leader of Caravan Bryant, aspired to such levels, although we included a number of less experienced and less disciplined wagons which hampered his efforts.

The center of the ring of wagons left ample space for dancing, the large circle enclosed with a ring of logs that provided seating for anyone disinclined to join the colorful, moving throng. Behind the logs, a second circle of campfires provided warmth for their backs and light for the revelers. The spring nights were still cool enough that their warmth was welcome for anyone not involved in the energetic movement of the dance.

Everyone else had dressed in their finest party outfits, the bright colors and fine material brightening the scene and giving life to the night. I tried to scrub away a large streak of dirt thrown into stark relief by the flickering flames. My efforts only succeeded in spreading the dark patch further over the rough material of my most practical gown. I sighed and straightened my spine. My appearance didn't matter, anyway. I wasn't here to dance or to mingle.

"You go that way, and I'll go this way." Lilah pointed for me to move to our right around the circle.

I nodded and hurried off, already scanning the confusing mass of whirling bodies. If I could find Tallie first, I could at least prepare her for her mother's wrath—after I gave her a piece of my own mind for leaving without a single word to me.

I thrust aside my frustration with the younger girl. I had spent my whole life caring for children younger than myself, and I was more than familiar with the irritation caused by their poor decision making.

A few people called friendly greetings as I passed, and I smiled and nodded back at them dutifully, although my mind was occupied in searching for Tallie's dark hair. A couple of times I was squeezed against the surrounding logs by a surge of movement that momentarily pressed the dancers against one edge of the makeshift dance floor. I took each opportunity to examine the people laughing and singing as they moved, but I could see no sign of Tallie.

Twice I saw Percy swing past, laughing at the merchant girl he was guiding through the dance. I suppressed the ungenerous wish that he would have been too delayed in his return to join the festivities. Instead, I took care to duck out of view each time I caught sight of his bronzed skin and wind-swept hair.

I refused to ask myself why it mattered so much to me that he not see me in my current state, trying to force my mind to stay focused on my mission instead. I strained to hear Lilah's voice over the noise of the celebrating merchants, sure she would be berating Tallie if she found her. I heard no such altercation, however.

I had nearly made it halfway around the circle when a familiar giggle caught my straining ears. I whirled around, the brightness of the flames making it hard to see anything outside the circle.

But the giggle came again, along with a flash of bright skirt. I lunged between the two closest fires, popping out the other side in time to grasp the arm of the girl who was attempting to slip off into the surrounding woods with three other youngsters.

Another girl of a similar age to Tallie gave an exaggerated squeal at my sudden appearance, while the two boys stepped forward threateningly. I gave them both a stern look, and they stepped back, looking sheepish.

"What are you doing?" I hissed at Tallie who was attempting to pull away from my hold.

"Let me go!" She kept tugging despite my iron grip.

"Your mother is here with me, and she's furious." I gave her a significant look, but Tallie only increased her struggles.

"Then, quick, let go of me. Tell her you haven't seen me."

The memory of Percy's warning strengthened my determination, and I clung to her.

"Not a chance, Tallie. It's not safe to go wandering around out there at night."

She groaned loudly. "Not you too!" She gestured at her companions. "It's not like I was going alone."

One of the boys stepped forward, trying to look grown up despite his smooth chin. "I wouldn't let anything happen to her, ma'am."

I wanted to roll my eyes. I was only eighteen—hardly warranting a *ma'am*. But since I was attempting to project an authoritative manner, I didn't actually protest. Tallie, however, snorted in disgust.

"I'll protect *you*, you mean." She turned beseeching eyes on me. "Oh do, please, let me go, Dee."

I softened. Their attempts to play at being adults looked foolish to me who had been forced into the responsibilities of adulthood far too early. But for all my frustration, I didn't want that for Tallie. She was just being young, like everyone should have the chance to be.

But I didn't let go. A traitorous prince was somewhere in these woods trying to raise an army, and Tallie wasn't half as fierce as she thought she was or my hold wouldn't have kept her in check.

"I'm sorry," I said. "But I can't."

The other girl gave a squeak, drawing back into the arms of the other boy. Her movement caught the attention of all three of the others who followed her line of sight back toward the dancers. When Tallie slumped in my grip and the others all fled back toward the bright circle, I sighed. Lilah must have found us.

"The forest?" she cried, taking in the situation in a glance. "You were planning to go wandering around the forest? In the dark?"

She strode forward and seized Tallie's free arm, and I quickly dropped my hold on her other one. Lilah continued to berate her daughter as she dragged her back between the two closest fires. I trailed behind, my eyes on the ground and my hands clutched hard in my skirts. Of course she wasn't going to retreat surreptitiously outside of the firelight. She wanted the feeling of safety in the large group. But her angry mutterings to Tallie were being met with sullen replies, and already Lilah's volume was rising. Eventually she would become too incensed to care who heard her.

It was Tallie, however, who precipitated the scene. Twisting free of her mother's hold on the other side of the dance floor, she came to a sharp halt.

"I'm not a child anymore, Mother! Can't you see that? If you'd let me come to the dance in the first place, like everyone else, I wouldn't have had to sneak away."

Her eyes flashed in the firelight, and her slender, graceful form certainly looked close enough to full-grown. She had braided her hair in hundreds of thin braids before winding them into a complicated arrangement on top of her head that added a couple of years to her looks. No wonder she'd disappeared all afternoon. I sighed quietly to myself. Regardless of how she looked, her words betrayed her true age.

"If you were an adult," Lilah snapped loudly, "then you would know there are dangerous people lurking in the forest. All the true adults in the caravan know that."

"Dangerous people?" Tallie stared at her as if her mother had lost her senses.

I gulped, my eyes widening as I saw how many people had drawn away from us, their movements faltering as they stopped dancing to watch the exhibition. A large empty space had appeared around us, but it wasn't large enough to stop the angry words from reaching our interested audience.

A sharp murmur broke out among the younger members as they turned to ask questions of those beside them, while several of the older merchants glared at Lilah. I flushed on her behalf. She had let her emotions run away with her and said what the caravan leaders were clearly trying to keep from the younger members of the caravans. Were they trying to avoid alarming the youngsters, or were they worried one of us might be inspired to do something foolish and attempt to confront the traitors?

Tallie and Lilah continued to exchange acrid words without noticing the reaction going on around them. As they bickered, the empty space around us grew, as if no one wanted to risk being associated with us.

I drew on every ounce of my self-control to keep a straight face as we attracted more and more attention. A number of brows creased and noses wrinkled as eyes dwelt on my dirty dress and bedraggled hair. I wanted to sidle into the audience, but the empty space I would have to cross was large enough now to make such an action conspicuous. And for all their current poor behavior, Lilah and Tallie were the only family I had in the Four Kingdoms. I had to stand with them.

Forcing myself to move slowly and calmly, I crossed over to Lilah. Placing a hand on her arm, I spoke quietly into her ear.

"Perhaps this conversation would be better delayed until we've returned to our wagon?"

She turned on me with a frown, and I directed a pointed look over her shoulder. For a moment she continued to look incensed, but as her eyes traveled around our audience, she sagged, weariness overtaking her. When her eyes latched on Isambard who had pushed his way through to see what was going on, discomfort crossed her face.

"You don't suppose they heard me mention the—"

"I'm afraid they did." I cut her off, anxious to convince her to leave the dance as quickly as possible.

But as I turned slightly, I realized it was too late. My eyes met Percy's, his expression confused as he took in my unkempt appearance before traveling to my alleged stepfamily. I bit my lip and then forced my spine to straighten. He wasn't a merchant, or even Elamese. And he was a prince. We weren't likely to cross paths in the future, so it didn't matter what he thought of me.

Lilah hissed and took firm hold of Tallie's arm. The younger girl was now looking thoroughly chastened—not by her mother's words, I was sure, but because it had finally dawned on her that she had been making a spectacle of herself in front of everyone from Caravan Hargrove.

"We need to get out of here," I said, quietly but urgently, and even Lilah didn't dispute my words, although she had intended for us to wait and walk back with the larger group.

I shepherded them both toward the nearest logs while she kept a wary eye on Isambard, as if she feared our caravan leader might publicly rebuke us.

Please no, I thought. The night had been humiliating enough already.

We made it between the logs and out of the circle of light before a commotion started behind us. The loud rustle of voices, interspersed with exclamations, brought the remaining dancers to a standstill. Had Isambard decided to renounce us after all?

I spun, wanting to face this new calamity head on. But no one was looking in our direction. Instead people were standing in clumps or rushing hurriedly to and fro, calling various names as if searching for loved ones who had been separated from them in the dancing.

"What...?" I asked as someone hurried out of the circle, but they passed by without seeming to notice me.

Lilah held out a hand to detain them, speaking in louder, more commanding tones.

"What is going on?"

"It's the Traitor Prince," the man called over his shoulder, still not stopping. "Someone saw him in the forest."

CHAPTER 6

*L*ilah stiffened, her eyes widening, and Tallie let out a piercing scream.

"Hush." I gave her arm a shake. "He's not attacking the camp."

At least, I hoped he wasn't. Surely the commotion would be larger if so? I pushed the thought aside and assumed a confidence I didn't entirely feel. Lilah seemed too shocked to take charge, and it wouldn't help anything for Tallie to indulge in histrionics.

"Look." I pointed to one side. "It looks like Caravan Bryant is gathering around Isambard. We should join them."

Lilah nodded, snapping out of her surprise and looking carefully to each side.

"Yes, come on, girls. We'll be safer with the group." She ushered us toward the familiar faces of our own caravan.

"So you'd been told Prince Damon was in these woods?" I asked her as we hurried through the flickering darkness.

"Only yesterday."

"So that's why you didn't want us attending the dance." I frowned, speaking without thinking. "I'm surprised you sent us off into the woods to gather wood."

"There were supposed to be two of you together." Lilah directed narrowed eyes at her daughter. "And daytime is different from night, although we were assured there was no imminent danger regardless. They believed him to be in another part of the woods entirely."

I bit my lip. "Thus the consternation at this new piece of news." I shivered remembering the sounds I had heard in the woods while talking to Percy. Had there been someone there after all?

Sudden appreciation for his insistence on walking me back to camp overwhelmed me. I glanced around, looking for his already familiar figure. A gap in the crowd gave me a glimpse of him, a serious expression on his face as he spoke with Ariana and her Guardsmaster.

Arvin stood just behind Percy, but his attention wasn't focused on the conversation. Instead he was looking directly at me with a sour expression on his face. Almost as if he blamed me for this disruption.

I looked hurriedly away. I had certainly done nothing to bring Damon to us, and I couldn't imagine my supposed godmother had either.

We reached the group around our caravan leader just as Isambard let out a loud call for any remaining Bryant stragglers. Several people rushed up out of the darkness, swelling our numbers even further.

After a brief glance around the emptied dance floor and the surrounding area, Isambard gave a single nod, and turned for the road. We clumped tightly together behind him, the off-duty guards who had come over for the dance taking up positions on the outside of the group. Our own Guardsmaster had remained behind with the on-duty guards watching our wagons, but the guards with us didn't need direction to respond in such a situation.

Lilah seized my hand, gripping Tallie just as tightly on the other side as she ushered us into the center of the group. We walked in silence, alert for any unnatural sounds that might indicate the presence of people in the trees beside the road. Everyone else remained equally quiet, but just the noise of so many people breathing and walking made it impossible to discern anything from our surroundings.

By the time we reached our own campsite, every nerve felt wrung out and exhausted, and my hand was starting to lose feeling from Lilah's tight grip. We all streamed into our inner circle, and mine wasn't the only soft sigh of relief I heard.

Isambard called for the Guardsmaster, and they soon had every guard on duty in a watchful ring around the outside of our wagons. As soon as they were in place, he sternly ordered the rest of us to bed, informing us that we would be needed to assist with watch duties in the morning while the guards snatched some sleep.

"We won't move straight out, then?" One of our senior members asked, his voice displaying a faint hint of nerves.

Isambard shook his head. "We'll need to consult with Caravan Hargrove before we make any moves. There is no need to be unduly alarmed. The Traitor Prince has not been in the habit of raiding such well-guarded targets as a caravan like ours. Remember his conflict is with Queen Ava of Rangmere, not the traveling merchants, so we have no reason to believe ourselves in danger from him."

Nothing in his tense demeanor corroborated this hopeful perspective, and I found myself relieved at his caution. We might not expect Damon to attack us, but I didn't want us to be caught unprepared if the unexpected did happen.

I turned away obediently, however, preparing for bed as quickly as possible and raising no demur when Lilah announced we would all be sleeping on our pallets inside the caravan. Tallie objected, declaring she intended to sleep outside by the campfire on such a mild evening, but her protest seemed only a token one since she quickly bowed to her mother's overruling.

Lilah carefully closed us inside the wagon, and I lay on my pallet, staring at the roof and wishing it were really that easy to shut the rest of the world out.

I arose in the morning far from rested after a night spent sleeping in fits and starts. Every time I woke, I strained to hear any hint of unusual nighttime noises, but I could hear nothing but the occasional sound of a guard, moving past on some sort of patrol route.

But even with my lack of sleep, my spirits lifted as I stumbled blinking out of the wagon. In the brightness of day it was hard to remember the fears of the night before. The caravan guards carried their swords at their waists and their bows across their backs, ready for instant action. Only the most foolhardy party would attempt to raid such a well-prepared target.

I hurried straight to the stream, eager for a proper wash after my half-hearted attempts of the night before. It took me a little time to straighten my braids and be sure I was completely clean, but I was grateful for the effort when I turned from the stream bank straight into a broad chest.

"Steady there!" said a laughing voice as Percy braced my elbows before stepping back. "I didn't mean to catch you by surprise."

"What are you doing here?" I asked and then immediately flushed. He had caught me off guard or I wouldn't have blurted out such a question.

"I've come to join you," he said cheerfully.

"Join me?" I blinked, glancing back at the water. "At the stream?"

Are you sure you haven't hit your head? Arvin asked, thrusting his head over Percy's shoulder and eyeing me warily.

I glared at him while Percy looked between us in lively curiosity.

"Did he just speak to you?" he asked.

I frowned at him. "Of course. Couldn't you hear him?"

Percy shook his head. "You just get more and more interesting, Dee of the merchants." He glanced up at Arvin. "I don't suppose you mean to enlighten me about what's going on?"

If you needed to know, I would have spoken to you in the first place. Arvin trotted around the prince and down to the stream for a drink. *I don't need your permission to make new friends. I don't belong to you, remember.*

"How could I possibly forget?" Percy sounded wry as he watched the golden horse bend elegantly down to the water.

"If that's how he makes friends, I don't want to know how he makes enemies," I muttered, surprising a laugh out of Percy.

"Being rude was he? That sounds like Arvin." There was affection in his voice, though. "The easiest thing is not to get offended. It doesn't make any impression on him, anyway."

I chuckled. "Believe me, I have far more valuable things to do with my time than get offended at a horse. Even a talking one."

"Very wise." Percy's friendly smile brightened the morning. "I knew I liked you."

I bit my lip and turned my face slightly to the side, remembering the circumstances of our last encounter.

"I'm not entirely sure why, Your Highness."

He winced. "Someone mentioned that, did they?"

I said nothing, unwilling to correct his false assumption.

"I do hope you'll ignore it," he continued. "I've been roaming Arcadia and Rangmere for two years now, hunting down Damon, so I don't require any sort of special treatment. I prefer to be just Percy."

"Very well," I said, unable to resist the appeal in his brown eyes, despite my reluctance at adopting such informality with an unknown royal.

In the light of day, I could see the gold flecks within the brown of his eyes, and they seemed as bright as everything else about this all-too-appealing prince. But while he might be choosing to live like a commoner for the moment, it was only a role he had assumed for a short time. My friendship with Snow had taught me that royalty wasn't something you got to walk away from.

"Tell me then, Percy," I tried not to wince as I said his name, "what are you doing here at Caravan Bryant? Since I can't imagine you came to see me."

He grinned. "You might not be the reason for my presence, but I did hope I would have the chance to see you again. Does that count for anything?"

Reluctantly I smiled back before his face took on a more serious expression. "You're right, though, of course. These are serious times, and none of us have the luxury of indulging our own preferences too far. After consultation with Ariana and Isambard, we decided my sword arm would be better placed here. I have a small squad of highly trained guards who travel with me, and with our assistance, Caravan Bryant should remain safe for the rest of the trip to the capital."

My eyebrows rose. "You're to stay with us all the way to Rangmeros?" I had already heard this morning we were redirecting to the capital, but there had been no talk of this part of the plan.

He nodded. "Caravan Hargrove is a much bigger caravan, so they have a larger guard force of their own. Plus, they'll be moving more quickly."

I didn't question that statement, used to the fact that the larger, more established caravans took precedence over caravans like ours. Caravan Hargrove had already been on their way to the capital, and Ariana no doubt wanted to consult with Queen Ava. We would trail in their wake, far enough back not to be competing for the same campsites and grazing spots each night. We were just fortunate these new happenings meant we had been afforded permission to mirror their route.

"Thank you," I said instead. "We appreciate your willingness to aid in our protection." I hesitated, biting my lip. "Do you think it will be needed, though? Do you really think Prince Damon would go so far as to attack a merchant caravan?"

Percy looked grave. "I certainly hope not. And it wouldn't be in his interests to do so if he hopes to rule in Rangmeros one day. There's a reason none of the kingdoms will violate the merchant treaty since everyone needs your services."

He grimaced. "But from what I've seen he's been growing increasingly desperate. You've probably heard he raided two small villages on his way down from the mountains, taking whatever he could carry and trampling over anyone who tried to get in his way. He didn't expect to be reduced to these straits, since he intended to murder and deceive his way into the position of heir of Arcadia. He thought he would have all sorts of resources to draw on when he made his move against Rangmere." He gave an elegant shrug. "At this point I wouldn't want to make any bets as to what he would or wouldn't do. Thus my presence."

He smiled again as if wanting to lighten the mood, but I couldn't smile back.

"I hope it doesn't come to a fight," I said. "We have our elderly and children with us."

"I think you'll find Isambard has already issued instructions for them to be confined to camp until we finish the journey. We will ensure there are no easy pickings for Damon or his followers, don't worry."

I nodded, turning back toward the camp. He fell into step beside me, and when I glanced nervously over my shoulder at a strange sound, I discovered Arvin following almost as closely. For the first time I wondered about the reaction of the rest of the caravan to the presence of a prince and a talking horse. If Lilah had disapproved of their inclusion in Caravan Hargrove, what would she think when she discovered they were now going to be traveling with us?

CHAPTER 7

*W*e moved back through the circle of wagons together, and Lilah pounced on me as soon as I came into view.

"There you are, Dee!" Before she could say any more, Tallie pushed past her. The young girl's eyes grew round as they latched on to Percy's face.

"You're the prince!" She sounded delighted as she held out her hand to him as if she were a grand, court lady.

He responded laughingly, bowing graciously and even raising her fingers to his lips in the briefest salute.

"I'm Percy," he said. "And it's a pleasure to meet you..." He glanced at me, inviting an introduction.

"This is Tallie, and that's Lilah." I pointed at my supposed stepmother.

"A pleasure to meet you both," he said promptly, giving Lilah just as charming a smile as he gave the dazzled Tallie.

Lilah looked from me to him, clearly unhappy about something. But whether it was disapproval of Percy himself or a reluctance to remonstrate with me in his presence, I couldn't tell. I held my breath as the issue hung in the balance.

After a brief internal wrestle, she smiled at the prince.

"We appreciate your willingness to travel with us, Your Highness. Although we hope not to require your services."

I let out my breath.

"I join you in that hope," he replied, but Tallie spoke over the top of him.

"You're going to be traveling with us?" Somehow her eyes grew even wider. "Wait until I tell Aida."

Percy looked bemused, but Tallie caught sight of the other girl —her closest friend—and went dashing away with a vague farewell. I allowed myself a small grin as I watched her. No doubt she wanted to get to her friend with the exciting news before she heard it from someone else.

"I apologize for her, Your Highness," Lilah said, shaking her head. "Sometimes I don't know how I produced such a child."

I had sometimes wondered the same thing myself, but Percy merely chuckled.

"I well remember when my own sisters were her age. They're twins, so everything was twice as loud."

I frowned as I pulled up a vague memory of Princess Opal and Princess Pearl. They knew Snow from the infamous Princess Tourney and had traveled to her wedding, leaving Percy back in Talinos. I didn't remember them being loud, however. In fact, they had struck me as incredibly quiet and fearful. Had they changed so much?

I couldn't voice the question, however—not without raising questions I wasn't ready to answer. Damon was on our heels, and I wanted to preserve my anonymity a little longer.

"That's kind of you, Your Highness," Lilah said. "Tallie is a good girl at heart, if a trifle impulsive."

I suppressed a snort. Tallie was more than a trifle impulsive. But Lilah was right that she had a heart underneath her sometimes thoughtless behavior. She would grow more aware of how her actions affected those around her in time, no doubt.

63

"Please, just Percy."

Lilah found herself caught in the same charming smile that had overcome my own reluctance.

"Certainly, if you prefer it, Percy," she said with calm dignity, reminding me that she had been raised as a traveling merchant.

A proud people, the traveling merchants didn't bow to any crown. Instead they were bound by a complicated set of laws administered by each caravan leader but determined by the merchant council. Comprised of the merchants' most senior leaders, the merchant council met only as needed and had been responsible for the ancient treaty that permitted the merchants free passage through the kingdoms and freedom from persecution by local authorities.

The merchants valued their freedom and independent status highly, and the monarchs of all four kingdoms respected the treaty under fear of having their kingdom placed under a merchant ban. Rangmere had briefly found themselves under such a ban before Queen Ava's ascension to the throne, over ten years ago, and I still heard talk of it among the towns we visited.

Lilah showed no discomfort about consorting with royalty, and any concern over Percy's foreign origins were not in evidence. Had she ever felt such concern, or had it just been an excuse to cover her inability to tell us about Damon and his men?

The Guardsmaster called to Percy, and he waved a casual farewell to us as he strode over to join the grizzled older man. Lilah watched him go, shaking her head.

"These are strange times, Dee." She turned to look at me, her expression troubled.

I reached forward and wrapped her in an impulsive hug. I could see in her eyes she was thinking of me and the strange circumstances of my arrival with them. She had never pressed me for details about the trouble that sent me flying into their arms, respecting my silence. And she had quickly come to act as if I truly were her older daughter. But every now and again, at moments such as this, I read remembrance in her eyes and concern for my safety.

A part of me longed to unburden myself to her, but I knew it would only increase the already overwhelming load of fear she carried. I couldn't do that to someone who had provided me with shelter all this time. Instead I limited myself to a tight squeeze which she returned before telling me to take myself off and do something useful. But there was a lingering smile on her face as she said it.

Percy's presence told me our consultation with Caravan Hargrove was already completed, but we lingered the rest of the day anyway. We needed to give them a head start before we could continue in their wake.

I spent the day cleaning and cooking and completing various chores that were difficult to accomplish while we were on the move. I wasn't the only one taking advantage of the opportunity, so Percy and his men were assigned to stand guard over the stream where a number of us had carried large tubs for washing clothes.

The prince introduced me to his men, and I noted with interest they were a mix of Talinosians and Rangmerans. When I questioned him on this fact, he shrugged.

"I've spent time in Rangmeros as a guest of Ava and Hans. As Damon's primary targets, naturally they are supportive of my efforts. I refused a larger force, since they would impede my speed and flexibility, but I was grateful to accept the assistance of a small team. Only a few of my men opted to stay with me when my ship sailed back to Talinos, so we were in need of support. The Rangmerans assigned me by Ava and Hans are experienced fighters and trackers, and only those with no families to leave behind were allowed to volunteer. Their Majesties swore to their loyalty."

"Aye," one of his men called out from across the stream, "but they didn't warn us we'd have to put up with that horse."

I don't know what you're talking about. Arvin achieved a dignified tone that should have been impossible for a neigh. *Anyone might consider themselves fortunate to travel with me.*

"You're harmless enough," another of the men said from Arvin's other side. "It's the infernal good cheer of His Highness I needed warning about. Who wants to be greeted with a smile before breakfast, I ask you? As if sleeping on the ground wasn't bad enough."

Harmless?!

Percy ignored Arvin's spluttering and snorting to show us the cheerful grin his guard was complaining about.

"The real wonder is how I put up with the moaning and complaining of all you old codgers." He shook his head, giving me a look of mock suffering. "When I said I wanted experienced guards only, I didn't realize I would be saddling myself with such ancients."

The guard across the stream laughed. "Oh, aye, I feel ancient enough after a string of nights with the hard ground beneath me."

A number of the other women uttered shocked protests, the oldest of them shaking her white head.

"Babies the lot of you. You can come to me complaining of a life on the road when you've another three decades or so on your bones."

Percy gave her a gallant bow. "I'm sure we could not match your endurance, ma'am. And in truth, I could not ask for better companions to fight and ride beside me. I've had plenty of chances to be grateful for their good humor and steady sword arms."

I shivered, hiding the movement by bending over my washing and scrubbing the dress I held with extra vigor. What was wrong with me? I barely knew Percy, and there was no reason for me to be affected by the thought of him in danger. I resolved to avoid the prince for a while in order to give my usual calm a chance to reassert itself.

Percy made that task difficult, however. At the midday meal, he seated himself on the log beside Tallie, accepting a bowl of food from Lilah with a cheeky smile and a laughing rejoinder to her joke about men who claimed to have empty stomachs after doing nothing but standing around half the day. A quick glance around the campsite showed his men had spread themselves around the various family groupings for the meal. Isambard had clearly pledged Caravan Bryant to provide for their new guards.

My vague assumption that Percy meant to circulate among the various campfires for the different meals was proved false when he joined us again at the evening meal. He even sat talking after we'd cleared away the food, asking Lilah questions about the jewelry she was working on by the firelight. No one else commented on it, despite the fact we had walked into camp together after breakfast and then chatted by the stream as well.

When I overheard a casual conversation at the wagon next to us, I discovered no one was surprised at Percy's attaching himself to us. Apparently he had managed to create the impression we were already acquainted. When I challenged him on it, he reminded me that we were—if you counted the chance meeting in the forest before the dance. I shook my head but didn't dispute his version of events. As always it was hard to deny the hopeful expression in his eyes.

When we moved out the next morning, I rode on the seat at the front of the wagon. The uninterrupted peace of the previous day had done much to calm everyone's fears, and cheerful calls passed up and down the long train of wagons. The sun shone brightly, warming the air enough to resemble a late summer, and my mood lifted in consequence. The occasional flash of Percy's smile as he rode beside the caravan only lifted it further, although I told myself any friendly face would have had the same effect.

Tallie had invited Aida to ride in the back of the wagon with her, leaving me free to chat idly with Lilah. She had spent time in Rangmeros as a girl, it turned out, and was full of stories about the city. Since this would be my first visit to a capital in these kingdoms, I listened with interest.

"The city is vastly different from in my girlhood, of course," she told me. "Oh, not the buildings themselves," she added in response to my questioning look. "But the feel of the city is changed. Queen Ava is responsible for that. It used to be a hard, gray place with that cliff looming over it, but now…" She trailed off, shaking her head and smiling. "Well, I'll leave you to see for yourself."

My curiosity increased, but she refused to be drawn, turning the conversation instead to a discussion of the latest additions to the caravan. When she commented with a teasing note about how often she saw Percy in my company, all humor dropped off my face.

"For all he chooses to act like one of his guards, I haven't forgotten he's a prince."

She sighed. "Very wise, of course. But then, you always have seemed wise for your years, Dee."

If there was an implied question in her words, I chose to ignore it, turning the conversation firmly to safer topics.

We continued on for several days, moving slowly so as not to nip at Caravan Hargrove's heels. We made camp every night in sites that showed the detritus of the larger caravan's passage. With no further sign of anyone beyond the normal travelers on the road, everyone relaxed further.

Percy continued to eat with us, sometimes going as far as riding beside our wagon at a close enough distance to maintain a conversation. I tried to pump him for further information on Rangmeros, but he entered fully into Lilah's plans to let me be surprised. When I complained, he only laughed.

On the fifth day on the road, I admitted to myself that despite the vague threat, I had rarely enjoyed a journey more. I looked forward to meals now in a way I never had before, and if I was honest, the change was due to Percy's presence. With him around, I felt peaceful and safe. It was only in the evenings, when the merchants drew close around the various campfires and talk often turned to Prince Damon, that I felt the prick of uncertainty and fear.

And it wasn't just fear of the Traitor Prince. For two years now, my existence had been ordered and calm. Although I had set out with the intention of staying only until the caravan reached a coastal city, I had easily settled into life with the merchants. My old life—where no one needed me any longer—felt more and more distant as the time passed.

But now I felt the approaching disruption of that settled life, and I found myself shying away from the question of what awaited me back in Eliam. There were loved ones, of course— friends, and the family I had made for myself—but I no longer belonged with them. The other children had Captain Tarver and Willow, and Snow had Alexander and a kingdom to run.

I was an orphan girl with no official title or role, and I had no place at court. Snow's kindness had led her to try to include me there, but I had never felt at ease. While I had been a child myself, I could accept Snow's generous provision, but during my time here I had grown up. An adult now, what place could I find in Eliam?

But what did it mean to abandon the idea of returning to my original kingdom? I couldn't stay here forever, pretending to a family I had no true right to. I had justified my lack of openness with them with the thought that it was only a temporary situation, and I would tell them the full truth before I left. I couldn't stay forever with such a barrier between us. And I was practical enough to recognize that Percy's arrival would eventually mean the destruction of my current persona. Once my full identity was revealed, would he feel honor-bound to return me to Snow and Eliam?

Perhaps that was why I clung so hard to this final journey when I was free to be Dee of the merchants and nothing more.

As I gathered water from a stream one evening, I was exerting great effort not to think of the future, or to let myself dwell on Percy's handsome face. The sun had started to set, but there was still plenty of light, which was why I saw the rustling of some leaves across the water. Movement in a forest was hardly unusual, and I felt no particular alarm. But it caught my eye just the same, and I glanced that way again as I straightened with the full jug.

A flash of white from glistening eyes made me gasp, the jug slipping from my fingers. I didn't even notice the splash as it hit the water and began to float downstream. Stumbling backward, I couldn't tear my gaze from the figure who emerged from the bush, his focus just as firmly on me as mine was on him.

I gulped, trying to find my voice as I took in the many weapons strapped to his person. But the breath was knocked out of me when my gaze returned to his face and I identified the expression on his hardened countenance. Recognition. He was looking at me with surprised recognition.

He took a step toward me, and I finally unlocked my tongue. With a loud scream, I turned and fled for the wagons.

$\mathcal{P}$ercy met me before I was fully inside the circle, several of his men hard on his heels.

"Dee!" he shouted. "What is it?"

"I saw someone." I pointed back the way I had come. "On the other side of the stream. One of Damon's men. I'm sure of it."

Thankfully he didn't stop to ask me how I was sure. But he didn't go racing after the man either, as I expected. Instead he began to call orders.

His men obeyed him without question or hesitation, and the caravan guards responded to his air of command with similar obedience. Even the Guardsmaster didn't protest, merely adding his instructions to the shouts racing through the air.

Within an unbelievably short amount of time, a ring of guards surrounded the wagons, blades drawn, while archers scaled the closest trees. The merchants showed their mettle, no one screaming or getting in the guards' way.

Children were scooped up by protective parents and bustled into wagons, the older youngsters shooed in after them. The able-bodied adults took up weapons or bandages—depending on their inclination—and formed a clump in the center of the camp.

They would be a secondary line of defense if any attackers broke through the ranks of the official guards.

I seized a roll of bandages and moved to join them. Lilah opened her mouth to protest, but I gave her a stern look, and she jerked a quick nod. When Tallie went to follow me, however, she stood firm, and I left them arguing beside the wagon as Lilah attempted to force Tallie inside.

The order of the camp lasted only brief moments before a loud shout came from those facing the stream. Seconds later the clash of steel against steel rang through the clearing. Shouts now came from every side, along with the whistle of arrows and several screams. I tensed, my mouth suddenly dry. The skirmish on the road two years ago was my only previous experience of battle, and I had run from that.

A guard, blood pouring from one arm, staggered back, but other, more experienced nurses leaped forward to meet him. Bile rose in my throat as another guard sought assistance, a jagged head wound making it hard for him to stay on his feet.

I slipped back and then back again, not wanting to get in the way of those with actual experience. With my eyes on the makeshift hospital, I nearly backed into a wagon. I froze, not realizing how close I had come to the edge of the ring, even if it was away from the shouts and clanging of the small struggle going on near the stream.

A small squeak made me jump. Whirling, I breathed a sigh of relief at the sight of Tallie. But a moment later, I stiffened.

"You're supposed to be inside, out of sight."

"Would you want to be in there? Shut up, unable to see, every moment expecting some brigand to come bursting through to end you?" Her words were belligerent, but her voice was small and her eyes round as she stared at the injured being tended on the other side of camp.

I grimaced, sympathetic to her argument. It was just such visions that had driven me to pick up the roll of bandage which hung uselessly in my hands. I had doctored countless bumps and scrapes in my years of caring for children, but I had never encountered injuries like this.

Tallie and I stood side-by-side, our eyes focused across the messy campsite at the conflict on the other side. A loud clang and an even louder shout to our right caught us both by surprise. I jumped, and Tallie screamed, both of us whirling to face a trio of attackers. The guard who had been defending that approach lay flat on the ground, bleeding heavily, and nothing stood between the men and us.

I thrust Tallie behind me, scooping up an abandoned log and wielding it like a club. One of the men barked a derisive laugh, but the one in front didn't break focus, his piercing gray eyes spearing into me.

"Which one is she?" he threw back at the two men behind him.

"I don't know," one of them replied, uneasily. "We should have brought Dastin with us."

"He's otherwise occupied," the one in front said, his eyes briefly flicking toward the main fight. "We take them both."

A new level of fear pulsed through me. Take us? These men meant to abduct us? They advanced closer, weapons drawn and aimed in our direction.

Tallie, who had been babbling incomprehensibly since they appeared, didn't seem to have heard their brief interchange, but she chose that moment to let out another piercing scream.

A loud echoing whinny sounded over the chaos of battle, drawing my eyes instinctively toward the large, golden horse. Percy, fighting at his side, spun in our direction. Arvin had already started to move, but somehow, impossibly, Percy wheeled, lunged, and managed to grab hold of Arvin's mane, swinging himself onto his back.

The horse leaped the obstacles between us, carrying the prince to our side in a matter of seconds. As soon as he reached us, Arvin gave an equine scream and reared onto his hind legs, bringing his front hooves down hard on the man with the gray eyes.

A horrible cracking sound made me gulp and turn my face hurriedly away. But the man didn't cry out, and his companions didn't even pause, one of them evading my makeshift club and seizing Tallie by the arm.

She screamed again, and Lilah appeared from nowhere shouting furiously and falling on the man holding her daughter with nothing but her bare fists. Punching and kicking him, she drove him off Tallie. The other man left me and turned to aid his companion, bringing his sword up.

Before I could interpose myself between them, movement on my other side caught my eyes. Against my will, my head spun around to see what was happening. But instead of the mangled body I expected to see, Arvin's victim was in the process of righting himself, scrambling to his feet with all of his limbs intact and not a drop of blood to be seen.

My mouth dropped open, but Percy didn't hesitate, leaning down from Arvin's back to spear the man through with his blade. The man stumbled, driven backward by the sword, and his hands flashed to his chest.

This time, when he pulled them away, they were covered in red. Arvin whinnied loudly, and Percy gave a shout of what sounded like triumph, although the man didn't go down. Instead, the flow of blood slowed and stopped, the man appearing uninjured despite the deadly blow.

He looked tense now, however, as he had not looked at anything previously. His eyes flashed between Percy and the rest of us, before he called an order to retreat.

His words jolted me out of my shock, and I spun around to find both Tallie and Lilah each now held in the grip of one of the attackers. I rushed forward and whacked one of them across the shoulder with my stick.

He shouted, his grip with that hand slackening, allowing Lilah to pull free. Hooves sounded behind me, and Percy appeared, his sword flashing through the air.

The leader shouted another, sharper order to retreat, and the man in front of me turned and ran from Percy's attack. The third man let Tallie go, and she turned and kicked him hard in the shin, tears pouring down her cheeks. He cursed at her but didn't stop for retribution before sprinting after the others.

The call to retreat must have been heard on the other side of camp as well because the sounds of battle died off completely. Glancing in that direction, I saw the attackers melting away, and the caravan guards looking to the Guardsmaster for direction.

One of Percy's guards sprinted toward us.

"We'll go after them?" he called up at the prince.

Percy, the light of battle still shining in his eyes, nodded. "Move out!" he yelled, his voice ringing across camp. "In pursuit."

Our own guards remained, but all of the ones who answered to Percy went sprinting into the trees after the disappearing attackers. Percy, still riding bareback, wheeled Arvin to follow, pulling up at the last minute to look down at me.

"You're not harmed?"

I shook my head. "No. Thanks to you."

He nodded once before Arvin took off, streaking impossibly quickly across the camp and plunging into the trees.

A hand grabbed me from behind, pulling me backward, but it was only Lilah. She pulled the stick from my slack grip, propelling me toward Tallie and taking up a protective stance in front of us both, my makeshift weapon raised.

"I think they're gone," I said, but she didn't relax her position.

Two women ran to the guard who still lay on the ground a short distance from us. Together they lifted him up, displaying the muscles honed by a lifetime of hauling merchandise. I angled my body so that Tallie, who was now clinging to me, was turned away, but to my surprise, the man groaned. He still lived, then.

One of the women, Maris, glanced over at us.

"Do you have water?" she called to Lilah.

Lilah shook her head, and I remembered guiltily that our jug was gone, washed away down the stream.

"It's safe now," her companion, Anthea, said as the two of them shuffled past us, bearing their burden toward the space someone had cleared in the center of the circle. Several other wounded already lay there, being tended by Aida's mother who had undergone medical training before marrying into the caravan.

"They tried to take my girls." Lilah sounded grim and determined. "I'll wait a little longer before I judge it safe, thank you."

Maris's and Anthea's shuffling steps hitched as they exchanged a startled look.

"They tried to abduct Tallie and Dee?" Maris asked.

"That's right." Lilah nodded. "And they might have succeeded, too, if it wasn't for that prince and his strange horse."

The two women resumed their walk, but as soon as they reached the other wounded, they deposited their burden and turned away, scanning the camp. Others leaped to tend the man while Maris ran to Isambard. The caravan leader was in consultation with the Guardsmaster, his bronze face creased with deep lines of concern.

They were too far away for me to hear the hurried words Maris spoke to him, but she gestured in our direction, and all three of them looked our way.

"Perhaps we should move closer to the others," Tallie said in an uncharacteristically hesitant voice.

"That's a good idea," I said, injecting a brisk note into my tone to try to chase away any potential wobble. "Perhaps we can even be of help."

Lilah nodded her agreement, shepherding us ahead of her while her head swiveled in all directions as she maintained a watchful vigilance. As soon as we approached, the Guardsmaster broke away from the others to speak to us.

"Is it true?" he asked. "They tried to take you girls?"

"And nearly succeeded," Lilah snapped. Her hand had started to shake slightly.

Tallie gulped and nodded, fresh tears spilling over her cheeks. I hesitated, torn about what I should say. Did I have a responsibility to inform them it had been me Damon's men were after?

But the Guardsmaster was already turning away. With quick strides he crossed to a nearby clump of three guards watching over the injured. He spoke quickly, but I made out the words, *go after them.*

One of the guards nodded, running to a nearby horse and swinging himself up onto his back. Kicking his flank, the guard directed his mount toward the stream.

I watched them go, my bottom lip clenched between my teeth. What did I really know? It was only supposition on my part that the guard at the stream had recognized me and those other three men had come after me as a consequence.

Wanting to be useful—and desperate to keep my circling thoughts at bay—I offered my assistance to those doing the nursing. Anthea paused on her way to the stream to give me a friendly smile.

"It's a big enough shock you've had for one evening. You sit down, dear. There's enough of us adults to do what needs doing."

I forced a return smile, although inside I was wincing. Apparently my near abduction had relegated me to the status of youngster who needed to be kept safely in the confines of the camp.

And maybe they're right about that, an inner voice said softly.

I thrust it away, looking desperately for some occupation until my eyes fell on Tallie. She had managed to stop the tears, but she was standing frozen, her arms wrapped around her middle, and her eyes staring blankly at nothing.

Lilah reached her before I did, encircling her in a hug. Our eyes met over her head in a silent message of shared concern and purpose.

"Will you make her some hot tea?" Lilah asked softly. "We could all do with a mug, I suspect."

I nodded, springing eagerly to the task, although I had to borrow our neighbor's jug of water to accomplish it. Soon I had enough tea brewed to hand out to anyone who had a free hand to take some. I was still scooping the drink into mugs when the guard returned, Arvin close behind him. An ordered line of men strode into camp in their wake, their expressions ranging from disappointed to alert.

At a word from Percy, they spread out, bolstering the able-bodied caravan guards who remained on duty around the wagons. Percy himself slid down from Arvin's back and hurried over to consult with the Guardsmaster. He ran a hand through his hair as they spoke, at one point glancing in my direction with what looked strangely like guilt.

So he wanted you. The neigh beside me made me jump. *Interesting.*

"That's not how I would describe it," I said shortly, and then grimaced. The fright of the battle was getting to me.

"My apologies," I said stiffly to the horse.

He looked down his nose at me before softening and reaching forward to blow a whuffling snort into my hair.

You'll do, small one. It was bravely enough done in the moment.

I looked up at him, surprised by his kindness and nearly undone by it, too. I fought back the tears gathering in my eyes.

"You heard us," I said. "You're the one who alerted Percy we were in trouble."

Of course. His dignified manner had returned. *I am a superior being, after all.*

"How could we possibly forget it?" Percy appeared on Arvin's other side. But the concern in his eyes was at variance with his joking tone.

"I'm sorry for running off like that," he said to me. "I got caught up in the moment. After two years chasing him, that's the first time I've been that close to getting my hands on Damon at last."

"Damon?" I stared at him. "That was the Traitor Prince himself?" Sudden certainty filled me. "The one with the gray eyes."

Percy nodded, seeming to watch me extra closely. My eyes widened as I remembered what I had nearly forgotten amid the chaos and fear.

"He—"

Percy cut me off. "I wondered if you'd noticed that. I can explain, but not here."

I barely contained my patience, trusting he must have a reason for his reticence.

"I'm sorry you had to abandon the chase. I take it the Guardsmaster called you back?"

Percy nodded, looking rueful. "He was concerned, and understandably so. He wants us here, guarding the caravan, not wandering around the forest where Damon might elude us and double back. A raid for supplies is bad enough, but if they're after the caravan's girls, that's far more concerning. I should have thought of the danger myself and not gone haring off in such a fashion."

I looked down at my ladle, filling another mug to hide the emotions in my eyes. Everything had been loud and chaotic and terrifying—had I misheard or misunderstood Damon and his men? Had they really been after only me?

"It's a pity, though," I managed, once I trusted my voice again. "To come so close and have him slip away again."

"More than a pity." Percy's frustration sounded in his voice. "But it's no surprise either." He sighed. "And in truth, they'd slipped away from us before the messenger arrived to call us back. It shouldn't have been possible given how close we were on their tail, but…" He shook his head. "Damon is an expert at disappearing in such a way. If there's one thing I've learned in two years, it's that he never appears anywhere unless he has a clear route of escape."

His words relieved my mind a little. It would have been awful if Percy had been on the brink of capturing Damon when he was called back to guard me.

Anthea approached for a cup of tea, her shoulders slumped in weary lines. Percy asked after the wounded guards, and I was relieved to hear they were all expected to live.

"Only thanks to Dee here." Percy gave me a warm smile that made me squirm inside. "We would have fared far worse without those few moments of warning."

I wished I could banish the lingering feeling the attack had only happened because of me.

Anthea accepted the cup I handed her, full of agreement with Percy but also grateful for the role he and his men had played in our defense. She bore the prince away to cast his eye over their nursing efforts. But a single backward glance over his shoulder reassured me he hadn't forgotten his promise of an explanation when we could find a more private moment.

CHAPTER 9

*I*n the aftermath of battle, privacy was in short supply. All the younger women, in particular, were watched with a close eye.

Isambard had the wagons drawn into a closer circle, and we all passed a night of tense watchfulness, punctuated by the occasional groans of the wounded. I volunteered to stay up and help with the nursing overnight but was once again turned down.

"We've more willing nurses than wounded, thankfully," Aida's mother told me. "And the guards will benefit from having loved ones close."

The next morning, Isambard departed, two tense guards in attendance. They galloped out of sight along the road, heading in the direction of the capital.

"Isambard rides the fastest horse in the caravan," Maris told me when she saw me gazing down the now empty road with concern. "He'll make it to Caravan Hargrove and back before anyone else could." She glanced toward the center of camp where two of the wounded remained, still too injured to move. "And we couldn't be traveling on this morning anyway."

"Will another night do it?" I asked, following her gaze.

"I've no experience with such injuries myself, but that's what I'm told."

"My men don't have much in the way of medical training, but some of them have seen such wounds before." Percy smiled at us both. "They agree we should be ready to move out by tomorrow. It's a smooth, well-established road, so the injured shouldn't be jostled to an excessive degree."

"Isambard will see them placed in his own wagon," Maris said. "And there isn't a better made one in all the kingdoms."

Someone called to her, and she moved away with a nod in our direction, leaving Percy and me alone. I glanced from side to side before fixing him with a steady stare.

"I hope you haven't forgotten you promised me answers."

He nodded, taking my hand and pulling me into the shadowed gap between two empty wagons. He let it drop as soon as we were out of sight of the rest of the caravan, and I tried to pretend I wasn't intensely aware of his momentary touch.

"Do you think your stepmother and sister saw what happened?" he asked.

"I don't think so." I tried to focus, replaying my memory of the brief scuffle. "They were distracted at the time."

He sighed. "There's enough fear around the Traitor Prince, as the people call him, without feeding the tales, so we've kept the truth quiet."

I pressed my hands together, trying to keep my own fears at bay. "That he's impervious to injury? How is such a thing possible? And how are you ever to stop him if he can't be harmed? It must be an enormous help in his constant escapes."

Percy reached forward, taking both my hands in his and looking into my eyes with a serious gaze.

"We will stop him, Dee, don't worry. I won't let him harm you. He might not be able to be wounded or killed, but he can be locked up like anyone else, and that's what we intend to do. I

82

won't rest until he's no longer free to roam around, stealing and killing at whim."

"But why?" I asked, momentarily distracted by the intensity of his reassurance. "You aren't even from these kingdoms."

He hesitated for a brief second. "I had a chance to stop him once. Back at the beginning. But I failed. I don't intend to fail again."

I shook my head. "Whatever happened then, this isn't your fight. You don't have to dedicate your life to it."

He dropped my hands, turning away slightly. "You might not have heard about it over here, but when I was younger, my own kingdom was affected by a curse. A creeping paralysis of heart that sapped our courage. We were powerless to fight it, and in the end it was someone from outside who saved us. And Lanover's Princess Celine did the same thing for Eldon." He shrugged. "Maybe it's arrogance on my part, or foolishness, but if I can do the same thing for another kingdom, it will feel like paying back the great debt I can never otherwise repay."

I nodded, respecting his desire to help others as he himself had once been helped. I remembered the affliction that had gripped Talinos, although I had heard only dim rumors of it at the time. I had been absorbed enough in Eliam's own troubles back then, an orphan who didn't even dream of consorting with royalty.

"I'm sure both Arcadia and Rangmere appreciate your efforts," I said softly, but he brushed the comment aside, apparently uninterested in receiving praise.

"I'm just sorry to have missed my chance on this occasion. But the encounter wasn't entirely without value. I've never heard tell of him bleeding before."

"I still don't understand how it's possible." I swallowed. "He should have been dead after Arvin crushed him."

Percy nodded. "I wouldn't care to receive a blow from even

one of those hooves. But his body knit back together before a single drop could be spilled."

"But not after you stabbed him," I said. "He bled then. I saw it clearly."

"Not for long." Percy sounded enthusiastic now. "But he did bleed. The question is why. If we can determine how to replicate the effect, we'll have a significant advantage." He paced up and down the tiny space, his eyes alight with the puzzle I still didn't fully understand.

"But how is it possible?" I repeated.

He paused, his brows creasing. "I didn't explain that?"

"Not at all." I smiled and shook my head. "I think you were distracted by the puzzle of his bleeding."

Percy's lip twisted in an amused grimace. "My apologies. It's a rather morbid topic, but one that has absorbed a great deal of my mental energies, as you can imagine. According to information from one of Damon's former allies, he inherited a godmother object from his mother. You'll have heard she was Princess Mina of Arcadia before her marriage, of course."

I nodded, and he continued. "I believe it was originally intended to be used to heal someone in case of dire illness or injury and had been kept for generations, used only in great need. However, Damon used it to gift himself its powers, imbuing himself with indestructibility but leaving it useless."

"He would do something so selfish," I said, indignation coloring my voice.

Percy smiled. "I've seen enough of you already, Dee of the merchants, to know such selfishness is foreign to your nature."

I flushed. "I'm as capable of self-absorption as anyone else, I'm sure."

He shook his head. "One only has to look at Damon to see that isn't true. No one is perfect, but you are more selfless than most."

I looked down, uncomfortable with the turn the conversation

had taken. "So Damon can heal instantly. Except we both saw that didn't happen when you stabbed him." I considered the matter. "So is the gift wearing off? Does it have a limited number of uses?"

"That would be ideal," he said. "The other option is that it might need time to replenish its power between uses, so to speak."

"Either way, he can be worn down," I said.

Percy nodded, his eyes full of excitement again. "And that is a very valuable piece of knowledge. Knowledge we have thanks to you."

He turned the full force of those bright eyes on me, the gold flecks in the brown seeming to glow. I bit my lip. It might be thanks to me in a greater part than he knew. He had just been open with me. Should I repay his honesty with my own truths?

Before I could make up my mind, however, someone turned into the gap we were occupying. They paused, startled, but Percy smiled and greeted them, smoothing over the awkward moment as we stepped back into the center of camp. If I wanted to confide in Percy, I would have to find another opportunity.

Isambard arrived back before dark, his horse showing signs of hard riding. Word soon passed around the caravan that we would break camp and leave first thing in the morning. If we moved at pace, we could reach Caravan Hargrove in a single day since they had agreed to wait for us. It would be awkward to travel with such a large group, but our numbers would provide greater safety against another such attack.

The rumblings that had been swirling around the caravan all day reached their peak at this announcement. A number of the more senior members demanded to hear what had been discussed with Ariana.

"A blatant attack on a peaceful caravan!" one cried.

"This violates the treaty," another added. "Rangmere will find itself under another ban. Do we really want to trap ourselves in Rangmeros? Shouldn't we be turning around and making for the border?"

Mutterings swept the caravan at the mention of a ban, concern filling many eyes. It wasn't only the offending kingdom that suffered when one was in effect, but the traveling merchants could not allow themselves to be attacked with impunity.

"Obviously I cannot speak for the council," Isambard said, "but I spent a long time in consultation with Ariana and her senior merchants."

Everyone quieted to hear the wisdom of Caravan Hargrove. Unlike Isambard, who had not yet attained enough seniority to even sit on the merchant council, Ariana had been its chair for almost a decade.

"Naturally Caravan Hargrove were horrified to hear of the attack, and there was some talk of sanctions against Rangmere. But Ariana insisted that since Damon leads a rebel force in direct opposition to Rangmere's current rulers, they cannot be held responsible for his actions."

"It's their kingdom, and their responsibility to keep the roads safe," Maris said with a frown.

Isambard nodded in her direction. "Attacks on travelers has not been the Traitor Prince's pattern before now. We must give Queen Ava and King Hans a chance to respond. But at the same time, we cannot ignore such a blatant attack against the merchants. We travel for Rangmeros to join forces with the king and queen, and together we will eliminate this threat to both the kingdoms and the caravans."

The guards and many of the younger caravan members let out a cheer at these ringing words, so any further objections were swallowed. Working together, the merchants threw their full efforts into preparing for a hurried flight to the safety of the bigger caravan.

We reached Caravan Hargrove as the sun was setting the next day. We were welcomed with glad cries and expressions of sympathy and concern. The larger caravan had the luxury of their own doctor, and he stood waiting to examine the recovering wounded.

Others rushed forward to help us maneuver our wagons into the tight spaces they had created for them and to care for our exhausted animals. We had pushed the horses far harder than we would ordinarily consider doing, and I heard Isambard telling Ariana that the enlarged caravan wouldn't be able to travel far the next day.

We soon discovered we would not be moving at a great pace on any of the days. Although the doctor reported his patients had been well tended and could expect a smooth healing, speed just wasn't possible with such a large group. Breaking camp and getting on the road took a long time each morning, and we had to take what campsites we could find that offered enough room, even if there were hours of daylight still available when we reached them.

As I had learned when I first joined Caravan Bryant, a merchant caravan had an ordered rhythm that allowed them to set up and pack down camp smoothly and efficiently each day. Each person knew their role and each wagon knew its place. All of that was thrown into chaos now, however, as we attempted to blend the two groups.

Despite the occasional small squabble, there were no larger complaints, however. Even the members of the larger caravan seemed to appreciate the extra feeling of security from greater numbers.

Tallie, much to my relief, recovered from her shock in the excitement of our temporary merge with Caravan Hargrove. She and Aida disappeared into the crowd at every opportunity, off to spend time with the Hargrove youngsters. Several times I passed her holding court as she described her terrifying ordeal to an interested audience. And it wasn't only others her age who asked to hear the tale. As one of those who had nearly been taken, she found herself an object of unprecedented interest.

In such an environment, I was hardly surprised to find myself doing her share of the chores each morning and evening. I had time to offer only the briefest of replies to anyone who asked me for an account of the incident, and interested parties soon learned to direct their questions at Tallie. Of course, I could have told them more than she could, but I had no desire to do so.

My legs ached one evening as I bent over yet another stream, scrubbing at some washing. I had spent the day on the hard seat of the wagon, and every muscle and joint seemed to be conspiring against me. Normally we saved washing for rest days, but there would be no rest days until we reached Rangmeros.

A number of others worked beside me, the usual bright chatter of washing sessions intermittent given the general exhaustion and the sense of alert tension that was a constant undercurrent to our journey.

Percy and Arvin's arrival brought a wave of smiles, however. Few people could resist the charm of the Talinosian prince since it came from a genuinely warm heart.

"Working again?" he asked, affecting dismay at finding me thus occupied. "Do you ever do anything but work?"

"Mayhap she could work less if some people worked more," Maris muttered beside me.

I gave her a brief glare at her criticism of my adopted family before forcing a smile onto my tired face for Percy.

"We'll all be able to rest when we reach the safety of Rang-meros's walls."

"I was born and bred a merchant," Anthea said from my other side. "Usually being inside four solid walls makes me itchy. But

I'll confess I'm straining for a sight of that gray stone just like everybody else."

"These are unusual happenings—I'm glad to say," Maris said gravely, and a ripple of agreement passed up and down the line of merchants.

"What about you, Arvin?" I looked over at the horse who had found a patch of lush grass beside the stream. "Do you prefer life on the open road to four walls?"

"Ha!" Percy snorted. "Arvin loves nothing better than the royal stables. He has them well-trained and will accept only oats, corn, and apples."

And sugar cubes.

Percy chuckled. "How could I forget?" He looked back at me, eyes twinkling. "We have an agreement—he accepts a diet of primarily grass while we're on the road so long as I keep him well supplied with sugar cubes."

I shook my head and adopted a serious air. "Arvin, I'm disappointed. You embrace being caged by walls for the sake of your stomach?"

No walls could cage me, he neighed calmly before moving to a fresh patch of grass a little further down the stream.

"He's telling the truth," Percy said ruefully in answer to my surprised look. "I have no idea how he does it, but I've yet to find a stall or door that could hold him."

"Well, he is a talking horse," I said. "I suppose nothing should surprise me."

"Don't speak so loudly." Percy gave a mock groan. "He hears far too much praise as it is. We can't go anywhere without people exclaiming and admiring him—and that's regardless of whether he lets them hear him talk."

I eyed Arvin. "You can hardly blame them. Merchants pride themselves on their animals, but I've never seen another one like him."

Percy looked from side to side before lowering his voice, as if about to make a confession. "In the early days after we started traveling together, I was convinced he was going to sprout wings if we ever found ourselves in a tight spot."

I laughed. "And I can just imagine how he would react if you showed surprise at such an event."

"*I am a superior being from the Palace of Light,*" Percy said in a poor imitation of Arvin. "*Did you expect any less?*" He dropped back into his normal tones. "You can see why I became obsessed with the idea. I wouldn't let it go for a full year."

"Maybe you just haven't been in a tight enough spot?" I suggested.

Percy's eyes lit up, and then he groaned. "Now don't go putting that idea into my head. Just because I had a childhood dream of riding a flying horse, doesn't mean Arvin is going to grow wings just to please me."

Certainly I shall not do so, Arvin whuffed, walking back over to us. *I am not a performing animal.*

Percy couldn't keep a bright spark from appearing in his eyes. "You mean you could do so, if you wanted to?"

Arvin turned a disapproving eye on him. *I am not a bird. Why do all you humans insist on being obsessed with nonsensical things?*

"We can't help it," I said in my most humble tone. "Not when faced with your magnificence."

Arvin relaxed, giving me an approving look. *That is a good point. I—*

Percy betrayed me by bursting into laughter which set me giggling as well. Arvin immediately stiffened.

I see you are determined to jest. A strange attitude for one engaged in laundry.

"Quite the opposite," I told him. "Such an attitude is entirely necessary in order to face such vast quantities of washing."

I expected Arvin to take further offense, but instead he fixed his attention on me for a long, silent moment. *Perhaps you are right,* he conceded at last. *Thankfully it's not something I've had occa-*

sion to think on before. He turned his attention to Percy. *I cannot say laundry is a topic that interests me. Are you done here?*

Percy looked at me, and I told myself I was imagining the reluctance on his face.

"I suppose you'll be working later as well." I wasn't imagining his disheartened tone.

"There's always work in a merchant caravan." I kept my voice light, telling myself it was for the best when he slung an arm over Arvin's neck and wandered away with a brief farewell for us all.

"It's good to make them work for it," one of the Caravan Hargrove women said with a twinkle in her eye once he disappeared from sight. "Especially handsome ones like that prince."

I stared at her blankly, and another woman let out a chuckle. "He's got hard work ahead of him, all right, if she doesn't even realize he's pining for a chance to take her walking."

This time Anthea joined their gentle laughter, while I stopped scrubbing to stare at them.

"What are you talking about? Percy is a prince, remember. Princes don't go walking, like us commoners—they do their courting at balls and such."

"A man first and a prince second, I think you'll find," the first woman said. "And I haven't noticed any balls for him to attend hereabouts, have you?"

"He's more sense than I'd credit for one of his rank—setting his sights on a good, sensible girl like you," another of the women added. "We've all seen how hard you work."

"Percy is a prince." I wished I didn't sound so stiff. "You're letting your imaginations run away with you. Circumstances may place him with us for a time, but he'll return to the world of balls soon enough. And he'll find himself a princess from that world as well."

The first woman gave a gusty sigh. "Mayhap you're right." She looked at me sideways. "But a girl can be too sensible, you know. It does a body good to dream on occasion."

"There is too much work to be done to leave time for dreaming," I said, producing a wave of murmurs and light-hearted complaints about the never-ending work of life on the road.

Satisfied to have turned attention away from me, I bent my head over my washing, scrubbing as hard as I could. I wished it were true that mind-numbing work like this could drive away unwanted thoughts and the kind of insidious dreams that would leave me unsatisfied with the reality of life. But I had proof enough lately that no chore was sufficient to banish the bright eyes that insisted on invading my thoughts.

CHAPTER 10

That night at the campfire, Tallie was in her brightest, most sparkling, mood. Her mother watched her with a suspicious eye, and I shared her concern. Such high spirits usually presaged some particularly outrageous behavior.

"I think this might be your best stew yet, Dee!" She gave a sigh of satisfaction. "Your cooking might even surpass Mother's these days."

"Thank you, my dear," Lilah said, but there was a laugh in her voice.

"I'm not sure I can claim any credit," I admitted, a little sheepishly. "I was so tired when I was putting in the ingredients I wasn't paying enough attention. I accidentally added sage instead of basil. So then I thought I'd better throw in some rosemary and thyme as well. It turns out it's a perfect combination."

Tallie went off into giggles at the image of me frantically throwing random herbs into the stew. I had no doubt I had looked frantic since I was sure I'd ruined our meal. I grew up cooking plain, serviceable food in bulk, and I hadn't learned the subtleties of fine cooking.

"I refuse to cede my crown to a mistake," Lilah said with a

chuckle of her own. "But if you can replicate it again, then I'll make way for the new queen with pleasure."

Tallie sat up, stretching and rubbing her belly with a feline look of contentment. "Where did you put the clean washing?" she asked me.

"It's folded in the wagon," I replied absently, busy gathering the empty bowls. "I haven't had time to put it away in the drawers yet."

She clambered inside and began rummaging around. From the sounds she was making, I would have to do the folding again. I suppressed a sigh. There was no point remonstrating with her. She would look guilty, promise to remember to be more careful next time, and then forget all over again. It wasn't worth the energy.

"Where's my yellow dress?" she called, a sharp note entering her voice.

"I didn't get to it," I called back. "There wasn't time to do everything."

"What?" Her screech easily reached us outside the wagon. Her head popped back out, her eyes flashing with anger. "What do you mean you didn't wash it?! I *need* that dress!"

"Whatever for?" I stared at her blankly. Her yellow dress was one of her finest, and there wasn't a dance or any other entertainment planned.

"Because I want to wear it! You should have known it was my favorite and washed it first. How could you be so thoughtless?"

"Thoughtless?" My normally cool temper, strained from the constant tension of the last few days, snapped. "Are you sure you want to get into a debate about thoughtlessness? If you needed that dress so desperately, you should have washed it yourself!"

"Girls." Lilah gave us both a reproving look. "That's no way to talk to your sister."

I drew a deep breath, struggling to regain my equanimity.

When neither of us responded, Lilah turned to Tallie. "Really,

Tallie," she said, and I was ashamed of the bloom of satisfaction that she was going to take Tallie to task for her failure to help with the chores. "You can just as easily wear your green dress, you know. As long as you look neat, Ariana likely won't even notice what you're wearing."

The sharp spear of disappointment at the lack of rebuke dissolved at her mention of Ariana, replaced by curiosity.

"Ariana?" I looked back and forth between them. "Is something happening tonight?"

Lilah smiled proudly. "Ariana has invited Tallie to join her at her campfire after the meal."

"She wants to hear my story about the attack," Tallie said proudly.

So that's why she wanted to look her best. No wonder she had been so bright throughout the meal. Her enthusiasm faded now, however, replaced by doubt as she looked at me.

"I suppose you'll want to come as well, Dee. I didn't realize you didn't know about the invitation."

I could read her emotions as clearly as if she'd named them. Tallie was well aware I had more claim than she did to tell the story of the attack, and she saw her shining moment as the center of attention slipping away.

She said nothing to dissuade me from joining her, however, and my remaining irritation melted away. The overwhelming emotions of youth were heightening her legitimate excitement at being singled out for such an honor. In the midst of that, her willingness to include me—despite her strong personal inclination against doing so—meant more than her carping earlier.

"You go without me," I said. "It will take me a while to clean up here."

Tallie immediately brightened, throwing her arms impulsively around my neck and promising to help when she returned. I laughed and returned her embrace, refraining from pointing out that the chore would be completed well before then.

"Oh no," Lilah said, "of course you must come, Dee."

We turned to her with identical frowns.

"Honestly, I would prefer not to," I said. "I don't want the attention, I promise."

But Lilah continued as if she hadn't heard me. "You can't stay here alone. Not at night. You need to stay where I can see you."

"Mother!" Tallie cried. "She's just going to be right here in camp." She whirled on me. "That's right, isn't it? You're not going anywhere?"

"No, of course not. The guards wouldn't let me, anyway."

Tallie spun back to her mother. "There, you see! I'm going to change, and then we need to get going. We don't want to be late."

"No, it wouldn't do to offend Ariana," Lilah was quick to agree, but I could see the shade of doubt lingering in her eyes as she watched me.

When Tallie had disappeared back into the wagon, she stepped closer. "You'll stay close to the wagon? If anything happens, we'll come straight back for you."

"I don't think we need to worry about an attack tonight," I said. "There are double guards on watch at all times now, remember."

She chewed on her lip. "Yes, but—"

"Go and enjoy yourself," I said firmly. "I'll be right here when you get back."

Tallie stuck her head out of the wagon. "You could stay here with Dee if you like."

She sounded innocent, but Lilah just raised an eyebrow. "Nice try. I'm not letting you out of my sight after dark. Now hurry up."

Tallie reappeared in her green dress, her earlier tantrum over the yellow gown seemingly forgotten. I waved them both off and turned back to the clean up. But when I moved toward the wagon, my hands full, Percy appeared in front of me.

I cut off a shriek, jumping back half a step and nearly dropping all the bowls.

"Where did you come from?"

"Never mind that." He pulled the dirty crockery from my reluctant fingers and deposited it in the back of our wagon. "This time I'm not allowing you to use chores as an excuse. No one should have to work all the time."

"I don't work all the time," I protested.

"No," he said dryly. "You spend long, boring hours sitting on the front seat of your wagon. That's not the same as time off." He gave me a cheeky grin. "And it's definitely not the same as time off with yours truly."

I frowned at the mess now piled in the back of the wagon. "I can't just leave that."

"Of course you can." He put a hand under my elbow and began to gently guide me away. "It's not going to grow legs. It'll be there when you get back." He dropped his voice to a mutter. "Because your stepfamily sure aren't going to clean up their own mess."

"That's not fair," I said with stiff dignity. "My stepmother works every day driving the wagon, and then she spends her free time designing and crafting the jewelry we sell. Just because you don't see it, doesn't mean they don't do anything for me."

"Consider me suitably chastised." He looked at me sideways. "But I reserve the right to dislike how much they make you do. You're not their servant."

I sighed. "It's partially my fault. I know that."

"Your fault?" He turned to look at me fully, a crease between his brows. "That's definitely not what I'm saying."

I grimaced. "It's true, though. Tallie isn't callous—she's just young. And if she gets away with too much, it's because I let her."

"Or because her mother lets her, perhaps?"

"Lilah does let her get away with a lot in some areas, it's true. But not enough in others. Tallie would do better with a little more freedom and a little more discipline at the same time." I sighed. "But her mother can't correct what she doesn't know about."

"Then tell her."

We reached a nearby campfire, and Percy dropped my arm, bowing me gallantly onto a well-placed log.

"Your seat, my lady."

I rolled my eyes, plonking myself down. "You know we have a perfectly good fire over there as well."

"Ah yes, but that fire came with a heavy weight of responsibility and the reminder of duties and chores to be accomplished. This one comes with...warmth."

I shook my head, but secretly I was touched. We'd gone only steps away—we were so close I didn't even feel I was flouting my promise to my stepmother—but he was right that it felt different here.

"So?" he prompted, sitting on the ground and leaning his back on the log I was using as a seat. "Why don't you tell Lilah how often Tallie leaves you to do all the chores?"

I bit my lip. "You've noticed that?"

"You fascinate me, Dee of the merchants. There's something about you I can't quite put my finger on—and it's not just that Arvin has some interest in you he won't explain to me."

My pulse jumped, heat suffusing my face at the idea that I intrigued him. I didn't even try to tell myself the warmth came from the fire, but I did steer the conversation firmly onto safer ground.

"I think, if I'm honest, I let her do it because she's young, and this is her one chance to be free of such responsibilities. They'll seize her soon enough, and then she'll never be rid of them." I shrugged. "Perhaps I'm doing her a disservice, but I can't seem to help it."

"Because you never got it." He said the words quietly, and I flinched, my heart racing for an entirely different reason.

"What...what do you mean?" I stammered. Had Arvin told

him who I was? But he'd just said Arvin wouldn't explain his interest in me. How could Percy know about my past?

Percy ignored my discomfort, looking into the fire as if to give me time to recover my composure.

"I hope one day you'll tell me all about your past, but it's obvious you're far too used to carrying a weight of responsibility for someone your age. Tallie isn't that much younger than you, and yet you talk as if she's a mere child, while you're an experienced adult."

"I...I suppose I do." I hesitated. "Maybe one day I will tell you my whole history. But you're right. It's been a very long time since I was a child, if I ever truly was one. I think that's the cause of some of my problems with my stepmother as well. I'm used to being the responsible adult—not answering to one."

He glanced up at me. "I'm sorry you didn't get to be a child, Dee. You deserved that chance just like everyone else."

I shrugged. "I made a home and a family for myself, and there are far worse fates than that." I hesitated but decided if he could pry, I could too. "Like being cursed, for instance. I may not have had an idyllic childhood, but I didn't spend years bound by a curse."

The firelight flickered over his grimace. "Sometimes I think the worst part is how hazy those years seem. It's like I lost a whole chunk of my youth. I'll admit, when the curse was first lifted, I leaned too far the other way. I became reckless in my desire to prove to myself that the timidity of the curse had no true reflection in my nature or character."

I watched him with curiosity. "It's hard to believe you could ever have thought yourself naturally timid."

He grinned up at me. "Are you trying to remind me of my impulsivity the other day at the battle? You needn't rake me over the coals, you know. Your Guardsmaster already did it for you."

"Of course I don't mean to do so. I wasn't thinking of the battle at all."

"Now you've roused my curiosity. What feats of courageous daring have I completed recently? I confess I can't think of any."

"Courage is used for more than just battle. You sought me out earlier in a positive fortress of laundry and gossip." I glanced back at the campfire where he'd found me. "And you never seem daunted by rejection."

"Ah, but you're forgetting," he said with an impish grin. "I wasn't alone by the stream. I had Arvin with me, then. He has enough self-assurance to count for two or three extra people, at least."

I laughed. "That he does. And yet I don't see him here this evening. You can't fool me, Percy of Talinos. You're not fearful at all."

"I am, of course," he said, suddenly serious. "Sometimes, at least. But I refuse to let my fear rule me. Not anymore."

I bit my lip, gazing into the dancing flames. He made it sound so easy to cast fear aside.

"Tell me about your childhood," I said. "Before the curse, I mean."

If he was startled by the change of subject, he didn't show it, launching into an entertaining description of his younger twin sisters and his older brother, Gabe.

"I was determined to keep up with him, of course," he told me. "And his friends. I would follow them everywhere. So maybe it was for the best he was sent off to foster with the Trionian royal family when I was six. If I was free to follow him around all year long, I might have ended up doing worse than just breaking my arm."

"Your brother made you break your arm?"

He chuckled, as if the memory were a humorous one. "Well, to be fair, he broke his arm, too. But considering he's three years older than me, and I was only seven at the time, I'm lucky I didn't break something more serious. That was on one of our visits to Trione."

I shook my head. "It's a tale as old as time. The younger children are always determined to follow the older ones, even if it kills them. Mine were just the same."

"Yours?" He looked up with astonishment.

"Not mine by blood, of course," I amended, "but I already told you I made a family of my own."

"They were fortunate to have you," he said.

I snorted. "Tell that to Anthony."

"I hope one day I'll have the chance to do so," he said. "If you'll introduce me."

I stiffened. This firelight was just as dangerous as those warm brown eyes. I had nearly forgotten myself and the vast gulf that lay between me and this prince.

"Perhaps one day," I said in a stiff tone.

His face fell, a crease appearing between his eyes at my change in attitude, but before he could speak, a sharp cry propelled me to my feet.

"Dee! Dee, where are you?"

"I'm right here," I called back hurriedly, before Lilah could rouse half the caravan.

Percy sprang to his feet at the same moment as I did, but I shook my head at him.

"Thank you for a lovely break." I gave him a brief smile before sprinting away.

"You promised you'd stay right here." Lilah's eyes flashed angrily.

"And so I did." I kept my reply calm. "I was right there within view and earshot. I was with Percy, as well."

"Oh. Well, in that case…" The prince had been in high favor with her ever since he rescued Tallie and me from Damon.

"How was the visit with Ariana?" I asked, eager to turn her attention to other matters.

"We had a pleasant time, thank you." She glanced at the wagon. "Tallie has already retired for the evening. She's in a miff with me because I wouldn't let her go looking for Aida in order to spend half the night recounting her moments of triumph."

Tallie must have been riding high on elation and admiration if she thought she had any chance of convincing her mother of such a plan. But I kept such thoughts to myself, both from Lilah and later from Tallie, when I collected the dirty dishes from the wagon where they still sat.

CHAPTER 11

$\mathcal{W}$e drew closer and closer to the capital, the mood in the caravan lightening with every day that passed without sign of Damon or his followers. All the injured from our small battle were back on their feet—if not entirely healed—our necessarily slow pace of use to them, at least.

I grew increasingly exhausted, however. Most wagons housed larger family groupings who could share the extra workload created by our lack of rest days. I had let Percy convince me to put work aside for one evening, but when I collapsed exhausted into bed far too late that night, I promised myself I wouldn't be so beguiled again.

I remained firm in my refusal when he came searching for me the next night, but once he learned the cause of my change of heart, he was undaunted. Turning his charm on Lilah, he convinced her to let me out of her sight as long as I remained in his company. Together we carried the dishes to the closest stream, making the job of cleaning them far quicker, even before his assistance.

After that first night, he insisted on joining me for all my evening chores. Since he often still came to our fire for the morning or midday meals, he claimed it was only fair he take some share of the chores as well. When I tried to remind him he stood guard shifts all day, he brushed my words aside.

"We haven't sighted Damon since that unfortunate day, so it's hardly an onerous task. But, if he should appear, and I were to take an injury in the course of my duty, then I promise to allow you to complete the dishes alone that night."

I shook my head. "Now that I've seen your imperious ways, I've no doubt you would insist on my nursing you and feeding you grapes by hand."

"Only if you peeled them first," he said promptly. "I am a prince, after all."

I giggled at that, but underneath, his reminder stung. Out here on the road, it was far too easy to forget Percy belonged to a world of balls and courts—a world I had already unsuccessfully encountered as Snow's friend. I would do well to remind myself daily that I could be of no use among courtiers and royalty.

On our last night before our arrival at the city, a celebratory atmosphere pervaded the camp. After we finished our meal, I waited for Percy's arrival, but he didn't appear. I told myself it was hardly surprising given his true status. No doubt he was caught up with the caravan leadership who would be making plans for the next day.

But I had grown used to the freedom of washing the dishes at the stream, and I was loath to give that up just because Percy wasn't with me. Lilah had joined Tallie in the caravan, searching for something she had lost, and I decided to make my escape while I could.

Hurrying into the darkness between campfires, I made my way down to the stream at a quick walk. I would have the dishes washed and be back at the wagon before they found the missing item, in all likelihood. Tallie's ability to lose things within the limited confines of the wagon was legendary.

Percy and I usually encountered others down at the stream

completing the same task, but I must have spent too long waiting for him because I was alone. The solitude didn't bother me unduly, though. The moonlight and the campfires behind me combined to provide enough illumination, and guards patrolled the outside circle of camp constantly. I only had to call, and one of them would be with me.

I washed quickly anyway, however. If I didn't make it back before Lilah reemerged, she would be angry with me for having gone alone. The water made my task easier, flowing with more strength than many of the smaller creeks we had camped beside on other nights.

A rustle in the bushes to one side of the stream made me freeze. I must have been more on edge than I'd realized. Peering in the direction of the sound, I could make out nothing. I didn't want to call for a guard, only to discover it had been the wind or some small forest animal. My cheeks flushed at the thought of the embarrassment.

I was still staring hard at the offending bush when arms grabbed me from behind, hauling me to my feet. Shock rendered me silent for a moment, and when I finally tried to scream, the arms around my middle had tightened enough that I could produce only a muted sound.

Even so, a rough hand immediately covered my mouth.

"None of that, now," an equally rough voice said.

I struggled, thrashing wildly and trying to kick backward with my heels, but the man holding me stood immovable. A second man slipped out of the bush I had been watching. He strolled over to us as if making a social call, his manner much smoother than my captor's.

"I apologize for the rough methods, Daria," he said. "We just want to talk."

I struggled harder as he began his speech, incensed at the meaningless apology, but I froze when he spoke my name.

"Yes," he said, right in front of me now. "We know who you

are. And we've been watching you ever since you slipped through our hands earlier."

I remained still, trying to control the churning in my gut and think what to do. Surely there must be a way for me to break free.

The man must have read my intention in my eyes because he sighed. "We really do only want to talk. But I understand why you might have doubts about that after the unfortunate happenings of your last encounter with us."

I narrowed my eyes at him, swinging out my legs for another attempted kick.

"If you come with us, I swear it will be entirely different. Whatever rumors you've heard, they aren't true. Prince Damon is the rightful heir of Rangmere—his father was older than Queen Ava's father, you know. All he's been trying to do is reclaim his rightful position. But as soon as he made himself known, the royalty of the Four Kingdoms turned against him."

I tried to speak, muffled mumblings coming out as I thrashed again. I had more than rumors to go on where Damon was concerned—I had been attacked by his men myself, twice now.

"Desperate times call for desperate strategies, you know." The man flicked a glance toward the camp, and I willed one of the guards to appear.

No one did, however.

"Prince Damon was shocked to discover that after bringing you all this way, Princess Giselle just cast you aside. And both Eliam and Arcadia left you to fend for yourself. He feels responsible that you got unintentionally caught up in his conflict with the other royals—although he never imagined they would abandon you so."

I stared at him, too shocked by his words to struggle for a moment. A look of satisfaction greeted my stillness. He must think his words were finding roost.

"We've seen how you're used here among the merchants," he

continued. "Overworked like a common servant. Prince Damon wants to offer you the chance to be part of making a new world —one that has a place for someone like you." A nasty grin spread across his face. "Revenge on those who abandoned you is only a bonus."

I continued to stare at him. Revenge? If I had reason to want revenge, it was against his master who had driven me here.

Oblivious to my thoughts, the man commanded my captor to let me talk. I took a breath, relieved to have my airways clear again, and ready to give him a piece of my mind. Before I could actually speak, however, a loud, wordless whinny broke the night.

Arvin burst out of the camp, rearing at the sight of us. Both men pulled back, cursing and dragging me with them. I began to thrash again.

"Hold still, Dee!" Percy's voice called.

Arvin moved, revealing the prince, bow drawn and eyes fixed on us. I froze.

His arrow flew true, burying itself in the leg of my captor. The man swore again and thrust me away from him, apparently not committed enough to the abduction effort to ignore an arrow in the leg.

Caught by surprise, I staggered forward. The other man leaped to catch me by the shoulders.

"We won't have another chance to come for you before you reach the city," he said in a hurried whisper. "If you tell no one and come alone to the small eastern gate at sunset tomorrow evening, you can still join Damon. At sunset, mind. No later."

Arvin charged at us, and the man let me go, diving out of the way. He moved in the direction of the bush from earlier, retrieving a small, shallow canoe from behind it.

The injured man had drawn a sword and was barely holding Percy off. But at sight of the canoe, he abandoned the effort and threw himself into the boat. Before any of us could respond, the water had swept them both away.

Percy leaped forward to the bank, peering after the vanishing canoe. "Could we catch them, Arvin?" he called over his shoulder.

For once the horse didn't have a glib response. He trotted over to join Percy, looking at the water and then down the stream in a measuring way.

If it were only a matter of speed, yes. But further down, the trees and underbrush grow right up to the stream bank. Unless you have a boat handy, I think they're gone.

Percy groaned. "Escaped again. This is infuriating." He looked at me, fear replacing his anger. "Thank goodness Arvin has such good hearing. When he told me you were in trouble, I feared—"

"The Traitor Prince again?" Ariana's Guardsmaster reached us at a sprint, a clump of guards trailing behind him.

Percy shook his head. "Not this time. But two of his followers, I've no doubt." He looked at me. "Did they say…"

"Yes, they were his followers." I hesitated. "They wanted to take me to him."

The Caravan Bryant Guardsmaster, arriving belatedly, ground out an oath. "A last desperate try before we reach the capital. I don't like this new tactic of targeting our girls. Not one bit."

The Hargrove Guardsmaster frowned at me. "What's your name? Dee, isn't it? If I'm not getting mixed up, you've been at the center of two of these attacks now. You've a talent for being in the wrong place, do you?"

"Not generally, sir." I tried to ignore the cold sensation washing over me.

He frowned. "Did I hear someone saying you're a newcomer to Caravan Bryant?"

Our Guardsmaster rubbed his hand along his chin. "Wouldn't call Dee new. And she's never given any trouble."

"Not like that sister of hers," one of the other guards muttered.

The Guardsmaster ignored him. "She's Lilah's oldest, and Lilah has been with us for near fifteen years now. It's common enough for the children of traveling merchants to do a stint with more settled relatives while they're young."

The Hargrove Guardsmaster sighed. "Oh, aye, that it is. No offense meant."

I tried to ignore how much interest Percy was showing in this conversation. Did he have the same questions that had clearly been raised in the mind of the other caravan's Guardsmaster?

"You may ask anyone from Caravan Bryant about my older daughter," Lilah said in her coldest voice, appearing behind the massed guards.

"I've just been telling him, Lilah." Our Guardsmaster spoke in his most placating tones.

She marched forward and seized me by the arm, eyeing the area around the stream apprehensively, despite the presence of so many guards.

"And are you sure the rest of the campsite is safe?"

"I've extra guards checking all approaches, ma'am," the Hargrove Guardsmaster said. "You can be sure they'll raise a hue and cry if anything is found."

"Thank you," Lilah said with dignity. "I'll be glad to have the walls of the city around me for once. As will we all, no doubt. Now, if you'll excuse us, my daughter has been through quite enough for one night."

She put her arm around me and led me away. I threw a look back over my shoulder, locking eyes with Percy. But I didn't pull away from her hold. Everything had happened too fast, and I was still too overwhelmed by the words of Damon's messenger to know what I should say. If I told them the truth, would they suspect me of being allied with him somehow?

As soon as we were out of earshot, Lilah glared at me.

"What were you thinking? You know better than to go off alone like that! I was worried sick when I heard the guards shouting about the Traitor Prince seizing a girl again. You'd disappeared off, and I feared you were dead!"

She had worked herself up to a crescendo by the final word, stopping only to draw a much-needed breath.

"I'm sorry," I said, feeling impossibly small. "I thought I could do the dishes quickly and be back before anyone noticed I was gone. I didn't mean to cause any trouble."

"You can't go wandering off like that on your own! It's bad enough trying to keep an eye on Tallie without you trying to slip away as well."

"I'm sorry," I repeated, rubbing at my head.

When had the giant headache started forming? My heart still hadn't settled to its normal rhythm, and I shivered whenever I remembered the helpless feeling of being held immobile.

Lilah's anger melted off her face, replaced with a look of warm sympathy.

"You poor thing. I'll warrant you learned that lesson without any lecturing from me."

"Oh!" I cried, twisting to look behind us. "The dishes! I left them back by the stream."

"Never mind them. One of those guards will bring them back. And if they don't, we can do without them." Lilah shuddered. "None of us are going near that stream or the edge of camp again. We'll finally be safely off the road tomorrow, and we're not stirring away from our wagon until then."

She didn't stop fussing until she had me tucked in bed, Tallie peppering me with questions the entire time. The headache had blossomed into a pounding pain, and it was all I could do not to speak sharply to her.

Finally I was left alone, darkness enfolding me. At last I was free to think and to remember.

Damon didn't realize I had chosen to stay hidden. He thought

I had been abandoned by the royals who brought me over to these kingdoms. And he didn't understand the complicated bonds of gratitude, loyalty, and love which bound me to my new family. He thought I had been forced to seek a role as an over-worked servant—and that I must hate my previous companions as a result.

Damon would never hesitate to seize anything he believed his, no matter the risk or cost. And, in consequence, he couldn't fathom the idea I had remained here by choice. He believed I must have been cast off.

I shook my head against my soft pillow. He judged me by himself and came to entirely the wrong conclusion. But he had also told me how to contact him. I had to tell Percy about those final whispered words.

Discomfort filled me. What would he do with the information? Would he go to the gate himself and try to force the gate-keeper to take him to Damon?

A new thought sent ice cascading down my spine. Would he want me to go? To enact the charade Damon thought was real? Would I be asked to play the role of double agent?

It took all my control to keep my breathing even and pretend the peace of sleep for the other occupants of the wagon. I remained loyal to my friends, both old and new, but I wanted nothing to do with Damon. I couldn't take on such a role.

But how would I refuse if they asked? Maybe it was better if I didn't tell them the truth, after all.

CHAPTER 12

Twice in the night, I woke up panting, my blankets twisted around me and my mind full of a dream where I had gone to Damon to discover his plans only for him to announce it had all been a trap. Both times I woke up as he pointed a sword at my heart.

But in the light of day, I couldn't believe Damon would go to such an elaborate ploy just to kill me. If death was his aim, he could have delivered it by the stream when I was caught unaware.

Despite that certainty, however, I couldn't consider the idea of obeying his whispered instructions without a churning in my belly so severe I could only keep my breakfast in place through sheer force of will. I tried telling myself I might gain useful information that could save many lives, but it didn't matter. My body wouldn't cooperate.

At first I had little opportunity to dwell on the matter, caught up in the usual routine of breaking camp and getting on the road. Everything had to be done at double speed as the camp buzzed to be on the move—the attack of the night before adding extra tension to what would already have been an exciting day. We should pass through the gates of Rangmeros by midday.

The events of the night before had almost entirely eclipsed my eagerness to see the city, but a small seed of that earlier interest remained. Lilah still refused to tell me how the gray city had changed, and I hoped the sight of it would drive away some of the sick feeling that made it hard to concentrate.

All through the morning preparations, every time I turned around, I nearly tripped over Lilah. Despite the need for haste, everything seemed to take twice as long, and we kept a whole section of wagons waiting while we finished harnessing the horses.

"I'm not letting you out of my sight," Lilah said any time I looked the least bit frustrated at her nearness, and not even Tallie protested this statement. If fear was contagious, we had all caught it, and we clung together as if we were each other's only safe harbor from the storm around us.

But when it came time to climb onto the front seat of the wagon, Lilah shook her head.

"I want you two safely inside the wagon. Out of sight."

"It's so stuffy in there," Tallie complained, but her words lacked heat. I could read the indecision on her face, as her eyes darted around the campsite. The second attack had shaken her almost worse than the first, despite her lack of participation.

"Safety is more important than comfort," Lilah said firmly. "In the back." She hesitated. "Why don't you invite Aida to join you?"

Tallie instantly brightened at that suggestion, calling loudly to her friend who came bounding over eagerly. She always preferred to ride with us over riding with her younger siblings, And her parents were happy to pass her added weight over to our horses to pull.

The two girls clambered in the back, already chattering almost too fast to follow. I sighed and put my foot on the step. As I did, I looked up and saw Percy trotting past on Arvin. He didn't see me, but the horse gave me a look I swore was full of contempt.

I hesitated.

Just as I was debating whether to put in the effort of fighting Lilah, a spear of sunlight hit the wagon and the tree beside us, causing a bird to break into riotous song.

I took my foot down from the step. It was a glorious day, and I refused to be cooped up inside.

Straightening my spine, I walked around to the front of the wagon.

"I'm riding with you," I told Lilah.

She shook her head. "I need to know you're both safe. And that means being out of sight of Damon and his despicable followers."

I ignored her words and climbed up to sit beside her. She treated me like a child, and I usually let her. But I wasn't one, and I refused to give way on this point.

"I'll be safe enough here. With you."

I put a little emphasis on the final words, and she hesitated. Examining my determined face, she sighed.

"Very well. If you insist."

"I do."

She smiled, although it didn't quite reach the worry in her eyes. "In truth, I'll be glad enough for the company."

"I couldn't miss my first view of Rangmeros. Especially after you were so cruel as to refuse to describe it to me."

My reminder of our earlier conversation brought a real smile to her face. She chuckled.

"I keep forgetting you've never been there. It's an interesting city, and I'll be curious to see what you make of it."

The long caravan began to move, the sound of straining horses and turning wheels slowly making its way down the line until it was our turn. I tipped my face up to the sun, closing my eyes and breathing deeply of the fresh air. I had made the right decision being out here.

For the first little while we didn't talk, Lilah's attention focused on the team. They were always frisky first thing in the morning.

We soon left the trees behind us, coming out into open ground. Immediately, the cliff Lilah had mentioned seized my attention, dominating the scene. I stared at it in awe, acknowledging the genius of whoever had chosen to build Rangmeros at its foot. Not only did it provide an impregnable defense for one side of the city, but it created an overawing impression. Rangmere had always been known for its strength, and nothing communicated that impression more effectively than that cold, gray stone, looming over everything and everyone.

"The castle is flush against the rock," Lilah said quietly. "Almost as if it's an extension of the cliff itself."

I shivered suddenly, although the sun was still warm. "I'm glad I didn't come here back in King Josef's day. I don't think I would have liked Rangmeros then."

Lilah bit her lip. "If Prince Damon succeeds in claiming the throne, something tells me the city could end up just like it used to be."

"But surely that won't happen." I looked sideways at her. "Queen Ava is strong and well-liked, isn't she?"

"In general, yes. But there are always those who resist change. Damon started with only a few followers from that island of his, but his forces have grown large enough that they've resisted two years of attempts to squash them."

Guilt surged through me in response to her words. When had I ever hesitated to do what was right—or to help others?

Since you let your fear rule you, a small voice inside me whispered. *Just like Lilah does.*

I gazed ahead at the magnificent cliff, shining with reflected sunlight. I would have missed this incredible introduction to the city if I had cowered in the wagon like Lilah wanted. And I had nearly done it, too. Fear was contagious, and I had let Lilah's concerns amplify my own.

Damon assumed I had been abandoned because he couldn't imagine I would choose to hide here for two years. And sitting here in the sunlight, it was increasingly hard to remember just why I hadn't told Lilah and Tallie the truth about myself long ago. After two years, I knew I could trust them.

What had happened to me?

I could still remember so vividly my fear in the forest when I had been driven away from my traveling companions. It had been a valid response at the time and had lent me the strength to escape. But it had found a mirror in Lilah, and the more time passed, the more I let my fear control me.

Percy had said he felt fear, but he chose not to let it rule him. I had been doing the opposite. The longer I gave in to my fear, the stronger it grew—and the more power it had over me. If I didn't stop its growth, I would miss the rest of my life, cowering in the back of a wagon.

I wouldn't think about all the horrifying things that could go wrong in the future. I would think of Percy. He had shown himself to be caring and compassionate. He could be trusted.

I would tell him the instructions Damon had sent for me, and together we would work out what was best to be done. I didn't know enough about the efforts being made against Damon to make such a momentous decision on my own.

Contrary to my expectation, the churning in my center calmed at this decision. Fresh certainty that I was doing the right thing filled me.

The unexpected buoyant feeling carried me the rest of the way to the wide city gates. We were clearly expected because we didn't stop, waved through by the guards without pause.

Other travelers scattered to either side to make room for us, some even going so far as to cheer and call friendly greetings.

Traveling merchant caravans were always well-received with our load of fresh wares, news, and interesting stories from far-away places.

When we visited towns and villages, we camped just outside, using the same arrangement as we did on the road. But there was nowhere in a city like this for such a large camp. Instead our wagons were to be stored in several large warehouses co-opted for our use by the Rangmeran crown. From the rumors going around the caravan, the royals were eager to accommodate us, fearful of the results if we chose to place the blame for Damon's attacks at their feet.

Two inns had also been booked for our use, with Caravan Bryant to occupy the smaller one. As we passed through the gates, my thoughts turned to a proper bed and a hot bath, and I gave a soft sigh of anticipated pleasure.

As was to be expected with a city dominated by such a cliff, Rangmeros gave off a strong impression of gray stone, sharp edges, and ordered squares. But as I glanced around, I blinked, confusion creasing my brow.

"The residents are very fond of yellow," I said slowly, my eyes lingering on the many window boxes overflowing with almost exclusively yellow flowers. Another flash of yellow caught my eye as someone threw open a set of shutters, and a brightly painted yellow door further down the street banged closed in the wake of a small child.

Even the many central squares had yellow touches on the large fountains where women congregated to wash laundry, and the children playing an unfamiliar game in the square beside them were doing so with a yellow ball.

Lilah laughed. "Just wait."

I frowned at her, but before I could press her for an explanation of the strange phenomenon, we passed some sort of invisible delineation. Suddenly the window boxes were full of red.

I gaped around me at the smattering of red doors and roofs. "What does it signify?"

Lilah laughed again. "The city used to be all gray, or nearly all. But it's divided into six equal rectangles, and the different districts have always been known by color names. The Red District—where we are now—houses the military, for instance, and the merchants are found in the Green District. A few years after Queen Ava came to power, some shopkeepers in the Yellow District decided to decorate according to their color. The trend grew, and now the whole city is like this." She gestured around her. "Everyone is very proud of the district they hail from, and the king and queen have encouraged the move by instituting annual games."

"It's certainly unusual." I shook my head, unsure what I thought of the uniform color of the decorations. "I didn't recognize that game the children were playing in the last square. Is that what they play at these games?"

She nodded. "It's called quickball and has always been something of an obsession in Rangmere. I'm sure you could find plenty of children willing to teach you, if you want to learn." Her good cheer suddenly fell away, and she continued hurriedly on. "Not that now is a good time to be wandering around the city and talking to strangers, of course. Some other time, perhaps."

I said nothing, turning my gaze to the other side of the road so she wouldn't see the twist to my mouth. Her words only strengthened my determination. Fear would swallow my life if I let it.

Our path led us from the Red District into the Purple District where the subtle touches of color were noticeably less intrusive. Lilah explained the district contained the city residences of most of the Rangmeran nobles—the reason for the less garish decoration. This district grew out from the palace, but we turned right, instead of left, making our way to warehouses just inside the Green District.

The caravan guards took on a new role, directing the wagons as we maneuvered into the space one by one, unharnessing our horses and leading them out while the guards pushed the wagons into their places in neat lines. Caravan Bryant had never performed such an operation before, but it was clear from watching the Hargrove guards and drivers that they were more familiar with the exercise. No doubt most of their trade routes included the capital cities.

We didn't have far to go to reach the inns assigned for our use, which was fortunate given the amount of dashing back and forth being done as people realized they had forgotten this or that necessary article from their wagon.

Lilah oversaw Tallie and my hurried packing, warning us in stern tones that she would not be giving us permission to come back from the safety of the inn.

"But aren't we safe now?" Tallie asked. "We've reached the city."

Lilah frowned. "Cities have their own dangers—ones neither of you are used to."

I bit my lip to stop myself reminding her I had lived sixteen years before I joined Caravan Bryant and had some familiarity with large cities—and their dangers.

"Besides," she added. "The Traitor Prince is aiming to seize Rangmeros for his own. We're not out of the conflict yet."

I grimaced. No, I was far from out of it. But unlike Lilah, I wasn't willing to hide away anymore.

But before I could do anything else, I had to find Percy.

CHAPTER 13

As we walked to our assigned inn and waited to be shown to the room the three of us would share, I tried to spot Percy in the chaos of moving people. I saw no sign of him, however.

Excited members of Caravan Bryant filled the building, milling around in the common spaces and exclaiming over the rooms and the city itself. But I quickly realized not only Percy, but his men as well, were missing. When Lilah dragged us along to the attached stables when she went to check on our horses, I went readily. But I could see no sign of Arvin among the stalls.

Reluctantly I accepted that Percy and his men were no longer attached to Caravan Bryant. They must be housed with the inn holding the members of Hargrove.

I was still determined to speak with him, but the task would now be considerably more complicated. If only I'd seized the opportunity while we were all camped together. But everything had happened so quickly, I hadn't had time to think.

My concern grew as we ate our midday meal. I was too distracted to even appreciate the luxury of being served by the inn waiters. The clock on the wall ticked unnaturally loudly as the minutes slipped away. *Tonight*, the man had said. If we were going to make use of the information, someone needed to be at the eastern gate tonight.

Most of the other merchants were making plans to explore the city, their worries apparently lifted by the solid gray walls surrounding Rangmeros. When Lilah remained firm in the face of Tallie's pleading to be allowed to accompany Aida's family to a local market, I knew it was no use my saying I intended to visit the other inn alone.

I would have to slip away.

The goal was easier set than accomplished. Given Tallie's sulks, Lilah was alert, afraid she meant to sneak out while her back was turned. I could have left in the face of her protests, of course—she could hardly physically constrain me. But the last thing I wanted was to make a scene—especially after being at the center of both the recent attacks.

My opportunity came when Isambard finally arrived at the inn after accompanying Ariana to the palace for an audience with Queen Ava and King Hans. Everyone clustered around him, full of questions, most seeming cheered by the broad smile on his face.

"We've arrived in good timing," he said loudly to the packed dining room. "The palace is hosting a series of balls in honor of Lady Isabella's eighth birthday. The first is tonight, a masquerade —and every merchant from both caravans is invited!"

A great cheer went up followed by the loud hubbub of many excited voices exclaiming at once.

"Who is Lady Isabella?" I asked, but Tallie spoke over the top of me, focused on a more important question.

"We can go, can't we, Mother? Please tell me we can go!"

"Well…" Lilah hesitated alarmingly. "I can't see the harm. I'm sure it will be a select event and well guarded."

"And now we *have* to visit the markets," Tallie pressed. "We don't have shoes to wear to a ball!"

"What do you mean you don't have shoes?" Lilah asked. "Your dancing shoes were new only this year."

"I can't wear those!" Tallie cried. "Not to a royal ball in a palace. I need proper dancing slippers."

Merchant dances were always held outdoors, so even the most elaborate gown was worn with a pair of sensible shoes. Lilah glanced at the other merchants, most of whom were now discussing plans to visit local shops in search of items our own caravan couldn't supply—like dancing slippers. Fifteen-year-olds weren't the only ones who wanted to look their best for a ball.

"I suppose a short visit would be safe enough."

Tallie whooped and went speeding off to tell Aida.

I saw my opportunity. "I don't need to go. I'm happy to wear my normal dance shoes." I looked at Lilah. "That way you can keep your focus on Tallie. I'm sure she'll enjoy the time with you."

Lilah looked uncertain. "Are you sure?"

I nodded. "Go and enjoy yourselves."

She looked like she wanted to ask more questions, but Tallie reappeared, seizing her arm and babbling away about shops and shoes and jewelry.

"You're not sixteen yet, my girl," Lilah said. "You don't need jewelry. Some ribbons to wind through your braids will be perfectly sufficient."

"But Mother…"

"When you are old enough for jewelry, I'll design you some pieces myself."

Tallie accepted this peace offering, and the two of them moved away, pulled toward Aida by Tallie's insistent tugging.

Merchants poured out of the room, rushing to complete the various preparations they considered necessary for such an unusual event. Isambard looked slightly bemused at the effect of his announcement but also pleased to see the caravan's spirits restored. I turned to him with my original question.

"Who is Lady Isabella? Did you say she was turning eight? She must be important if she's getting an entire series of balls. She can't be Queen Ava's daughter because I'm sure the princess's name is Ellery."

At such close range, the worry lines on the caravan leader's face looked deeper than before, but he still projected an air of confidence and security. Solidly built, the older man wasn't much taller than me, but he gave an impression of much greater height. He smiled at me, erasing the underlying impression that he carried a heavy burden.

"Yes, Queen Ava's daughter is Princess Ellery. Isabella is the oldest child of the Earl and Countess of Lander. But the countess is also Princess Clarisse of Lanover, and before her marriage to the earl, she was married to Ava's older brother, Prince Konrad. So she's the queen's sister-in-law—in a way."

"Prince Konrad died before Ava ascended the throne, didn't he?" I asked, trying to make sense of this information. Damon claimed he was the true heir of Rangmere, but his claim came from his father, not from Prince Konrad.

Isambard hesitated and then nodded. "Not that the prince would have needed to die in order for her coronation to proceed. In Rangmere, the heir is chosen not through birth order but through the Monarchy Trials. After the death of the previous monarch, his sons are given the opportunity to register their claim to the throne. If more than one does so, they hold the Trials and crown the winner."

"Only princes? But you said it wasn't his death that won Ava the throne?"

"Well, it used to be only princes," Isambard amended. "Not that it will make a difference either way in this generation. Princess Ellery is an only child."

"And what about the Traitor Prince?" I asked, still struggling to remember the details of the Rangmeran royal family tree. "Why does he claim a right to the throne?"

Isambard frowned. "He has no right to the throne. He never

competed in the Trials—and he would never have been granted the opportunity to challenge Konrad and Ava regardless. He bases his claim on his father, Prince Friedrich, being King Josef's older brother. But King Josef won the Trials in their generation, and as victor he chose the fate of the losers. One of his brothers died from injuries received during the trial, but Friedrich was banished along with his wife, an Arcadian princess. No one even knew they had a son until he reappeared in the Four Kingdoms two years ago. He is not a lost heir—however much he might try to claim such a title."

I raised an eyebrow. One of them had died? It suddenly made all too much sense why Queen Ava had chosen to have only one child—an unusual decision for a monarch, especially one without living siblings.

But if I was faced with a tradition that would pit my children against each other in such a way, I would probably only have one as well.

"So Lady Isabella is a sort of substitute cousin for the young princess, I suppose," I said. "And by honoring her, they honor her mother—a Lanoverian princess. That makes more sense."

Isambard nodded. "Princess Ellery is only a year or so younger than Princess Clarisse's daughter, and I've heard they are close friends. Apparently the two had been promised a trip to Lanover for Lady Isabella's seventh birthday. But the trip has been delayed for two years now due to the unrest caused by Damon."

"Ah!" I grinned. "Now the extravagance of a series of balls makes a great deal more sense. Disappointed children must be handled gently."

Isambard shook his head. "My poor children were consoled with sugar cakes, I'm afraid. I never offered them anything half so grand as a ball."

"Maybe they would have loved you more if you did."

He barked a laugh. "I like you, Dee. I always have."

"Thank you, sir. I've always appreciated the welcome I received from Caravan Bryant."

Someone called for his attention from the other side of the room, and he departed with a nod and a smile. I watched him go. I didn't know what would happen after I told Percy about Damon's message, but the impending sense of change had strengthened. Caravan Bryant would eventually leave Rangmeros, but I was no longer sure I would be with it.

I shook off the suddenly melancholy mood when I realized I was the last one in the room. The afternoon was slipping away, and I needed to get moving.

I waved as Lilah and Tallie left for their shopping expedition, busying myself by laying out my nicest gown and my sensible dancing shoes. I didn't know how long I would be gone, and I might need to prepare for the ball in a hurry.

As soon as they were safely away, I searched out the innkeeper to request directions to the inn housing Caravan Hargrove. To my relief, the inn was close and the directions simple. I could only hope Percy would be easy to find once I reached it.

I hurried through the streets, calling an occasional greeting to fellow merchants on their way to or from one of the inns. When I arrived, however, I found the building almost as deserted as ours. Apparently the invitation had already been delivered here as well.

After roaming through the common rooms without any sign of Percy or any of his men, I stood in the inn yard, biting my lip. It was possible they were in private rooms. I eyed the large building of gray stone, enlivened with green shutters and a creeping vine. It was certainly large enough that the prince might be accommodated in a separate section.

With a sigh, I went back inside, looking for someone who might know about room allocations. The first person I encountered was a maid.

"Do you know which room Percy is in?" I asked. "And if he's here at the moment?"

"Percy?" She frowned. "I don't know everyone's names, sorry. You'd need to ask the caravan leader or one of the other merchants."

"He's not a merchant." I flushed a little. "He's actually a prince. He was just traveling with the caravan. Prince Percival of Talinos."

She raised an eyebrow, running her eyes up and down my unimpressive form. "Prince Percival? I don't know how such things are handled on the road, but here in Rangmeros our inns don't host princes." She shook her head. "His Highness will have rooms up at the palace, of course."

"The palace?" I stared at her blankly. "But I need to talk to him."

The eyebrow climbed even higher. "I wouldn't know anything about that, miss."

"No, of course..." I thanked her as quickly as I could, hurrying away before she could give me any more judging looks. Out in the sunshine, I mentally berated myself.

Of course Percy was up at the palace. I had forgotten for a moment he wasn't really one of us. He had joined us for a period on the road, but now we had reached Rangmeros, he had resumed the place appropriate to his station.

I thrust away the personal sting, unwilling to examine it when the sun was sinking lower and lower in the sky. Damon's sunset deadline was looming closer, and there was no time for self-reflection. I would have to go to the palace.

Finding my way was easy enough, since the castle was by far the largest building in the city. But with each step I trudged through the Purple District, my concern grew. Would I be turned away at the gate?

When I arrived, however, I soon realized I had been worried about the wrong thing. A parade of people moved freely in and out of the palace gates, busy on various errands for the ball that night. I slipped in among them without hindrance.

But once I was inside the courtyard of the castle, I discovered the gate had only been the first hurdle. People hurried everywhere, intent on tasks that gave them direction and purpose while I stood lost and confused. No one stopped to speak to me—a good thing since I had no idea what to say to anyone who did. None of these people would know about the housing arrangements of royal guests.

The enormous double doors of the main entrance would no doubt be thrown open for the ball itself, but for now they were firmly closed. After eyeing them for a few moments, I followed the flow of traffic around to the side of the building.

Deliveries were being made to a side entrance, and not knowing what else to do, I joined the line. A porter stood guard at the doorway, receiving the goods and marking them off against a long list before directing the delivery people where to go.

When I reached the door, he kept his eyes on his list.

"Your delivery?"

"Ah…I'm not making a delivery." I fumbled my words, feeling awkward and out of place.

The man looked up, his brows lowering. "Not making a delivery? This is the delivery entrance."

"I'm sorry," I said quickly. "I wasn't sure where else to go. I need to see a palace guest."

"A guest?" He looked me up and down. "If you're expected, then you'll be greeted at the main door."

I shook my head. "No, I'm not expected, but I need to speak to Prince Percival. I'm one of the invited guests tonight—from the merchant caravan. He's been traveling with us."

At my mention of the prince, the man gave a similar look of surprise to the maid at the inn, his eyes communicating doubt at my story. I reached for the leather cord around my neck, but before I could pull out my traveling merchant token as proof of my identity, he spoke again in a politely neutral tone.

"If you're invited to the ball, you'll have a chance to talk to His Highness this evening."

"But I need to speak to him before the ball!" I tried not to allow my voice to become heated, knowing it would only work against me. "It's important." I resisted looking up at the sinking sun.

"This isn't the entrance for guests," the man said. "I can't help you."

When I didn't move, he gave me a pointed stare, gesturing at the line of people now building up behind me. For a moment, I stayed, considering blurting out that I had valuable information about Prince Damon.

But after a moment, I shook my head and stepped away. If I mentioned the Traitor Prince, I might get an audience with Percy —but I might just as easily be arrested under suspicion of being in league with Damon and be required to tell my story to some unknown guard captain. And given the nature of my information, it was only likely to confirm any theory about my being in league with the Traitor Prince. I needed to find another way to get to Percy.

Snow's palace back in Eliam was much easier to access than this rectangular block pressed against a cliff, but there was one door that was always open. And I suspected I would find it open here in Rangmere as well.

Hurrying around the building, I watched the people around me closely. One man appeared to be carrying sacks of flour, so I fell into step behind him.

Clearly familiar with the palace, he proceeded directly to a sturdy wooden door which he thrust open with one foot. I slipped in behind him, entering a bustling kitchen, hot from an entire wall of roaring fires.

For a moment, I stood immobile, overwhelmed at the level of

chaos reigning in here. Chefs, cook's assistants, scullery maids, pastry chef's apprentices, and messenger boys all hurried from bench to bench, calling to each other in loud voices and carrying heavily laden trays and bowls.

The delivery man didn't pause, however, instead launching into a defensive speech as he dumped his load on the one bare stretch of bench remaining. From his various voluble excuses—given to the room at large—his delivery was late. The tardiness of the flour must be the reason he had been sent directly to the kitchen and not to some storeroom somewhere.

An authoritative woman appeared, her hair pulled tightly back under a white hat and her face in a scowl.

"I've no time for excuses today. Where's the rest of it?"

"I'll bring it directly, but it'll take a few loads. They wouldn't let me pull my cart all the way up."

"As well you might have expected on a day like today. If you'd brought it two days ago, like you promised…No, don't start in on your excuses again. Just get me my flour." Without pausing for breath, she swung her head toward me. "And you, get out of my kitchen!"

Taken by surprise, I gaped at her. "I just—"

"I don't care what you *just*, you're not doing it in my kitchen. Not today! Don't you know we have a ball tonight? I said no one in my kitchen who doesn't belong here, and I meant it."

"Very well, then." I strode forward, aiming for a door I could see on the other side of the room and trying to look like I belonged. But a burly arm appeared to bar my passage.

"Out the way you came!" the head cook said from behind the apprentice who had blocked my path. "We're not a thoroughfare either! I said no one, and I meant no one!"

With no other choice, I fled back outside, mumbling my apologies. How many people had tried to raid the delicacies being prepared for the ball? Too many, judging by the state of the head cook. Clearly she didn't miss a thing going on in her kitchen, so there was no hope I would find a passage through there.

The stream of delivery people entering the palace courtyard had slowed to a trickle, and I realized with a start that the sun was now below the level of the city walls. How much longer did I have until sunset?

Dread gripped me. Not long enough. Even if I could somehow force my way into the palace—and I still didn't know how to do that—I would never locate Percy in time to tell him the story and formulate a plan. If only he had been at the inn.

My mind filled with an image of his disappointment and frustration each time Damon slipped through his fingers. Percy saw more in me than I had ever seen in myself, and here was an opportunity for me to be of real use to him. I couldn't fail him now.

If there wasn't time to talk to Percy, then I would have to go myself. I would offer to be a double agent for Damon and convince him to tell me his plans. And then I would get back inside the city as quickly as I could.

I didn't give myself time to think about it, turning my feet east instead and running through the city streets—racing the sun.

PART II
THE TRAITOR PRINCE

CHAPTER 14

*I*t took me too long to find my way through the
unfamiliar city, and I had to stop twice to ask directions. By the time the eastern gate came in sight, I was sprinting.
Unable to see the sun on the horizon behind the barrier of the
wall, I couldn't be sure I had made it in time.

When I reached the gate, I doubled over, panting as I braced
my hands on my knees. No one guarded the gate, and I glanced
wildly left and right. Was I too late? Where was the guard?

Just as I was wishing Damon's man had given me more information, a voice spoke.

"Daria."

It wasn't a question, but I nodded anyway, peering into the
space where a building crowded up against the wall. A man
stepped out of the shadows.

"Is it sunset yet?" I asked. "Did I make it in time?"

"You cut it close." He hitched the bag he carried higher on his
shoulder. "I was about to leave." His brow, already lowered, knit
further. "No bag?"

I straightened, trusting to my exhaustion from my recent
exertion to hide the signs of my terror. "I don't expect I'll be gone

long. I'm sure Prince Damon wants me back here to serve as his agent—if not, I don't see what use I can be to him."

Pride at my calm, level tone helped keep my legs from buckling as the man opened the gate and gestured for me to precede him out of the city. I slipped out, turning to watch him close it again.

"Is it usually left unlocked?" I asked doubtfully. I just hoped there wasn't a dead guard stashed in the shadows somewhere.

The man grunted. "Not usually. And no doubt it will be locked again momentarily when the new guard shift arrives."

I licked my lips. "What happened to the old shift?"

"You're looking at him." He strode away, and I scrambled to catch up. "My sergeant started to get suspicious, so it was time for me to get out of the city. I would have left yesterday if..." He glanced back at me, and I guessed I had been the cause of the delay.

"Do we have far to go?" I asked, moving at an awkward half-trot to keep up with his fast pace.

He merely grunted, and I subsided, not wanting to push him too far. I soon realized we were heading for a small copse of trees, and as soon as we stepped beneath the branches, whickers gave away the presence of two horses.

Damon's man didn't ask if I knew how to ride, tossing me up into the saddle without a word. With efficient movements, he attached my horse to his with a leading line, before mounting himself.

Neither of us spoke as we cantered across the remaining open ground. Earlier that day I had approached the city from the south, but now we headed directly east into the foothills of the vast mountain range that curved around the top of the kingdom.

But the horses had barely started climbing uphill when we plunged into a deep layer of trees. Minutes later, we broke out into a large clearing, and I gasped aloud.

Spread out before me, and reaching back into the first few

layers of trees, was a large camp. Ordered rows of tents stretched in every direction, and disciplined soldiers moved among them, engaged in various practical tasks. A single patch of open ground had been left, a group of men using it for training.

I hadn't expected to find so many people—not within such easy reach of the city. The man who was leading me looked back with a satisfied smile and another grunt, obviously pleased with my shock.

"I'm to take you straight to the prince," he said, breaking our long silence.

I nodded, glad nothing was required of me while I processed the initial shock. What had I gotten myself into? If Damon didn't want to let me leave, this wasn't some ramshackle camp I might be able to slip away from. Too late I began to see how rash my decision had been. At the very least, I should have left a note explaining where I had gone and why.

But there was no use thinking of such things now. I would just have to convince Damon I was on his side.

The man led my horse through the camp to the largest tent. It stood at the center of the clearing, flying a flag from its tip as if we stood in a legitimate army encampment.

As soon as we stopped, I slipped down, not wanting to wait for assistance.

"Wait here." The man spoke in a gruff voice, fixing me with a threatening stare.

I shrugged, as if unaffected, and turned to look across the camp in a nonchalant way. If I was facing the other direction, perhaps he wouldn't see the fear on my face.

Almost no time passed before he reappeared, holding open the flap of the tent. "The prince will speak to you now."

I tried to read his expression, but it was neutral, giving nothing away. I tried to tell myself that was a good sign as I walked past him into the tent.

Even though it was past sunset outside, it still took a moment for my eyes to adjust to the dim light inside the canvas walls. A quick glance around showed a substantial table on one side of the large open space, and a basic sleeping pallet on the other with a chest at its foot.

"As you can see, I live like my men," said a suave voice from beside the table. "I am not seeking my own aggrandizement, but merely to prevent the corruption of my kingdom."

"Corruption?" I let the question slip out, wanting to keep him talking in order to gain myself another few moments to calm my racing heart.

"Rangmere is a strong kingdom—we always have been. It's our way. And yet a soft queen sits on our throne, and she is weakening the kingdom with every year that passes." He stepped forward, a contemptuous look twisting his handsome features. "Do you think I would have been able to gather strength and forces for two year under any of the old kings?"

I bit my lip to keep from speaking my thoughts. Probably those old kings had employed brutal tactics against their own people to flush out any traitors. It wasn't weakness to treat your people well.

But while my role called for some skepticism—that was to be expected—I couldn't speak my true thoughts. Damon had apparently forgotten he once sent his men combing the kingdoms for me bearing threats—or perhaps he thought his message had never been received. Either way, he now believed me an ally, and I needed to confirm that impression.

"I don't care about Rangmere," I said boldly, taking a gamble. "I'm just sick of always serving others. I've spent my whole life doing someone else's chores, and I'm ready to give the orders for once." I forced myself to meet his eyes. "Can you offer me that, Traitor Prince?"

He laughed at my taunt. "I can offer you better than that. You help me take my rightful throne, and I'll give you a title and lands of your own. You can have as many servants as you please. How does Countess of Anhalt sound?"

"I'm no soldier." I didn't have to fake the wariness in my voice. "A title will do me no good if I'm dead."

He smiled, the gesture carrying a hint of menace. "As you can see, I have plenty of soldiers. What I want from you is simple enough. The guard I had in place, the one who did shifts at the eastern gate, has had to flee. I need someone else trusted within the city. Someone who can get me past the walls and also into the palace itself."

"I'm only a merchant. I'm not staying at the palace." As my unsuccessful efforts earlier in the afternoon had shown.

His smile widened. "Ah, but I hear you have an invitation to a ball."

My mind raced as we regarded each other for a moment of silence.

"That's all I have to do?" I asked slowly. "I get you into a ball, and I become a countess?"

This time his grin showed all his teeth. "You get me into the palace, I kill the queen, and you become a countess. The ball is only the first step."

It took every bit of discipline I possessed to keep my face bland and agreeable. Years of keeping my true concerns hidden from the children who looked to me for protection came to my rescue now.

"The ball is tonight. Is there really time—"

"The first ball is tonight."

"You're planning your move for one of the other balls? When do you—"

He held up a hand to stop me. "We are alike, you and I, Daria. We have both been wronged by those who owed us their allegiance. But I am not, in general, a trusting man."

I froze, willing my heart not to beat so loudly as I forced myself to continue holding his gaze.

"You sought me out," I said with a suddenly dry mouth.

"And yet..." His smile dropped away. "If I'm going to share my plans with you, I need to know I can trust you. I need you to prove yourself."

"And how am I supposed to do that?"

"I need you to deliver a message for me."

"A message?" I frowned. "A message to who?"

"You go to the ball tonight, and you tell Queen Ava she has two weeks to abdicate her throne to me or I will take it—over her and her family's bodies."

I stared at him. "I can't just walk up to the queen and deliver such a message! I'll be locked away—and then what good can I do you?"

He quirked an eyebrow. "Perhaps you haven't heard that the first ball is to be a masquerade ball. Ava doesn't know you, she won't recognize you behind a mask. Deliver my message, take her signet ring as proof you spoke to her, and I will have an escape route waiting for you."

I frowned. "That sounds incredibly dangerous."

"It wouldn't be a test if there was no risk." He sounded brisk and businesslike now. "If you want to work with me, you have to prove yourself. There is no other way."

I swallowed, holding back the question on the tip of my tongue. I didn't think I would like the answer if I asked him what would happen next if I refused his request.

"Very well." I drew a deep breath. "I will deliver your message. Where will I find my escape?"

"Look for the man wearing a black band around his arm. He'll be there at midnight. Time your departure for then, or you're on your own. Now go. Your horse is still waiting outside. You'll need to move if you're going to make it to that ball."

He turned away to examine a map on the table in front of him. I dropped a quick curtsy, unsure what sort of protocol he demanded, and hurried for the exit. I had nearly reached it when he spoke again in a deceptively pleasant voice.

"Oh, and Daria, don't think to fool me."

I froze, my hand on the tent flap. When I looked back over my shoulder, his piercing gray eyes were locked on me with terrifying intensity.

"It would be a mistake to think that just because I lack someone to get me close enough to the queen, I also lack eyes at the ball. Fail to deliver my message—or show any signs of betraying me—and I'll know." He paused, the air heavy between us. "And you won't like the consequences."

I nodded once and stepped outside, letting the canvas fall closed behind me. I stopped to draw a single deep breath, but I wasn't safe yet.

The same man who had collected me from the city appeared leading the same mare. He threw me into the saddle in silence, this time handing me the reins.

"They're keeping the city gates open later than usual on account of nobles coming in from surrounding estates for the ball. But you'd better hurry."

"You're not coming with me?"

"I'm done with Rangmeros." He turned away. "For now."

I stared after him, but he was already striding away between two tents. I looked down at the mare's head.

"I guess it's just you and me, girl," I said softly.

She threw her head and whickered, which I interpreted as encouragement. "Come on, then."

I kicked her into motion, and she trotted off into the trees.

CHAPTER 15

$\mathcal{T}$hankfully the city loomed large as soon as I reached open ground. I ignored our previous route, since the eastern gate was presumably now barred to me. When Damon's traitor guard said they were holding the gates open, he must have meant the main ones I had entered that morning with the caravan.

Was it only that morning? It seemed a lifetime ago.

I urged my mare to a gallop, leaning low across her neck and shivering in the wind that whipped across me. The light was almost completely gone now, and we crossed unfamiliar ground, but I didn't dare slow.

Little traffic moved on the main road when I joined it, just short of the city. A carriage traveled ahead of me, lanterns attached to light its way, and a clump of three riders approached from behind, but I was otherwise alone. My horse dropped to a trot as it occurred to me for the first time to wonder what I was to do with her once I was back in the city.

"You're a good girl, aren't you?" I crooned, stroking her mane. "Maybe I can keep you."

I knew I was chattering to keep my frantic, terrified thoughts at bay, but it didn't stop me. I continued to murmur quietly to her until I reached the gates.

With the merchant caravans, I had passed through without hindrance, but this time a guard stepped forward, raising a hand to stop me.

"Halt!" he called, looking behind me as if he expected traveling companions to materialize. "It's after dark. What is your business in Rangmeros?"

"I am come to join my merchant caravan." I clamped down on the urge to babble further explanations. As a traveling merchant, the ancient treaty gave me free passage around the Four Kingdoms. I didn't need to explain myself.

The guard glanced at the other two on duty.

"A traveling merchant, you say?"

"We did have two caravans through this morning," one of the others said, stepping toward me. "You've got your merchant marker, I assume?"

I nodded, pulling on the leather strap and drawing free the smooth, round token. A hole in the middle had been used to attach the strap, and markings designated my caravan, although I doubted these guards knew how to interpret them.

The one who had asked to see it held out his hand, so I slipped the cord over my neck and handed the token to him. He stepped nearer to one of the lanterns which flanked the gate before looking toward his companions and shrugging.

"It's real enough. She's a merchant."

"Let her through, then," the third said. "There's more behind her."

The guard who had examined my token threw it back to me and gestured for me to proceed into the city. I kept my horse to a walk and my bearing relaxed, although inside everything was in tumult. I was starting to see why Damon thought I might be a valuable ally.

As soon as I judged myself safely away from the gate, I pushed my mount to a trot, hoping I could remember the way to our inn. Everything looked different in the dark, but we had followed large enough roads that I managed to retrace our steps without incident.

At the inn, I was saved having to make a decision about the horse when a groom appeared, ready to take her. After a brief hesitation, I let him lead her away without comment. For now he could stable her with the caravan horses. I could worry about what to do with her later.

Given the hour, most of the merchants had already headed to the palace, but a few stragglers were still leaving the inn. They called good-natured teases, telling me to hurry up or I would miss half the ball. I smiled, glad the dark hid the strain on my face. I wouldn't have come back to the inn at all, except I couldn't go to the ball in my dirty, everyday gown.

My mind was fully occupied with the matter of finding a mask when I pushed open the door to our room, so I was unprepared for the sight that greeted me. Lilah stood by the bed, her face more furious than I had ever seen it. I stopped, staring at her, trying to change tracks in my head at lightning pace.

"What are you doing here?" I asked. "Shouldn't you be at the ball already?"

"Shouldn't I be at the ball?" She enunciated each word with frightening force. "I returned from our shopping expedition to find you missing. No one had any idea where you'd gone—and you thought I would simply depart for a ball?"

"I—" My words stuttered out since I could hardly say the words that sprang to my mind. I hadn't thought of her at all.

"Where have you been?" she asked again, with the same unnatural calm.

"I—" Again I didn't get far. I could hardly tell her the truth. If she was like this now, how would she react if she knew the truth of the risk I had taken—and still intended to take?

"Really, Dee?" she asked. "Nothing? You age years off my life, and you don't even have the decency to tell me where you've been? I can see now why you were so eager not to go shopping."

"I'm sorry, Lilah," I finally managed to get out. "I truly didn't mean to worry you. I didn't think I'd be gone so long." She didn't move, and I tried to edge around her. "I need to be getting ready for the ball now, though. Maybe we can talk about this later."

Maybe later I would be able to tell her the whole truth.

"The ball?" She sounded incredulous. "You think I would allow you to go to the ball after this?"

The bed, previously hidden by her body, came into view, and I whirled back to face her.

"My dresses!" I gasped. "What have you done to them?"

"Clearly you cannot be trusted to consider your own safety," she said. "And so I've done what I must to keep you safe. Any mother would do the same."

"You're not my mother!" Fury swept over me. How dare she? But a moment later, a more important thought asserted itself. "I have to go to that ball."

All her anger drained away suddenly, replaced by sadness. She looked at me, and my heart broke.

"I've tried to be a mother to you, Dee. Because I could see you needed one. I suppose I haven't done a very good job if you can treat me like this."

"No. Oh no." I reached out, stepping toward her, but she turned away, stiffening again.

"I must go. Tallie has already gone ahead with Aida and her family, and I must be there to supervise her. We will talk more tomorrow, and I hope by then you'll be more ready to consider your own good."

She swept out of the room, leaving me to stare in dismay at all my nicest dresses, strewn across the bed. Lilah appeared to have taken scissors to them—or perhaps a knife. Either way, they were all now in pieces. Lilah had always been restrictive, but she had never been destructive like this before. The stress of the attacks appeared to have pushed her anxiety to a whole new level.

I sank down onto the bed, fingering one of them blankly. What could I do now? Any pleasure I had anticipated in the ball had vanished hours ago, but Damon had threatened dire consequences if I failed to complete his test. I had to go.

The sadness in Lilah's eyes kept intruding on my thoughts and making it hard to think. How ironic that she had placed me in desperate danger by her efforts to keep me safe. She loved me, in her own way, almost as she did Tallie. Every one of these dresses had been purchased by her and gifted to me after I arrived at her wagon without coins or baggage. She had never once begrudged me anything she gave her own daughter.

A single, deep sob shook me before I gulped and pressed the following ones down. I couldn't cry now. I didn't have time.

I had started down this path, and now I had no choice but to follow it. I had to cling to the hope that good might even come from my choices—as long as I could succeed in the complicated deception before me.

I thought of Percy and his unfailing good humor and kindness, letting my desire to help him refill some of my strength. He had spent two years tracking Damon, and now I had the chance to help him find the fugitive. I could do this. I had to do this.

But when I looked back at the bed, fresh despair washed over me. How could I go to the ball when I had nothing to wear?

A knock on the door startled me into emitting a small squeak. Kicking myself, I jumped up and opened it, peering cautiously into the corridor.

"A parcel for you, miss." The maid bobbed her head, holding out a large, wrapped package.

"For me?" I stared at her.

"Yes, the messenger who came for your horse said you would be waiting for it?"

144

"The messenger who came for my horse?"

She faltered. "You were expecting someone to come for your horse, weren't you?" She looked suddenly concerned that the inn had allowed a brazen thief to escape with my animal.

"Oh. Oh, yes, of course. Sorry. I forgot for a moment..." I let my weak words trail off, but they were enough to bring relief to her face.

She held out the package again, and I took it from her, mystified. Whisking myself back into the room, I closed the door and dropped the parcel on the bed, staring at it.

Someone had come for my horse and left this in her place. It had to be one of Damon's people, of course. No one else even knew about the animal. But what would he have sent me?

Despite myself, curiosity overwhelmed me, and I tore open the wrappings. When I exposed the contents, I gasped. Folded carefully inside, lay a purple satin gown. I lifted it gently to expose a fitted bodice, cap sleeves, and a long flowing skirt. This dress was far, far finer than any of the ones Lilah had destroyed —and it had the added advantage that no one would recognize it.

My hand shook slightly as I placed the gown on the bed and drew out a matching mask of purple satin with black embroidered embellishments. The elegant creation would cover most of my face.

The last item in the package was a long, black cloak. It would cover the dress completely, making sure no one would see me leaving the inn in the distinctive dress.

I shook my head. This hadn't been planned and executed in the last hour. Damon had been confident enough of my acquiescence to set everything in place for my success.

For a long moment I did nothing but breathe. If he had done this, he must also have set in place an escape plan, like he had promised. Ever since I rode away from his camp, I had been debating if I could actually go through with his request. If I told the whole tale to Percy, he would believe me. They could ride out tonight and try to catch Damon.

But Percy had said Damon always had an escape plan. He always melted away like morning mist, no matter how confident they were of capturing him. If I gave Percy the information I had so far, Damon might still escape.

But if I brought him into the palace itself—into a waiting ambush—then there would be no escape. And I could do it. I just had to get him to trust me.

He hadn't actually asked me to hurt anyone. Ava could do without her ring for a night. I would return it to her as soon as I had the chance. If I succeeded, Rangmere would finally be free of Damon.

I would be free of him.

Percy would be free.

I threw myself into action. The only detail Damon appeared to have overlooked was shoes, so I slipped on my old, comfortable dancing pair. When I slid the gown over my head, it fit me like a glove. I shivered, trying not to think about how accurately Damon had estimated my size. I already knew he was having me watched, there was no reason to be worried about it now.

But as I hurried from the inn, the cloak wrapped tightly around me, and the mask tucked away in its folds, I realized with sudden clarity what had caused the surge of discomfort. It wasn't the thought of Damon watching me while we traveled, it was the knowledge that he could reach me here, now. Someone had come for my mount and left me this dress. Someone who knew where to find me, and even what size dress I wore.

Damon had said he would be watching, and if I tried to trick him, I'd be sorry. On some deeper level, I had dismissed his words as bluffing. His guard from the gate was gone, and he needed me to get him inside. Some underlying part of me had thought I would be secure in the palace, whatever I decided to do.

But that layer of comfort was gone now. I couldn't be confident of the games Damon was playing, or who he had under his control. If I had any hope of fooling him, I must play the charade he had orchestrated down to the last move.

CHAPTER 16

By the time I reached the palace gates for the second time that day, all the other guests had already arrived. The guards at the gate showed no surprise at my late appearance, however, merely checking the merchant token I held out. All the traveling merchants had been invited, so it served in place of a written invitation.

Only once I had safely passed them, did I unwrap my cloak. Rolling it into a ball, I looked around the courtyard for somewhere to stash it. I might have need of it when I made a quick exit later in the evening. Eventually I had to be satisfied with stuffing it behind a small stack of barrels. At least its dark color should help keep it hidden.

Lingering in the shadows, I tied the mask around my face, checking twice that the knot was secure. Only the other merchants knew me well enough to potentially recognize me behind its protection, and they would be thrown off track by my gown. Merchants always assessed the value of items they saw—it was second nature to them. Masked as I was now, they would see the dress first and me second.

Percy might recognize you, a small voice whispered, but I thrust it aside. The ball must be a large one. I would simply have to make sure I didn't cross paths with the Talinosian prince.

My heart beat just as fast stepping into the ballroom as it had riding into Damon's camp. Enormous chandeliers made the room sparkle, the gowns and jewels of the guests reflecting light in every direction.

A small orchestra played on a dais at one end of the room, and couples circled the floor in tight embraces. Everywhere I looked, masked faces loomed like threats. I wasn't sure I would even recognize Lilah or Tallie in such a throng.

I could only hope I was similarly invisible.

But even as the thought formed, whispers spread around me as guests turned to take in the new arrival. Damon had blundered when he gave me a gown of such quality. It made me conspicuous.

Or was that his intention? a more devious part of me wondered. It didn't matter if everyone remembered the girl in the purple gown—as long as no one could recognize Dee of the merchants behind the mask.

My discomfort continued, however. I didn't like being the center of attention. So when a young man came forward and offered me his hand with a bow, I took it, eager to disappear among the dancers.

Before I had time to consider whether I even knew the dance, he pulled me into his arms and twirled me onto the dance floor. I stumbled for a single step before finding my feet and the rhythm. As long as I let him lead, the steps proved easy enough to pick up.

"I consider myself fortunate to secure the first dance with such a vision of loveliness," he said in a deep baritone.

"You can't even see my face," I protested.

"Not yet. But I hope to do so at midnight."

"We shall see." I lowered my eyes, mimicking a bashful reaction to hide my surprise.

There was to be an unmasking at midnight. No wonder

Damon had set such a specific time for my escape. He must have wanted to give me the maximum amount of time to get back and into the ball while knowing I would be no use to him after the unmasking revealed my identity. I had to be gone before it took place.

We were circling—both as a couple and around the room—and with each rotation, I searched the walls for a clock. Would I find one in a ballroom?

Finally I located an elaborate one, encrusted with what looked like diamonds. It took a second circuit before I managed to read the time.

Half an hour until midnight. I smiled at my partner, hoping he wasn't saying anything that required a more substantial response. I couldn't make sense of his words while my brain was busy formulating a plan.

I would have to time my approach to the queen just right. I assessed the length of the room, making note of every available exit. Would ten minutes be enough time to get back to the courtyard? Or too much time, perhaps? Surely Damon's man would be there for a short period before midnight. I couldn't be expected to time my escape down to the minute.

We completed another circuit, and I looked at the clock again. How could time move so slowly? As I spun back around, I looked for Queen Ava. She stood out in the crowd despite her height since not only did she wear a crown, but she was the only lady present not wearing a mask. I eventually located her on the dance floor.

I suppressed a grimace, pasting a smile on my face in its place while inside my mind scrambled. It would be difficult to approach her on the dance floor. But perhaps she would stop dancing soon in anticipation of the unmasking. If she didn't, I would have to act anyway.

Distracted by my thoughts, I failed to notice another man approaching. Cutting a nimble path through the dancers, he appeared at our side. Before either of us could protest, he had cut in, sweeping me out of my dance partner's arms and into his own.

"I think this is my dance," he said, a laugh in his familiar voice.

I closed my eyes for a brief second, intense emotion flooding me. The one person I had sworn to avoid was now gazing straight into my mask. Fear filled me, but it couldn't entirely account for the heat that now radiated through my body. Being held in Percy's arms was nothing like the impersonal grasp of my previous partner. Every nerve told me to be afraid, but something deeper whispered I was safe.

I said nothing as Percy spun me down the room, leaving my earlier partner behind.

"You look familiar, fair lady," he said, a quizzical note to his voice. "Have me met before?"

I shook my head, afraid to speak lest he recognize my voice.

"A mystery then." He gave me his familiar, friendly smile. "The rumor in the ballroom is that you're a foreign princess, waiting to announce your state visit until the unmasking."

When I still said nothing, he continued, undaunted. "But Queen Ava swears it isn't so. And surely she, at least, would know if foreign royalty had arrived in her kingdom. Plus there is the matter of an invitation."

He smiled gallantly. "Although I cannot imagine anyone refusing entry to someone of your beauty."

"I wear a mask," I said, betrayed by my indignation into speech. He was the second person to wax lyrical about my appearance, despite knowing nothing of how I looked.

But as soon as I spoke, I bit my tongue. I couldn't permit myself even the smallest slip tonight.

"It's your elegant bearing," he said promptly. "Your face is only one aspect of beauty."

I suspected my true *beauty*, as they called it, came from my mystery, given the way it made everyone fall all over themselves.

But I kept the thought to myself. I couldn't make another mistake.

"You cannot be so cruel as to refuse me conversation entirely," Percy said, in his most charming manner. "I have just learned that the person I most wanted to dance with tonight is not coming after all, and if my other dance partners won't even speak to me, it will be a miserable night indeed."

My steps faltered slightly before I caught myself. The person he most wanted to dance with? Was Percy talking about me? Had he just been speaking with Lilah, or perhaps Tallie?

I looked around, trying to spot either of them, but we were moving too fast for me pick anyone out of the crowd. My emotions jangled, the contradictory feelings jarring. The earlier sensation of security had persisted, despite the constant layer of fear underlying my every thought.

What if I told Percy everything? I could tell him right now and ask his help. Determination filled me. I would confess who I was and explain my situation. He could help me fool Damon.

Our turns had brought us to the edge of the dancers, and a servant stepped forward slightly, actually onto the dance floor, to hold out a tray of drinks.

"Can I offer you some refreshment?" he asked, his eyes on me.

Percy regarded him with mild surprise, but a shot of fear jolted me into action. Tearing myself from Percy's grasp, I shook my head and fled down the room before he could catch me again.

Eyes everywhere. Damon had eyes everywhere, and they could be anyone. Had I only imagined the threatening look in the servant's eyes? I had nearly let Percy's familiar presence lull me into forgetting my situation.

My eyes searched for the clock, my anchor in this turbulent night. I gasped when I saw the time. Before the seconds had ticked impossibly slowly, now time had sped up, racing past while I wasn't paying attention.

It was nearly midnight, and I had no more time to waste.

I spun, surveying the room. Where was the queen?

At first I couldn't see her anywhere, and my panic mounted. She must be here somewhere. She wouldn't leave her own ball.

There! I spotted her, at last. She had left the dance floor and taken a seat on an elegant chair placed on a second raised dais. I swallowed. In full view of the room.

But there was no time for thinking or doubting. I had to act now or never.

Clutching my skirt, I dashed across the room. People moved aside, murmurs and raised eyebrows following behind me.

I ignored them all.

Arriving at the simple throne, I stopped, suddenly gripped by the impossibility of the moment. Could I really do this?

The warmth of Percy's arms seemed to surround me again. He had dedicated himself to chasing Damon, and he wouldn't be free until he was caught. I could do this for Percy.

"Is something wrong?" the queen asked, and for the first time, I properly saw her.

Her short stature belied the strength of purpose that radiated from her and flashed from her deep blue eyes. At least ten years older than me, her face spoke of wisdom and experience far beyond my own, although I could see no visible lines. This tiny woman carried heavy burdens as if her shoulders had been designed for them.

Damon had described her as weak, but I saw nothing but strength. My heart lifted. Here was a woman who could face his raging storm and emerge victorious.

I dropped to one knee.

"Your Majesty."

Instinctively she held out one hand, and I took it as if I meant to place a kiss of fealty on her knuckles. But instead I gripped her fingers, holding firm as I looked up at her.

"I have a message from Prince Damon. You have two weeks to abdicate your throne to him, or he will take it." My words fell over each other. "He will see you dead, Your Majesty, and your family with you."

She stiffened, trying to pull her hand away, but I was already standing, the ring wrenched from her finger.

"I'm sorry," I whispered, my words barely above a breath. And then I ran.

CHAPTER 17

*T*he queen stood, calling after me and shouting for her guards. Out of the corner of my eye, I saw a tall, elegant noblewoman leap to her side faster than any of her official guards.

I had no doubt the woman could have caught me, if I hadn't had timing on my side. Once again, Damon showed his mastery of the moment. As I fled through the room, the music reached a crescendo, overtaken by hundreds of clamoring voices. The dancers stopped their movements, turning to each other and transforming the room into one giant mass of moving people as guests began to remove their masks. On the other side of the room, the clock chimed the first note of midnight.

Any further calls to stop me were lost in the general chaos, my pursuers hampered by the crowds that surged in behind me. I put on a new spurt of speed. Maybe I really could escape.

I almost tripped as I reached the doors of the ballroom, but I managed to catch myself in time. Taking a fresh grasp on my skirts, I hiked them up and ran faster. Gratitude for my sturdy merchant shoes flashed through my mind. They had been hidden by my skirts before, but now they aided my flight.

I reached the entrance of the palace as a voice called from the ballroom door.

"Wait!"

I turned involuntarily, everything in me responding to the familiar voice. For one brief instant our eyes locked across the distance before his gaze dropped to my shoes, a confused look crossing his face.

Nearly tripping for the second time, I stumbled down the stairs, the moment broken.

Somehow I arrived outside ahead of any alarm, although I likely had only seconds. I threw myself at the barrel where I had left my cloak, my terrified fingers fumbling as I shook it out and draped it over myself. As I moved, my eyes searched the vast space for a man with a black armband.

Several guards were starting to turn from the gate, alerted perhaps by the sounds of my arrival and the people clattering into the entranceway behind me, but the only other person I could see was a driver just inside the courtyard, loading a final pumpkin onto a cart.

He grumbled to himself as he worked, and I caught something about a mistaken order and lost earnings before my eyes focused on his arm. I sprinted toward him, half hidden in the shadows, only the bright splash of the orange pumpkins making him visible in the night.

He didn't turn to look at me or give any sign of having noticed my approach except that his words changed.

"In among the pumpkins and quick about it."

I vaulted into the back of the large cart, flinging myself face down between two mounds of pumpkins, my black cloak facing upward. The man leaned forward and rearranged his load, placing several pumpkins over me, their weight pressing uncomfortably against me. I didn't dare move, however, because I could hear others in the courtyard now.

"A girl! Did you see a girl in a purple dress?" one of them

called, and the man now climbing into the driver's seat of the cart paused.

"A noble lady?"

"Aye, that's the one!" He sounded like a guard.

"She ran that way, as if a whole team of hounds were after her," my driver said. "Strange thing to see a lady fleeing a dance." He gave a rough, choking sort of laugh, but I could hear his audience had already abandoned him—racing across the courtyard, no doubt thinking themselves hard on my heels.

"Gee up!" the man called to his horse, still showing no signs of hurry, and the cart creaked and began to roll ponderously forward.

My heart beat so loudly I could barely hear the complaints he called to the guards about the need to cart his wares away again.

"You should have come yesterday," one of them replied, clearly out of patience with what must have been a long running stream of complaints. "It's not our fault you got the day wrong. The ball is already underway, the dishes cooked and prepared. What would we do with so many pumpkins?"

"I was told today. I swear it," he said, but another guard called to him to hush and be on his way.

The man muttered a curse and called again to his horse to hurry up. I wanted to scream at him to move faster, but another, calmer, part of me applauded his cool head. No one would guess him to be aiding in a desperate escape.

Eventually, finally, we were free of the palace gates and rolling through the streets of the city. Still I didn't dare to move. Eventually the guards would determine I wasn't hiding in the palace grounds and come asking further questions of the gate guards. But with hundreds of masked guests and an entire palace, I had no way to guess how long that would take.

"Hold steady now," the man said, nothing in the cadence of his voice changing, although I felt sure the comment was directed at me and not his horse.

Nightmares were made of that slow journey through the streets, the pumpkins bouncing and jostling, no doubt bruising me all over, and my eyes covered. My ears strained for any sound, and twice I was sure I heard hooves behind us, only for the sound to fade away.

I tried to remind myself it was natural enough for a city this size to have some traffic, even at this late hour, but my racing heart refused to calm. I only hoped it didn't give out entirely before this awful night was over.

Finally the cart came to a complete stop. I still didn't move, however.

"You've still got your load," a bemused voice called.

"Aye, you were right." The driver sounded sullen. "After my wheel gave out on the way in, I should have just turned around. Not only did I arrive half into the night, but now they claim the order was for two days ago. Two days ago! I ain't in my dotage yet. I know the order was for today."

"No more of your complaints, please!" the guard said hurriedly. "I did try to warn you when you passed through earlier. And I heard quite enough then about your broken wheel."

"Easy enough for those with a cushy job and steady coin," the man said, once again calling for his horse to move.

"You try doing night duty, if you think it's so easy," the guard called after us.

We must have left through a side gate because I was sure we hadn't traveled in the direction of the main one, and I had heard only one guard. But knowing Damon, he wouldn't have been foolish enough to use the eastern gate after the desertion of its guard earlier in the day.

Sure enough, once we were far enough away to be covered by darkness, the wagon turned. Slowly we began a circle that would presumably take us around the city and toward Damon's camp.

Emboldened by the darkness, I pushed myself up to a sitting position, sending pumpkins cascading off me.

"Watch it back there," the driver called sharply, and I caught at the last rolling sphere.

Moving more cautiously, I tried to find a comfortable place to sit. Finding the task impossible, I settled for one that wouldn't bruise me further.

The moon came out from behind a cloud, providing feeble light as we pulled up beside a clump of several trees. Before I could ask the driver why we had stopped, the clomp of hooves sounded.

I stiffened, gripping the closest pumpkin as if it might be useful as a weapon—or a shield, at the very least—but my driver didn't respond.

Two horses appeared out of the darkness, one of them riderless.

"You got her out?" the mounted man asked, with some curiosity but no concern in his voice.

"She's back there, right enough. And my payment?"

"Girl? Are you there?" the man called.

I stood up, brushing myself off and clambering out of the cart. "I'm here."

The clink of coin changing hands sounded, and then the now-familiar, "Gee up!"

Before I could think of anything to say to my rescuer, he had disappeared into the surrounding darkness. I had thought him a follower of Damon, but perhaps he didn't even know what he had been involved in this night.

For a moment the new arrival and I both remained silent and motionless. He was the first to speak.

"Well, do you intend to come along, or do you want to stand there all night?"

"I'm wearing a ballgown. I'll need help mounting up." The long day and night were catching up to me, and I couldn't keep the irritation from my voice.

The man cursed, sliding down and throwing me into the saddle. I might be tired, but the night still wasn't over.

If I had thought the trip in the pumpkin wagon bad, the rest of the journey on horseback was even worse. Tension still filled me, but the release of immediate danger made it hard to keep my eyes open, and twice I nearly slid from my horse's back.

Only when we arrived back at Damon's camp did fresh fear return me to full alertness.

This time, when I entered his tent, I had to blink against the brightness within, numerous lanterns turning the interior almost as light as day. Did he create the contrast on purpose, to throw off anyone who entered?

"You're back." He sounded neither surprised nor satisfied.

"I did what you required." Reaching forward, I opened my fist to reveal the ring.

Damon strode over to me, reaching out to take it from my palm. It was the first time we had touched, and the hairs on the back of my neck stood up as my deepest instincts told me to back away from the predator before me.

I stood my ground.

"Yes, it's her ring," he said at last.

I snatched it back, and he narrowed his eyes.

"I won this prize," I said. "I shall keep it. As surety against your promises."

It was a bold move, but I had spent many years learning to read people so I could pass through life unheeded and unnoticed. It hadn't taken many dealings with Damon to grasp that he responded to strength and bold courage.

Sure enough, after a tense pause, he laughed.

"Keep it, if you will. It means nothing to me and has served my purpose."

I wrapped my fingers around it, whisking it out of sight.

"I must return," I said. "Immediately."

He raised an eyebrow. "So eager to leave my presence, Daria?"

I ignored the jibe. "If I am to be of use, no one can realize it was me at the ball tonight. Which means I have to be back in my bed before my stepmother and sister return. They will no doubt stay late, at my stepsister's urging, but time is already running short."

This time he didn't taunt me, nodding his agreement with my words.

"You must continue as normal, arousing no suspicions, until the night of the final ball in two weeks' time. No doubt they will be screening guests more closely on that occasion, so go to the ball with the merchants. When you leave again shortly afterward, you can tell them you're going to collect your partner for the evening. I'll be waiting just inside the eastern gate."

I nodded, and he continued.

"Invent some catastrophe that has delayed me. That way they won't question me when we enter together later. Once I'm inside the ballroom, undiscovered, your task will be completed and your reward sure."

"I will be there," I promised.

"And I will be watching," he said, piercing me with his steely gray eyes.

I let him hold my gaze for several heartbeats before I turned away.

"There is a small tent next to mine," he said, no longer looking at me. "You will find a plain dress in there. I recommend you not return to the city in that distinctive garb."

I nodded, although he wasn't looking at me, and hurried outside. I had no trouble finding the tent, soon emerging freshly gowned. Someone helped me onto the waiting horse, but I didn't take note of their face. All my remaining energy was now focused on getting back inside the city and into my bed. I couldn't imagine what Lilah would do if she beat me to our room. Perhaps I could claim I'd been hiding in the stables, taking comfort from the horses. I would certainly smell like one.

I let the horse have his head, not making an effort to guide him until we reached open ground. I kept nodding off on his back, too tired to attempt to see much through the predawn gloom until we had nearly reached the road. As we approached, a small build up of people loomed out of the dimness, halted at the main gates of the city. Several wagons were attempting to turn, their drivers calling insults as they obstructed each other's progress.

"What's going on?" I asked another rider who looked more alarmed than angry.

"They've barred the gates." He shook his head. "No one is allowed in or out."

CHAPTER 18

"*W*hat?" I stared at him before turning to look at the strong, gray walls. "For how long?"

He shrugged. "They won't say. There's been some sort of attack on the queen."

I swung back to look at him again, feigning surprise. "The queen?"

"She escaped unharmed, but King Hans ordered the gates closed. That's what the guards are saying anyway." He paused for a moment before bursting out explosively, "But what are we supposed to do? That's what I'd like to know."

"Go home, I suppose," I said absently. I was no longer attending to the conversation, my eyes scanning the walls.

These travelers, presumably here early for the markets, could return home. But I had to find a way into the city. And sooner, rather than later, or all my effort would be for nothing. If Damon heard I hadn't made it back into Rangmeros by morning, he would start to doubt me.

My mind spun, trying to latch on to any option, however tenuous. The walls were certainly too high for climbing, even if I had the necessary skill and equipment. But I hadn't actually been back to the east gate since leaving through it at sunset. What if the new guard shift had failed to check if it was secured? It might even now be sitting unlocked.

Even in my sleep deprived state, I knew it was a desperate hope. But I could think of nothing else to try.

Turning my horse in that direction, I left the road, making my way along the city wall. The sun still hadn't risen, but I could just make out the ground before me. I trusted to the horse's superior senses to guide our way, and he continued on happily enough.

The journey felt interminable, but the sun was still below the horizon when I reached the gate. Sliding down from my horse's back, I hoped I wouldn't have need to mount again since I doubted my ability to do so.

The gate in front of me more closely resembled a large wooden door, clearly not meant for use by vehicles. It looked as tightly barred as the main gates, but there was only one way to know if it was locked.

Holding my breath, I attempted to lift the handle that opened the gate. It rattled but wouldn't budge more than a few inches. I groaned. It was locked.

My shoulders slumped, and I slid down the door to sit in a huddle on the ground. Of course it was locked. I had known it was a forlorn hope, but I couldn't help feeling battered by the loss of it all the same. I had no idea what to do next.

A creaking was my only warning before the support behind me began to move. I nearly tipped backward, grabbing at the ground for balance and scrambling to my feet.

I faced the opening gate, readying my excuses and explanations for whatever guard appeared on the other side. But I still couldn't see inside when I heard a shout.

"Over here! I heard it again."

The tromp of feet sounded, and then the gate swung the rest of the way open to reveal…nothing. I stared at the empty space in front of me. Where were the guards? Who had let me in?

Don't just stand there! An irritated voice shocked me out of my confusion. *The guards will be back any minute.*

I hurried through the open doorway, making it several steps into the city when Arvin spoke again.

Don't just leave it hanging open! Shut and lock the gate, or they'll be combing the city for whoever managed to sneak inside.

Obediently I turned back and secured the lock, realizing a moment later that I had abandoned my mount on the other side.

"My horse!" I exclaimed, remembering only at the last minute to keep my voice low.

Never mind him. Arvin appeared in a narrow alley. *He'll turn his nose for home and his oats.*

I didn't question Arvin's knowledge of horses, racing across the cobblestones to throw my arms around his neck.

"What are you doing here? I'm so glad to see you!"

You'll be less glad if those guards catch you. I confused them enough to get them all turned around themselves, but they'll snap out of it and be back in a minute.

"Sorry." I started down the alley, the golden horse following behind. "Do you know the fastest way to the inn where I'm staying?"

Naturally. I have an excellent sense of direction.

We emerged from the alley into a broader street, making Arvin halt. Reluctance sounded in his voice as he spoke.

You had better take my lead rope. People are starting to stir in the city.

For the first time I noticed a rope trailing behind him. I scooped it up, holding it as loosely as possible. Arvin began to walk, and I kept pace with him, trying to present the image that I was leading him and not the other way around.

"I don't like to seem ungrateful, but I don't quite understand what's happening right now. What were you doing at that gate?"

Letting you back into the city. He spoke with slight impatience, as if the answer was obvious.

My mind whirled strangely, the lack of sleep making my confused jumble of thoughts hard to follow. I fixated on the least important element of the situation.

"But *how* did you open the gate?" I stared down at his clopping hooves as if expecting them to suddenly sprout fingers.

I told you no walls can cage me, he whickered.

My tired brain couldn't decide if that was an answer or not, but I let the question go for more important ones.

"How did you know I needed help? How did you know I was even outside the city?"

I followed you last night from the palace.

I nearly tripped over a patch of uneven paving. "You were there? In the courtyard?"

I was in the stables, but I heard the racket and came to investigate. While it didn't seem immediately obvious why you would be hiding in a cart full of pumpkins, it seemed an odd enough choice to warrant investigation.

"And so you followed me." I shook my head. "I thought I heard something behind us." A frown grew as I considered the previous evening. "But we didn't leave by the same gate, so you can't have been waiting there all night for me to return."

It seemed unlikely you would return by the same gate. But your scent was on this gate, so I decided it was the most likely candidate. Naturally once they locked down the city, you would need help gaining entry.

"How did you know I hadn't left for good? And why did you come to help me, anyway? You said you didn't want to be involved with whatever the godmothers have planned for me."

He hesitated. *While I have, in general, superior sense in all matters, I have on occasion in the past shown the smallest element of poor judgment when it comes to people.*

I raised an eyebrow. Was Arvin admitting weakness? I wished Percy was present to hear such a miraculous occurrence.

In the past two years, I have endeavored to put my vast mental *faculties toward this issue. I have learned much. And though your manner could do with some improvement...*he paused to give me a stern look...*your character is loyal and good. I am certain of it. And so, I decided to assist you.* His eye brightened. *I'm sure you'll explain yourself.*

So there was an element of curiosity driving him. But it wasn't the biggest factor. Impulsively, I put out a hand to rest on his mane.

"Thank you. I don't think I said that yet. Thank you for helping me."

Arvin tossed his mane in reply, and for a while we walked through the streets in silence. Although it made no sense, instead of growing more tired with the continued exertion, my energy slowly replenished—as if strength flowed through Arvin's golden coat to me.

As I gradually woke up, my awareness of our surroundings grew. I frowned, looking around us in confusion.

"Where are we going? I don't think this is the way to the inn."

No, certainly not. We are going to the palace.

"The palace?" I drew back, the rope I still held pulling against the horse when he tried to continue on. "You told me you knew the way to the inn."

He turned and gave me an impatient look. *Certainly I do.*

"But we're not going there?"

No. You are needed at the palace.

"Me? At the palace?" My brain was functioning more effectively now, but his words still made no sense. "No, I need to get back to my bed before Lilah comes back and discovers I'm gone."

Even as I said the words, a sinking sense of inevitability told me she must already have returned. Dawn had fully broken now, and I had no trouble seeing my surroundings.

She cannot return. She is still at the palace. I told you—you are needed.

"I still don't understand. What do you mean she *can't* return?

167

Has something happened to her?" Anxiety propelled my feet forward again, and Arvin immediately resumed walking.

Not to her individually, but to all the merchants. They have not been permitted to leave the palace.

"What?!"

Percy saw your shoes and reported you were likely a merchant. Since the Rangmerans are unaware you made it out of the palace grounds, they have detained all the merchants at the ball for examination and questioning.

"Examination?" I gaped at him, a slightly hysterical giggle rising up and threatening to burst out. "You mean they're looking at all of their shoes, trying to work out which one is me?"

I don't know if that is an exact description of what is happening, Arvin also sounded amused, *but I believe the essentials are correct.*

My sudden humor dropped away. "What's happening to them is my fault. I hope they haven't been harmed in any way."

Of course not. The Rangmerans seem civilized. And, besides, it is a delicate situation. The merchants don't come under the authority of the king and queen, so they don't really have the right to detain them at all. The only reason the merchants have put up with it so far is that they are also concerned to find the culprit. The treaty would soon break down if it was believed merchants were using their privilege to attack royalty in their own castles.

I gulped. "So now I'm endangering the entire merchant treaty! I need to go and explain everything. I was going to do it tomorrow, but clearly it can't wait."

Which is why we're going to the palace.

"I just hope I don't bring even more trouble down on the merchants' heads." Unease gripped me as I remembered the various uses I had made of my merchant token.

Naturally you will not. You are not a traveling merchant but an Elamese.

I considered trying to explain why that might only make the situation worse since it meant the merchants had given their token too freely, but I decided against it. The time for the truth had long since passed, and I would simply have to accept whatever consequences resulted from it.

I expected to be stopped at the palace gates, but although they were closed, a guard opened them readily enough for me.

"There you are!" he said.

I blinked at him in surprise until Arvin replied, and I realized the man hadn't been talking to me.

Here I am, indeed.

The guard chuckled. "A talking horse." He shook his head. "It doesn't matter how many times I hear it...But His Highness has been asking after you. He'll be glad to see you safe back."

Percy need not concern himself with my safety. I am the one who keeps him safe.

"Aye, I've no doubt," the guard on the other side said. "Mayhap that's why he'll be glad to see you returned."

Neither of them so much as questioned me. Clearly the respectability of a talking horse from the Palace of Light covered his companions as well. Arvin trotted through the narrow opening made for us, and I slipped in beside him.

A stablehand ran up to us before we had made it across the courtyard.

"Thanks for returning him, miss," he said, panting. "I'll take him from here."

It is I who take her, Arvin whinnied, glaring at the boy.

He fell back, whitening beneath the dirt on his face. "I'm sorry, Your Lordship, sir. Of...of course."

I snorted, but Arvin looked instantly mollified. *See it doesn't happen again.*

Arvin led me to a side door, indicating with a toss of his head that I should knock on it. I did so, my heart pounding the same rhythm as my hands. A long moment stretched out before the door swung open.

The suspicious face of the porter from the day before peered out at us.

"You're the girl from yesterday," he said, taking me by surprise. He had a good memory for faces if he remembered me amid all the chaos of the day before. Perhaps it was that skill that had won him the position.

"Yes. I still need to speak to Prince Percival."

"His Highness is otherwise occupied."

"Then I need to speak to Queen Ava," I said in my firmest voice. "Or King Hans."

The porter drew himself up. "Their Majesties are most certainly not available. If you haven't heard what happened here last night, you must be the only one in the city. They certainly do not have time to be bothered by some commoner girl who is out of sorts at being turned away."

Losing patience, Arvin thrust me out of the way with his long nose and fixed a large eye on the porter. *She needs to see the human rulers. Now.*

The man hesitated, his own eyes going wide as his throat convulsed. He had likely heard talk of Arvin, but hearing the reality of it for yourself was something entirely different.

"I..." He hesitated. While he was certain of where I fit in the social hierarchy, a talking horse was a great deal harder to classify. "If you will vouch for the necessity, I will ask if she can be granted an audience."

Good.

The man turned, clearly meaning to leave us at the door while he went to make inquiries, but Arvin pushed the door open and trotted straight into the building. I followed, closing the door behind me.

The porter gazed at us in some alarm, but obviously didn't feel up to the task of expelling a talking horse from the palace. Muttering inaudibly, he hurried down various corridors until he reached a large, solid door of dark wood, embellished and strengthened with some sort of black metal.

He hesitated again outside it, clearly reluctant to disturb whoever was inside. Before he could work up the courage to knock, a woman came striding down the corridor toward us. Clothed in leather and with a sword strapped to her waist, it took me a moment to recognize her as the tall noblewoman who had sprung to Ava's side at the ball.

The porter recognized her, however, immediately bowing and murmuring, "Your Ladyship."

The woman looked only vaguely surprised at encountering a horse inside the castle. Although she briefly surveyed me, she seemed to find nothing of interest because she turned back to the porter.

"Their Majesties are not to be disturbed. I thought the message had been circulated."

He bowed again. "Certainly, Lady Anhalt. But *the horse* said this girl needed urgent speech with either Prince Percival or Their Majesties. I didn't feel I had the authority to gainsay..." I didn't hear the rest of his excuses, my attention once more focused on the woman.

Lady Anhalt the porter had called her. Countess of Anhalt was the position Damon had offered me. Did he have some special grudge against her? From her behavior at the ball, she must be close to the queen.

She turned to me. "You need to speak to Prince Percival?"

I nodded. "As quickly as possible. I'm afraid it's urgent."

She raised a brow, her manner having lost none of its confident calm, despite the strangeness of the circumstances.

"I'm afraid this is not a good time. But if Arvin insists, I know Percy would not want him turned away. But I doubt you will be able to get an audience with the king or queen right now."

"Percy—Prince Percival—will be fine," I said, with a tinge of relief. I would rather tell my story to him than to intimidating strangers.

Her eyebrows quirked slightly at my use of his name, but she dismissed the porter without comment and turned to the door. Gesturing for us to wait, she swung it open.

Through the doorway, I could see a large, sturdy table of rough wood. Parchment covered most of its surface, and a glimpse of a map put me forcibly in mind of the inside of Damon's tent. Except Queen Ava and King Hans were not alone. A number of people stood around the table, involved in a lively debate.

"The message said two weeks, and that can't be a coincidence," said a grizzled older man, slapping his hand against the wood of the table. "He has something planned for the day of the final ball."

"That much is obvious," said another man. He was the opposite of the first speaker, tall and thin and dressed with careful, understated elegance. And yet he spoke with equal command and intelligence. "The question before us is precisely what those plans might be."

I stepped forward, pushing past the countess.

"I can tell you that."

CHAPTER 19

$\mathcal{M}$y sudden burst of confidence faltered when every eye in the room turned to me with varying expressions of surprise and disbelief. Lady Anhalt brushed past me, entering the room to range herself with those already inside.

"Apologies, Ava," she said. "I don't know who this girl is, but Arvin said she needed to speak to Percy. I was just coming to fetch him."

"Dee!" Percy stepped forward. "What are you doing here?"

"This isn't a time for games, girl," the grizzled man said, ignoring the prince. "That's a serious claim."

I squared my shoulders and met his eyes. "I know. But it's true. I wouldn't have come otherwise."

"You're asking us to believe the Traitor Prince confided in you of all people?"

Other faces mirrored his open skepticism, and Percy looked utterly astonished, but Queen Ava leaned forward, gazing at me across the length of the table with keen interest.

"Information can come from surprising sources, Captain. Surely you know that."

So the grizzled man must be her captain of the guard, then.

He subsided at her words, and the other man spoke instead, his voice calm and his gaze sharp.

"We do not have time to waste. I assume you can back up your claim?"

I nodded, stepping forward. Both the captain and the countess stiffened at my movement, their muscles tensed for action, but no one else moved. I pulled my fisted hand from the pocket of my gown, and opened it to show the room what I held.

For a moment there was silence as everyone stared at the ring on my palm. And then the room exploded into action.

"Seize her!" the king cried, thrusting Queen Ava behind him.

Both the captain of the guard and the countess rushed forward, but quicker than both of them was Percy. Interposing himself between me and my would-be arrestors, he held up both hands in a placatory gesture.

"No! I trust Dee. We have to give her a chance to explain."

"An explanation would certainly be welcome," said the older nobleman, the only one in the room not to have given any visible reaction to my reveal.

Percy grinned at him. "You were always a cool customer, Lord Adelmar."

"A product of my advanced years, young prince," Ava's Chief Advisor said with a hint of humor in his voice.

The queen pushed her husband out of the way, giving him a reproachful look.

"I would also appreciate an explanation. Whatever this girl may or may not have done, you cannot consider her a threat to me at this moment."

"Evelyn said the talking horse is in league with her," the captain said, clearly determined not to overlook a potential risk.

Arvin thrust his way into the room, looking at the captain with dislike.

I am not in league *with anyone, unless you mean the High King himself.* He gave the man such a pointed look that the captain actually muttered an apology. Arvin then turned to Percy. *You were wondering where she was. I found her for you.*

"Thank you." Percy looked half-taken aback, half-sheepish.

Despite the gravity of the moment, I felt heat fill my cheeks as Percy carefully avoided my eyes. He'd been looking for me? That must have been yesterday when I didn't show up at the ball.

"Interesting." The queen looked from Percy to me. "I can see there are several layers to whatever is going on here." She assessed me with a piercing gaze. "You are the one who delivered my cousin's message at the ball." It wasn't a question.

I nodded, causing the captain to mutter and the countess's hand to stray to her sword hilt.

"I knew those were the shoes of a traveling merchant!" For a moment Percy was caught up in a boy's satisfaction at being proven right. But a moment later adult considerations reasserted themselves, and he gave me a confused, rather hurt look. "But why, Dee? And how? When have you ever spoken to Damon?"

"Clearly she is in league with him," the captain said. "I don't know why we would trust anything she says."

"Because I know she would not mean us harm," Percy snapped back. "Dee is loyal and true—and she has twice been the target of Damon."

The captain merely raised an eyebrow as if he thought this evidence of my treachery.

"Thank you, Percy," I said, moved by his trust in me, despite the circumstances. I turned slightly to include the rest of the room in my next words. "I can't make you trust me, but I can start by telling the whole truth. It's actually three times now I have been the target of Damon and his men, and the more recent two were because one of his men recognized me from the first."

I drew a deep breath, feeling a heavy weight lift from my shoulders.

"Dee is a nickname that I gave to the merchants when I joined them two years ago after fleeing from Damon's guards. My full name is Daria of Eliam."

This pronouncement was greeted with a strong enough reaction to prove my name was known to every person in the room—despite their status and rank. A collective gasp sounded from multiple lips, and Percy started violently.

"Daria? *You're* Daria? But I've been searching for you for two years! And all this time, you were…" His words dropped away, shock apparently overcoming him.

"I'm sorry I didn't tell you the truth earlier," I said to him. "I've been hiding with the traveling merchants all this time out of fear of Damon—and it turns out fear isn't something that's easy to throw off in a single moment. Not when it's been building for years."

"Do you have proof of your identity?" Lord Adelmar asked.

I bit my lip. "I have nothing but the information in my head. Ask me anything of my history, or of Queen Blanche of Eliam, and I will answer you."

Certainly this is Daria, Arvin interposed. *I would hardly have brought her here otherwise.*

"You recognize her?" Percy stared at him before shaking his head. "But of course you do! Why didn't you say anything? All this time we've been traveling together, and you knew I was looking for Daria."

I do not need to explain myself to anyone—even you, Arvin said with dignity.

"He said he wasn't getting involved with another girl caught up in the scheming of the godmothers," I said.

Arvin's head whipped around to glare at me.

Percy groaned. "You really must let your grudge against the godmothers go, Arvin! They'll never let you return to the Palace of Light otherwise."

The decision is not up to them.

"Never mind that," Queen Ava said in commanding tones.

"You say you were hiding from Damon, so how did you come to be his messenger last night?"

I explained the false assumption Damon had made, and Percy jumped in to back me up with an account of how hard I worked. I fought down the flush that crept up at his words, trying to keep my focus on my story. As succinctly as possible, I described the message I had received from Damon and my subsequent actions.

"I wouldn't have done it if he had asked me to hurt anyone," I said quickly at the end. "But I thought, if given the choice, you would sacrifice your ring for one day in order to gain an advantage."

I held it out to the queen, and she rounded the table to take it from me, the king keeping close behind her.

"You would be correct, Daria of Eliam. You chose a dangerous path, but it seems you have played your part well."

"Not that your part is over," King Hans said, speaking to me for the first time. He looked at me with something like concern, although I couldn't tell if it was for me or merely for the consequences if I failed.

"I know. And I'm ready to do whatever you all think best," I said.

"First you must tell us what you know of Damon's plans," Lord Adelmar said. "And then we may formulate plans of our own."

"And when my cousin has been safely locked away, you will be returned to Eliam. You have my word on it," the queen said.

"But before that happens, we're going to have a talk." Percy sounded determined, and I reluctantly nodded, unsure how he felt about my deception.

I told them the little I knew of Damon's plans, and a lively discussion followed. The captain of the guard wanted to ride out immediately for his camp, but Percy spoke against that idea with the same concern that had worried me.

"If Damon has a camp that close to the city, he also has a

warning system and an escape route. Believe me, I speak from experience." He sounded grim. "We'll never catch him that way, and we'll lose the advantage we've finally gained, thanks to Daria." For a brief moment his face lightened as he looked at me.

"I agree with Percy," Queen Ava said, and her pronouncement ended that point of discussion.

"Who saw you enter the palace?" Lord Adelmar asked, and I tried to list every servant I had seen on my way in.

"The guards and the stableboy barely seemed to notice me, though."

"Let us hope not," he said. "Our one saving grace is that no one has any particular reason to link you and Arvin."

The queen looked at her advisor. "So you agree we need her to remain in place with the merchants until after the third ball?"

Adelmar nodded. "Damon says he has eyes in the city, and we must believe him. Indeed, the delivery of the dress strongly supports the claim, although it would appear his ability to find supporters in the city has been greatly diminished since we exposed Leuthar as one of his followers and cleared Rangmeros of his people. Damon wouldn't need Daria otherwise. But still, we must be careful."

He nodded at the queen. "I will ensure there is no loose talk about Daria's presence here today, and none of us can be seen to talk to her again. Which means we need our plans to be certain before she is slipped back out to her inn. It's fortunate we detained the merchants following the ball. Word of that will get back to Damon and make it more believable that she was able to return to her stepfamily without raising questions."

"Even with warning, he won't be an easy man to subdue." The captain rubbed his chin. "That enchantment of his will still cause us trouble."

"He's played into our hands there," the countess said. "By coming in the guise of an assassin, he's left us free to weight the numbers against him. With the new information from the prince," she nodded at Percy, "we have hope of wearing the enchantment down completely."

"I agree," the king said. "If Daria leads him to the green receiving room that opens into the ballroom, we'll have plenty of room for a full squad in there. Ten experienced soldiers will be plenty of back up."

Ava gave him a sharp look. "We?"

He grinned at her. "Of course. My guard days might be long gone, but you don't expect me to miss something like this, do you? Your cousin has threatened you, and I will see him dealt with myself."

"I will be there, too, of course." The countess met his eyes, wordless understanding passing between them. I suddenly felt certain the king wasn't the only noble present with a history as a guard.

"I almost pity my cousin if he is to face both of you," the queen said lightly, but I sensed concern behind her words.

"With twelve of us, we can wear him down for as long as necessary," Lady Anhalt said.

"And with any luck, that will be an end to his protections." Percy's face held a dark look of satisfaction. "I warrant we'll find some of his confidence disappears once he no longer has the enchantment in place. He'll give up his followers to gain any advantage for himself that he can."

The plan was repeated several times, and fine-tuned. Finally Lady Anhalt was given the task of escorting me out of the palace through a secret tunnel kept for the use of the royals when they wished to enter their city without being observed.

"I'll show you the green reception room on the way, so you know where to go the night of the ball," she told me.

I hoped my nerves didn't show on my face. It would have been preferable to have more than one opportunity to study the layout of the palace, so I would have to pay attention to this single lesson.

179

I thought nothing could make my mind wander from this important task, but as I curtsied farewell to the illustrious group in the strategy room, Percy slipped up beside me.

"I'm not staying away for two whole weeks," he murmured. "So be warned. I'll keep out of sight, but you'll be seeing me."

As I walked out of the room, shivers chased over my body. I followed in the countess's wake, telling myself it wasn't the time to analyze just what emotions those shivers signified.

CHAPTER 20

*L*ady Anhalt didn't have a warm or gushing presence, keeping her conversation restrained to the practical necessities of the moment. But nothing in her manner could be considered hostile. At times I even sensed a certain respect in the way she looked at me.

Before she left me—several streets into the city so I didn't appear to be coming from the palace—she informed me the other merchants would be released within the hour.

"We'll let the servants hear us discussing how we couldn't keep them any longer due to their protected status. No doubt the news will be discussed in every city tavern by nightfall." Her voice carried more wry humor than disgust at this fact of life, and my certainty that she hadn't started life as a noblewoman grew.

"I don't want to cause trouble between the merchants and Rangmere," I said. "They've been nothing but kind to me."

"Don't worry about that. I'll talk to Ariana—if Ava doesn't do so herself."

"You'll tell her the truth?" I asked, surprised.

"Of course. Ariana is trustworthy." The countess smiled at my expression. "I can see you don't know that I was raised as a member of Caravan Hargrove and served as a guard with them before I joined Ava's court."

I came to a stop and then had to jog to catch up when Lady Anhalt outpaced me. "*You* were a traveling merchant? And now you're a countess?"

She grinned. "There's no accounting for love. Although Jake had a difficult time convincing me to accept such a fate." She smiled reminiscently. "Now, here we are." Her voice turned brisk. "Remember, you must act as normally as possible. The other merchants won't know the truth."

I was still gaping when she disappeared back the way she had come. But I shook myself a moment later and hurried toward the inn.

The innkeeper hailed me, concern on his face as he asked after his other guests. I hesitated.

"I believe they will be following shortly." I gave him a beseeching look. "I would appreciate if you wouldn't mention having seen me to my stepmother."

He chuckled. "Oh, aye, an innkeeper knows how to be discreet. And I was young once, too, though you might scarce credit it now."

I thanked him and hurried up the stairs.

My intention had been to feign sleep until Lilah and Tallie returned. However, as soon as my head hit the pillow, real sleep claimed me.

Despite the deepness of my sleep, Lilah and Tallie's return woke me. Tallie looked exhausted, but she buzzed with the unexpected happenings of the ball. She was torn between disappointment at finding me still asleep, rather than awake and worrying over their lack of return, and excitement that I hadn't yet heard about the momentous events.

She rushed through a breathless tale of my doings at the ball and the examination of the merchants that had followed. Any lingering fears that my adopted family might have recognized me faded at her account of the beautiful, mysterious, and dangerous agent who had infiltrated the ball. This imaginary woman bore little resemblance to me, and Tallie clearly didn't credit the idea she might be a merchant.

"I am shocked the Rangmerans could suspect us of having been complicit in such an attack." Lilah looked almost as exhausted as Tallie but without the heady exhilaration that buoyed the younger girl. "As you can see, Dee, I was correct about the wisdom of your staying home. If I had been wiser, your sister and I would have kept away as well."

"Oh no, Mother!" Tallie cried. "I wouldn't have missed it for anything. It will be all anyone will talk about now."

She was right, of course. And, even worse, since I was the only person in the caravan who supposedly hadn't been present, everyone wanted to describe the events to me. I heard I was tall, short, elegant, strange, ominous, deceptively friendly...I remembered speaking to only three people that night, but somehow everyone had an impression to share. On only two things did everyone agree—my dress had been expensive, and I hadn't been a merchant.

The other primary topic of interest was the next ball, scheduled for only a week after the first one. Everyone had an opinion on whether or not it would still be held, whether they themselves would attend, and what Damon might do if it were to proceed.

I knew from the conversation of the royals that it wouldn't be canceled since they didn't want to do anything to disrupt Damon's plans—and neither did they want to give their people the impression they were unduly rattled by his threats.

I said nothing about my knowledge to the other merchants,

however. And by the second day, definite word had arrived that the ball would go ahead as planned, and that Ariana had ruled the merchants were free to attend.

I hoped her position signaled she had been told the truth of the various happenings of the last ball. But either way, it left the members of Caravan Bryant free to pursue their own wishes on the matter of the second one.

Tallie had fallen into bed and slept through two deliveries to the inn, a fight between a couple of angry cats just outside our window, and a riotous game of hide-and-seek which finished with a pair of maids shouting at the children involved. She woke to intense disappointment. Lilah had declared none of us would attend the second ball, regardless of the decision of the rest of the caravan. And she would not be moved.

While I gave Tallie what sympathy I could muster, for myself I felt only relief. Just the thought of attending the ball made me want to dive back into bed and never come out. The idea of dancing and smiling for hours while I tried to avoid doing or saying anything Damon might consider suspicious was hideous. Hiding in our rooms sounded like a far more appealing option—and completely in keeping with Damon's impression of me as an ill-used servant.

One benefit of the merchants' uncomfortable night was that Lilah had entirely forgiven me for going out alone the day before. Her guilt over ruining all my dresses had likely played a significant part in her change of heart, and she decided we would spend the week of enforced rest working to repair them.

Even at the height of her anger, Lilah was still a merchant, and she hadn't been able to bring herself to completely destroy the gowns. When I had time to examine them more closely, I realized they had all been torn along the seams, making their repair possible.

Naturally Tallie could not meekly accept spending her days sitting inside sewing. She would have protested it if we had still been on the road, but she found it entirely insupportable given we found ourselves unexpectedly in a large and bustling city. Lilah was deaf to her persuasions, however, merely reminding her again and again that Damon could reach all the way into the palace itself. Even in the inn she often stirred restlessly, peering into every corner as if expecting to find the prince hiding in one of them.

The common room was generally bustling with people, despite the greater freedom enjoyed by the rest of our caravan. For once, the merchants found themselves in the role of customers only, since Caravan Bryant wasn't scheduled to do business in Rangmeros, and the change in status left many at a loose end.

Lilah skipped the meeting of wagon leaders called by Isambard because she didn't want to leave Tallie and me alone. But she was in full agreement with their decision. We had been given a rare opportunity to travel with a more senior caravan and to enjoy a stay in a capital city at the expense of the royal purse. We would not endanger our caravan's standing by attempting to do business on Caravan Hargrove's turf.

Usually I would have enjoyed the unexpected reprieve from cooking and cleaning and the other chores of a merchant caravan. But time now hung heavy on my hands, and I longed for something more active to keep me busy. I had trouble sleeping at night, and the need to keep my restless insomnia from my roommates only made the experience worse.

I had expected my thoughts to be full of the coming ball and all the ways our plan could go wrong. But to my surprise, my mind was almost as obsessed with what came afterward.

Queen Ava had promised she would return me safely to Eliam, and I could no longer hide from thoughts of that future, like I had on the road. After long sleepless hours in the still and dark of night, I finally admitted to myself I had no interest in returning to my old life.

The short time I had spent in the ball reminded me of the many royal events I once attended as Snow's guest. She had invited me as her friend, in the hope I would enjoy myself, but I rarely did. I hadn't belonged there, just as I had not belonged at the ball in Rangmere—although for very different reasons.

And I only had to picture Anthony as a trainee guard, and even young Poppy nearing youth to know I wasn't needed by the children I had once raised either. I would like to visit them all again one day and see how their lives progressed—but I knew with certainty their lives were proceeding successfully without me.

Lilah might be frustrating at times—and Tallie infuriating—but they needed me. I had no idea how they managed before my arrival, but it couldn't have been a comfortable life. And now Lilah was demonstrating every day how much she cared about me—even if she showed her love in a strange way.

With the truth of my identity revealed, everyone would soon know I wasn't truly Lilah's stepdaughter. Could she forgive me my reticence? And could the caravan forgive our joint deception? I had never claimed to be Lilah's blood. If I had a place in Caravan Bryant as her stepdaughter, couldn't I have one as her adopted daughter just as easily?

The day before the second ball, Ariana called a meeting for the heads of all the merchant families from both caravans to discuss the upcoming ball. Lilah insisted Tallie accompany her—knowing she would flee to the markets the moment her mother's back was turned if given the opportunity—but she left me behind at the inn.

It was an apology and a test all in one, and this time I had no intention of moving anywhere. With many of our number at the meeting, and most of the others at the shops, picking up last minute items before the ball, I was alone in the inn's dining room when the door swung open.

When I saw who walked through it, I sprang to my feet, my

sewing falling from my fingers. Almost immediately I sat back down, only to realize my hands were now empty. Since I couldn't handle the embarrassment of leaping back to my feet again, I sat there foolishly instead, and it was Percy who fetched the material I had dropped.

He handed it to me with an elegant bow and a smile, but for the first time, his smile didn't reach his eyes.

"I'm glad to find you alone." He hesitated almost imperceptibly before adding, "Daria."

"What are you doing here?" My fingers clenched around the material now bunched in my lap. "The king and queen said none of us should have any contact."

"And I said I wasn't waiting two weeks. As you can see, I meant it." He sat on the chair beside me. "I was careful. I don't believe anyone saw me arrive."

I bit my lip. "I'm sorry I didn't tell you the truth about who I am. I didn't understand why Damon's people went after me two years ago, and I was afraid of what would happen if word spread about my location now." I frowned into my lap. "I actually still don't know exactly what happened back then."

"That at least I can enlighten you on," he said in an uncharacteristically grave voice before giving a succinct account of Damon's attempt to use Princess Giselle to establish himself in Arcadia and use his position there to launch an attack on Rangmere.

"His whole plan relied on keeping anyone who knew Princess Giselle far away from Arcadie, which is why he went after you and the other girls. All he cared about was that you didn't turn up at an inconvenient moment. We knew he had scared you away, and from your letter to Snow, we hoped you were safe. It didn't occur to us you might not know Damon's interest in you had ended, though. When things turned against him in Arcadia, his plans changed, and he fled to Rangmere. This is the kingdom he most values because its history of brutal strength aligns with his own character. And he feels he's the true heir."

He shook his head. "It's ironic, really, because if he had actually grown up here, he would understand the role of the Trials and his father's lack of claim to the throne."

"It seems that some at least of those who grew up here agree with him, however," I said softly.

He sighed, running a hand through his hair and looking more tired than I had ever seen him. "They don't think he's the true heir, they just dislike Queen Ava and the change she's brought. They don't care about legitimacy."

Silence fell for a moment before further words burst out of him. "But I don't care about Rangmere!"

I stared at him. "What do you mean? You've devoted two years of your life to tracking down Damon."

He sighed. "It started off as an adventure—one fueled partially by hurt pride and partially by a desire to see right done. And the longer he eluded me, the more I let myself become obsessed with the hunt."

He leaned forward, and I had the impression he would have taken my hands if I hadn't kept them firmly buried in the material in my lap. "But for some time now, I've found myself thinking more and more of home. And I think the timing coincides with when I met you, Dee." The earnest, melting look in his eyes hardened, and he pulled back. "I mean, Daria."

I swallowed, fighting back tears. "Dee is fine. It's a nickname. It's still me."

But the hurt didn't leave his eyes.

"You could have trusted me." His voice was quiet, but at the same time, all too loud in the empty room. "You seem to have trusted an entire caravan."

I shook my head. "They don't know who I am. None of them do. Not even Lilah and Tallie."

His expression changed to shock. "How is that possible?"

"Tallie saw me in trouble, and she reacted." I chuckled. "That's just her nature—and it's how I know she has a good heart underneath her youthful self-absorption. And Lilah took me in as soon as she knew I was alone and friendless. She told everyone in the caravan I was her older daughter, and sometimes I think she's forgotten I'm not."

He frowned. "But how is it possible they all accepted that? They all vouched for you as if they'd known you their whole lives."

"They haven't known me their whole lives, but they've always known Lilah has an older daughter. Apparently she often mentioned her before I arrived. You heard the Guardsmaster say how common it is for the children of traveling merchants to stay with family elsewhere. It was a simple enough matter for Lilah to explain I was a stepdaughter only, staying with family who were no longer able to care for me. She said we had lost contact after I was abandoned by the relatives, and that I had only just managed to find them. It explained my abrupt arrival well enough to quiet any questions."

"So where is her real daughter?"

I shrugged. "I have no idea. Lilah doesn't like to talk about her to me, apart from saying she's with family, and she was gone before Tallie was born, apparently. I've heard Lilah mention how difficult her pregnancies were. I think the older daughter might have been sent away when Lilah was pregnant with Tallie. The family joined Caravan Bryant soon after that, so no one else knows anything." I grimaced. "Not that I could have asked them questions when they thought I *was* the absent daughter."

Some of the hurt had faded from his face, but a shadow of it still lingered. "I still wish you'd realized you could trust me, at least."

"I should have. I can see that now, so clearly." Now I was the one leaning forward. "I realized it before we reached Rangmeros. I went to the palace to try to find you, but they wouldn't let me in, and then I was out of time." The final words sounded only in my head. *I did it all for you.*

He jumped to his feet, his hands balling into fists. "I hate that you went through all that alone. That you felt you had to run from me." He strode across to a nearby table, looking down at the small potted plant in its center before turning abruptly back toward me.

"I care about you, D—Daria. I can see why Snow values you so much. But I keep going over everything you've said, all our conversations, and realizing that you clearly don't value me the same way."

"No!" I leaped to my feet, taking two hurried steps toward him before slowing and coming to a stop. "I care about you too. And I trust you. I just…I let my fear hold me back. You were the one who helped me to see that—who helped me decide I couldn't let my fear rule me."

He looked across the space between us, the conflict clear in his eyes.

"It was always my own issues," I said. "It was never about you."

A light flared in his brown eyes, making the gold flecks glow. He strode forward, catching my hands in his before I could whisk them out of reach.

"I shouldn't be so hard on you. For two years you've been on the run in a strange kingdom, without friends or resources. You did what you felt you had to do to stay safe. How can I fault that?"

I shifted, uncomfortable with his praise. "I wasn't exactly friendless. I had Lilah and Tallie, remember. I owe them a great debt."

"Perhaps," he said softly. "But they also owe you. I've seen you, Daria—truly seen you. Despite everything life has thrown your way, you still respond with dignity and kindness again and again. You still put others before yourself day after day. I've never met anyone quite like you."

He caught my eyes with his. "I never want to be parted from

you, Daria—or Dee, or whatever nickname you choose. Will you come back with me to Talinos and marry me and make a life with me?"

I gasped, caught in his gaze and overwhelmed by the turn of the conversation. For a long moment there was silence as the ardor in his eyes dimmed, replaced by concern at my silence.

"No." The word was torn from me. "I can't, Percy. Soon Damon will be captured, and then you'll return to your true life. And I don't belong in the court of Talinos any more than in Eliam or Rangmere. I can't be who you need me to be. But I *can* be who Lilah and Tallie need me to be. I can be the missing part of their family."

Anger sprang into his eyes. "What nonsense is this? You would grace any court. You have kindness and love for others at your core, and that could never be out of place."

I shook my head. "You say that, but you forget I have experience with courts."

He pulled me closer, his grip on my hands remaining firm. "If courts sometimes lack in kindness, that's all the more reason they need people like you. But I don't care what they need, anyway. I just want to be with you. You say you care about me, but if you truly did, then you would be willing to fight for me. To fight for us."

For a moment, I was caught in the intensity of his eyes. I swayed toward him, and he drew a ragged half breath, leaning forward to close the distance between us.

An image of his face as it had appeared earlier in the conversation—colored with disappointment—filled my mind. His false life of the last two years had clouded his thinking. I seemed to fit now, but it would be a different story when he returned to Talinos. Back in his court, he would soon discover I could be of no use to him in his real life. He would thank me then for saying no now.

I pulled back. "I am thinking of you. You'll see one day."

His usually glowing bronze face turned pallid. "That's your final answer then?"

A tremor ran through me. "It is."

For a moment he looked like he was going to say more, but with a quick shake of his head, he released my hands and stepped back.

"Then I will see you at the final ball. Remind me afterward that I have a letter for you from Snow that didn't seem wise to bring to this inn. It's a reply to your own message, and I've been carrying it around for a long time. I didn't know where to deliver it."

I opened my mouth, but I didn't know what to say to the hurt and cold in his face and voice. I still hadn't come up with anything when he disappeared out the door, leaving me alone once again.

PART III
THE THIRD BALL

CHAPTER 21

*W*hen Lilah and Tallie returned, I had finished crying and washed my face. My years of practice at concealing my emotional state once again came to my rescue, and neither of them appeared to notice any difference in me.

But as the days passed, it became harder and harder to maintain the facade. In the inn, my only distractions came from Tallie's increasing despair at being refused permission to attend the second ball, and then—after it occurred without our presence —the endless descriptions of the event from the other merchants. Tallie, who had attempted to slip away on the night of the ball but been stopped by Lilah, took some small comfort in the lack of drama at the second dance.

But this apparent absence of excitement didn't prevent endless discussion on the topic anyway, with occasional comments on the wisdom of the king and queen in holding the ball as planned. Apparently the two week delay planned by Damon was bearing fruit in terms of concern and unrest among the populace. The people were afraid, and some were worried enough about the eventual outcome to even defect, slipping out of the city and not coming back. But the continuation of the planned festivities projected a sense of confidence from Rang-mere's rulers, and for many residents, the success of the second ball had eased their fears.

For me, the delay only chafed. The enjoyment of being waited on by the inn servants had long ago palled given the pain that now accompanied such forced inactivity. I had relived my conversation with Percy too many times to count, one moment buoyed by the memory of his tender words and the next crushed by the knowledge that we could never be together. Percy was a prince, and I was far from being a princess.

Weighed down by the constant presence of my thoughts, I greeted the necessity of completing our own washing with favor. Tallie, who was still sulking over her exclusion from the ball, ignored me as I gathered up our laundry, but Lilah attempted to stop me.

"I'm happy to do that, Dee. Why don't you have some time off?"

I caught a hint of concern in her eyes as she tried to take the pile of clothing from my arms. Perhaps I hadn't completely concealed my pain after all.

"Oh no, please!" More than a hint of desperation came out in the words, and she let her hands drop, her concern deepening. I tried to modulate my tone. "I've spent far too many days cooped up in this inn. I'm looking forward to getting outside and being active."

"Where will you wash them?" Tallie asked, showing the first bit of interest in my activity.

"A couple of the other merchant women are also doing washing today. They promised to show me the best place."

"But don't think you're going," Lilah said sternly to her daughter. "I know that look in your eye. You're hoping you can slip away to the markets or some other mischief once Dee gets absorbed in the chore. You're staying right here where I can keep an eye on you."

I smiled at her gratefully. Being responsible for Tallie under the circumstances would turn a pleasant outing into a high stress occasion. The younger girl was certainly not likely to be useful with the washing—something Lilah acknowledged without question. Whatever she might have been like in the past, she was no longer turning a blind eye to her daughter's self-absorbed ways.

"But Dee gets to go," Tallie said. "I thought you didn't want her wandering around on her own."

"She won't be on her own," Lilah said calmly. "You heard her. She's going with some of the other caravan women."

"Yes, in fact, I'd better hurry." I rushed over to the door before adding, "I shouldn't be more than a few hours."

"Take as much time as you need," Lilah called as I crossed out into the corridor.

I managed a brief smile back over my shoulder as I turned toward the stairs. Clearly I had passed the tests Lilah had been setting for me and had once again earned her trust. Now I just needed to convince her I wasn't an object of compassion, needing special treatment.

But I wasn't sure how to convince her I wasn't in pain when I felt a deep ache whenever I heard mention of Percy, thought of something I wanted to share with him, or was hit with the memory of his smile.

Once again I shoved such thoughts aside, trying to focus on the task at hand. At least I would be active for once.

Maris and Anthea met me just outside the inn door, their own bundles hoisted over their shoulders. Their greetings contained the usual amount of cheer, but I detected a faint sympathetic note in their eyes which made me tense. How many people in Caravan Bryant had discerned my mood?

The two women led me down an unfamiliar street, keeping up a constant stream of light conversation. Unlike me, they had spent their days exploring Rangmeros, and their steps didn't falter as they negotiated the occasional turn.

"There are other fountains here and there, of course," Maris said. "But the Square of Fountains is the best place to go. Lots of people gather there, but there are so many fountains, it's always possible to find a spot."

As she finished her words, we stepped into a large open space that took up a full block. Fountains filled the area, children racing between them, laughing, splashing each other, and playing a half-familiar game I recognized as the Rangmeran quickball.

Their mothers watched over them, calling the occasional correction but mostly enjoying a comfortable chat with the other women busy cleaning household laundry at the various fountains.

The closest fountains had a fair number of women already, so Anthea took us on a wending way through the square.

"There, that one's open." I pointed at one that had no washers, although a couple of women sat on its lip, talking to a small collection of children who gathered close around them.

Anthea looked at the women a little doubtfully but led us over to the fountain in question. As we got closer, I realized the source of her discomfort. Although the women looked relaxed in the casual setting, their clothing set them apart from the others who filled the square. These women came from the court.

I stiffened, but it was too late to pull back now without making my concern obvious. I cast a quick look around but could see no one who seemed to be paying us undue attention. Surely Damon couldn't have eyes in this particular square at this particular moment?

Unless he was having me watched and followed? It took all my willpower not to look back over my shoulder. As we set ourselves up and began to wash, I watched the two women out of the corner of my eye. I felt fairly certain I had never seen either of them before, and yet a vague sense of familiarity niggled at me whenever I looked at the older of the two. I examined her golden skin, long, sleek black hair, and deep brown eyes without sparking a memory.

I scrubbed my way through several garments before it suddenly hit me. Stiffening, I glanced sideways to find the woman in question watching me. Now that I had made the connection, I couldn't escape the similarities between this woman and the younger sister I had once shared a ship voyage with. She was stunningly beautiful, just like Princess Celine—although according to the tales, one of their middle sisters, Princess Celeste, was even more beautiful still.

When our eyes met, she smiled, sliding around the rim of the fountain until she sat close enough for easy conversation.

"You must be Daria, I think," she said in soft tones. "I've been coming every day in the hope you might appear here."

I cast a frantic look around the square.

"Their Majesties said I wasn't to have any contact with—"

"What could be more natural than women meeting over washing?" she said, cutting me off. "It is the sort of thing not at all likely to draw the attention of a male, I assure you. Especially since you won't see me in any war councils."

"I apologize, Your Highness, I didn't mean…"

She waved a hand, giving a musical chuckle.

"No, please, no apologies are necessary. I come to the Square of Fountains to forget I'm a princess—or even a countess, as I'm more commonly known in Rangmeros these days."

I managed a smile as I continued to surreptitiously examine the eldest daughter of the king of Lanover. She had a restful air I admired despite the close eye she kept on the children playing just beside the fountain.

When she said nothing for some time, I spoke tentatively, awkward in the knowledge she had come looking for me specifically.

"Did you have a message for me, Princess Clarisse?"

"Just Clarisse is fine," she said. "And I'm not here on any official business."

My hand slowed, a crease between my brows until I remembered we needed to maintain the appearance of this being a casual meeting. I returned to vigorous scrubbing.

"I'm afraid I don't understand. You said you've been coming here looking for me?"

"Yes." She glanced at the children before looking back at me. "My husband, Charles, and I are especial friends of Prince Percy. He often dines with our family when he's in Rangmeros, and I have come to view him much as I do my younger brother Rafe." A smile lit her face. "Maybe because he has a similarly reckless, charming air about him."

I sucked in a breath. "Percy sent you?"

She quickly shook her head. "No, he has no idea I'm here. I came entirely on my own. You see, he told Charles and me about what happened between you."

I scrubbed my arm up and down, carefully not meeting her eyes. Had she come to berate me for my decision?

I immediately rejected the ungenerous thought. Nothing in the friendly manner of this elegant, dignified royal gave credence to such an accusation. But I couldn't think why else she might be here.

"I'm glad Percy has some adopted family here," I said. "He's been away from home a long time."

She nodded. "We're extremely grateful for his efforts on Rangmere's behalf. As we are grateful you found a family of your own. We have all been concerned for you—and for Cassandra and Princess Daisy."

I glanced at Anthea and Maris, but somehow I had drifted closer to Clarisse as we talked, and with the falling water of the fountain providing background noise, we were no longer in earshot of the merchant women.

"I was disappointed to hear they're both still missing. I was hoping they might have been found and word just hadn't made its way to Caravan Bryant."

"We are assured the godmothers have their eye on them," Clarisse said. "As they do on you."

I raised an eyebrow. Apparently Arvin's fears hadn't been entirely groundless, although I had yet to see any sign of a godmother in my own life. Unless the dramatic and unlikely happenings of the last few weeks were signs of one working in the background.

The idea made me squirm. I wasn't a princess, and my happiness didn't affect the fate of kingdoms. I wasn't any more deserving of a godmother's attention than anyone else.

"Percy is hurting," Clarisse said in a soft voice. "It's hard for us to watch."

I tried to turn away before she could see the pain that lanced through me at her words, but I must not have turned quickly enough because she sat up straighter.

"Ah! So you do care."

"Of course I care." I still wouldn't look at her. "How could anyone know Percy and not care? I care too much to let him shackle his life to mine. I'm no princess, and I don't belong in a court."

She regarded me with a small crease between her brows. "If you truly don't want to live the life of a princess, then there is no hope for the two of you. He cannot change who he is, and there is no denying it's a heavy burden to ask you to shoulder."

I bit my lip to stop myself from saying I would bear any burden for Percy if only it wouldn't end up causing him greater pain.

"You are probably aware that royal children sometimes receive godmother gifts at their Christenings," she said, and I tried to keep the confusion from my face at the abrupt change of topic.

"Certainly," I said. "Although it has not been the case in our kingdoms until the recent return of the godmothers."

She nodded. "You are probably not, however, aware of the gift I received."

I glanced sideways at her, straining my memory for any mention of it. But she continued on without waiting for me to speak.

"I received courage."

"Courage? An unusual gift for a princess." I tried not to envy her the possession of such a useful trait.

"Is it?" She frowned. "If it is, it shouldn't be. Princesses need a great deal of courage."

I bit the inside of my cheek, remembering the stories about her first husband.

"I certainly needed to draw on my gift when I agreed to a marriage alliance with Prince Konrad of Rangmere," she said. "I didn't know him at all, but I had always expected to make a political marriage, and I was willing enough." She sighed. "If I had known him, not even my godmother's courage would have been enough for me to agree to marry a monster."

I winced at the word.

"I'm sorry to put it so baldly," she said, "but it's the truth. His desire for power overset his reason in the end. While my title and connections back home in Lanover protected me from overt abuse, he was an expert at exerting power and making me miserable. Eventually I stood up to him and escaped, and when he was subsequently killed, I credited my godmother with my relative wholeness."

"I'm sorry you had to go through that," I said, knowing the words were inadequate. I didn't know why this princess was confiding her story in a near stranger, but I couldn't deny my curiosity at her history.

"It seems a long time ago now," she said.

"I'm glad you were equipped."

"So I thought." She paused to call a warning to a boy who looked about five before turning back to me. "But it was more than a year before I realized the truth."

"The truth?" I frowned at her, unable to guess what she meant.

"There is more than one type of courage," she said. "And although I had used a great deal of it in my first marriage, deep scars still remained. While I told myself I had survived unharmed, in truth, I was harboring a deep fear."

"But Prince Konrad was deceased, wasn't he?" I asked. "Surely you weren't afraid Queen Ava would take out her revenge against her brother on you?"

Clarisse smiled and shook her head. "No, not that. Since Konrad's death, Ava and I have been more sisters than we were while he was alive. His presence had a way of poisoning everything." She sighed. "No, my fear only reared its head when I met Charles."

"Oh," I said softly, beginning to realize what she must mean.

"Charles has a title and status, but he's nothing like Konrad," she said. "His dry wit is never cruel, and his steady composure is enough for any situation. I feel peaceful and safe when I'm with him, and he manages the people under his care with dignity and compassion."

"He sounds wonderful." I smiled, glad that Celine's sister had found happiness at last.

"He is wonderful. And I was immediately attracted to him when we met. He had been away for several years as a diplomatic envoy to Northhelm, and we were only introduced after Ava took the crown."

"So you remained in Rangmere after Konrad's death?"

She nodded. "I wanted to support Ava in those early days when she was still consolidating her strength. She helped save me from Konrad, and I wanted to undo some of the damage he'd done, if I could."

I didn't bother protesting that his actions hadn't been her

fault. Her manner told me she'd already made her peace with that. But it warmed me to know she had made a family where she found herself, despite her circumstances—like I had done twice now.

"I'm glad you found a second chance at love," I said.

"I nearly didn't."

My hands stilled as my eyes flew to hers, confused. It was impossible to imagine the earl hadn't been as attracted to her as she was to him.

"What do you mean?"

"It turns out some things are even scarier than monsters."

I tried to breathe, but my throat seemed to be constricting as she continued.

"I had courage enough to survive Konrad, but it turned out opening my heart to love required a greater courage still. I didn't love Konrad, but he had stood beside me at our marriage and vowed to protect and love me—and then when I was alone and friendless in a new kingdom, he had betrayed those vows. I had been hurt—deeply—and my heart remembered. As Charles increased his attentions to me, I fled, afraid of my strong response to him. I had thought I found a home and a future when I married Konrad, but it had turned into a nightmare. I was afraid of a far greater pain if my second hope also turned false."

Home. The word resonated through every part of me. How many homes had I found now, only to lose them again, no matter how hard I worked? I could feel the fear she described all the way to my fingers and toes. It was a risk I couldn't take with Percy.

And yet, Clarisse had clearly taken the risk after all.

"What changed?" My voice squeaked, and I cleared my throat.

"Ava helped me, actually. She could see what was happening, and she stepped in. She grew up in a far more damaging environment than me, but she's been to the Palace of Light."

"What?" I stared at her. "Queen Ava has actually met the High King?"

"Yes. I found it hard to believe myself at first, until I saw the changes in her. There is a reason the High King decrees true love must rule the kingdoms. I had it the wrong way around. I thought love increased the fear, but it's love that defeats fear. Love is the foundation that lets us weather whatever storms come our way. True love sees us just as we are and loves us anyway—and it never wavers. I thought closing myself off from love would protect me, but it only made me weaker and more afraid."

"I'm not afraid to love Percy." I closed my eyes for a moment, willing myself to speak the truth. "I do love him."

"I'm glad to hear it." Her smile was radiant. "But our fears can take different forms. And sometimes it's not that we fear to love others, it's that we're afraid of not being enough to earn their love in return." She hesitated. "I couldn't accept that Percy has no chance of happiness with you until I had looked you in the eyes and asked you this question. Do you not want the life of a princess? Or is it that you're actually afraid—afraid of not being enough?"

"I—" I faltered, looking at the swirling waters of the fountain as I tried to sort out the chaos of my thoughts.

She continued in a confident voice. "Because you don't have to be afraid of that, Daria. The beauty of true love is that it's freely given. You don't have to earn it. All you have to do is have the courage to accept it. And the girl who walked alone into Damon's camp has the courage to love a prince—and the courage to be a princess. I don't doubt it." A smile warmed her voice. "I don't doubt you, Daria."

I tried to respond, but the lump in my throat seemed to be preventing any words from escaping. Flashes of my life spun through my mind as I thought of the failure of my parents and of all my attempts to build a family since. I had worked so hard each time to make a place for myself. Was she right? Had I been trying to earn a love that would have been freely given?

"Mama! Mama!" The voice of the young girl broke the moment, and we both turned to her.

"What is it, Izzy?"

"You said Ellery was going to be here. Where is she? I'm tired of playing only with Danton."

"You're not playing just with your brother." Clarisse slipped an arm around her daughter. "Sarah's children are here, too."

The other woman came hurrying over. "Sorry, Clarisse." She smiled at Lady Isabella. "It's hard always being the oldest, isn't it, Izzy?"

"Ellery isn't much younger," Isabella said. "She'll be seven this summer."

At this second mention of the young princess, I began to quietly gather my wet laundry. If the princess was coming, then I had to leave. I could hope my conversation with Clarisse had escaped notice, but the heir to the throne would attract too much attention.

"My apologies," Clarisse said, interrupting my task. "I haven't introduced you. Sarah, this is…Dee." She gave Sarah a significant look before turning back to me. "And this is Sarah. She's married to Lord Adelmar's son now, but she used to be a traveling merchant like you."

"Another one?" The question popped out before I realized it was coming. "Oh, I'm sorry." I bit my lip.

The young noblewoman just laughed. "I'm guessing that means you've met my cousin."

"You're cousins with Lady Anhalt?"

She laughed again. "I know we're different—practically opposites—but if you look a little closer, you'll see our coloring is the same, at least. We were raised like sisters in our caravan."

I gave her a closer look, noting her light skin, warm brown eyes, and light brown hair. "Oh, yes, and you have the same nose."

She fingered the article in question. "That's true. Although I wish I had her height." She sighed before brightening, her broad smile returning. "Except maybe it's for the best. If I was tall, they might have expected me to become a guard like her." She shivered dramatically. "I would have hated that."

I smiled, despite my unease. It was impossible not to like this irrepressible young woman.

"I won't bother introducing my brood. It's always impossible to keep other people's children straight when they get introduced in a whole horde, and Evelyn will be along anytime now with—oh! There she is!"

"Ellery!" Isabella screamed her friend's name and dashed across the square.

Her mother called a half-hearted protest before laughing across at Sarah.

"What can you do?" the merchant woman asked. "She'll be grown soon enough."

The look that passed between them told me, despite their light demeanor, these women understood the pressure that came with rank. Clarisse's earlier words continued to burn inside me as I considered their lives. Was I unwilling to accept Percy's love not because I disliked court but because it was the one place I hadn't found a way to be useful and earn my place? Was I really convinced that I had to earn—and keep earning—the love of any new family?

I gathered the last of the washing into the sack I had brought it in, although Anthea and Maris were still scrubbing on the other side of the fountain.

Lady Anhalt strolled up to us, a number of children in her wake, including Isabella and a younger girl who must be Crown Princess Ellery. The two had their heads close together whispering, while the others—all tall, lanky children—descended on Sarah's brood.

"Sorry I'm late," Lady Anhalt said with a smile that encompassed both Sarah and Clarisse. "We got caught..." Her voice trailed off as her eyes reached me. Caution immediately filled them.

"I'm just leaving," I blurted. I bobbed a quick curtsy to the group in general, before pausing for a brief second with my eyes on Clarisse. "Thank you for sharing your story with me. I'll think about what you said."

I didn't stop to talk to Anthea and Maris, fleeing across the square and out of earshot of the curious questions the countess was directing at Clarisse.

My feet flew over the cobblestones, but they couldn't outrun my thoughts. Was I fleeing from the potential of being seen in the presence of Lady Anhalt? Or was I fleeing from the truth in the princess's words?

I had determined not to let my fear rule me, but instead to live my life fully. And I had thought I threw that controlling fear aside when I faced Damon. But I could feel Clarisse's words in my bones. I was letting a different kind of fear rule me—the fear that if I stopped trying so hard, I would find myself alone once again. Even my courageous acts with Damon actually had their root in this deeper insecurity as I sought to find a way to be useful to Percy.

I was still letting fear rule me. And this fear was harder to cast aside.

CHAPTER 22

For the next few days, I could barely pay attention to what was going on around me, so deeply was I lost inside myself. But the more I searched, the more I found only the truth Clarisse had exposed.

In the back of my mind, a small part of me had been wondering if Arvin might be right, and a godmother might show up. Now I felt certain that instead they had sent Clarisse. The Lanoverian princess had enough hurt in her past to see straight to the heart of mine.

She had seen that the little girl who had been abandoned by both her parents had grown into a young woman full of fear that she too would fail those she loved. I had worked so hard to be enough for the other children I helped raise in our small cottage in the middle of the woods. And I had worked so hard to serve Lilah and Tallie. I had thought I succeeded on both counts, while I only failed to be a friend to Snow in the unfamiliar environment of her court.

And yet I had walked away from the families I built when I thought I was no longer of use to them, never considering that my absence might be enough to hurt them. Unable to believe I had a place with them beyond any capacity of mine to help them. And now I was planning to do the same thing to Percy.

I emerged from my thoughts the morning of the ball. Maybe I could accept Percy's love and hand, after all. Maybe he really meant it when he said he didn't care how useful I could be at court.

Hope filled me. I would go to the ball and tell him how I felt. If he still loved me after my rejection, I would go with him to Talinos or anywhere else our life might take us.

I went to breakfast as if walking on clouds, everything around me aglow from the sun. One look at Tallie's thunderous face sent me crashing back down to earth, however.

Lilah had forbidden either of us from attending the ball. And from her efforts before the first ball, she wasn't afraid to go to extreme lengths to ensure our compliance.

In my deep examination of my own heart, I had done the impossible and forgotten my mission to help capture Damon. I had meant to spend these days convincing Lilah to let me go to the ball—or devising a plan to go despite her. I had done neither, and now it was almost too late.

I served myself breakfast, determination filling me. I would find a way to get to Percy, no matter what. My hand paused over my bowl, a laugh filling me. Yet more proof that Clarisse had been right. Fear of Damon had crippled me, but love for Percy made me determined and strong.

"I don't know why you look so cheery," Tallie said in a sullen voice. "It's like you don't even want to go to the ball."

"I am going to the ball," I said with decision. "And so are you."

Tallie sat up a little straighter, a hint of hope filling her face. "You have a plan? A way for us to get past Mother?"

For a moment I considered the possibility. But I shook my head as I took a large bite of my food. I refused to creep out as if I was doing something shameful. I needed to go to that ball, and I would just have to make Lilah see that.

"No. I'm going to convince Lilah."

Tallie slumped back down. "That will never work. Don't you realize I've been trying that for *two weeks*?"

I considered telling her that her strategy of alternating between sulking and complaining wasn't likely to produce results but decided against it. I needed to focus my energy on Lilah.

I searched the dining hall for her, finding her deep in conversation with Maris. She glanced our way once or twice every minute, as if to reassure herself we were still there. I had let my fear drive me into a life of service no one had ever asked for, but Lilah was in far greater bondage.

I turned to Tallie. "We'll talk to her after the meal. Together."

Tallie frowned doubtfully. "I suppose it can't hurt." A slight lightening of her sour mood lifted her features. "Thanks, Dee. I was starting to think you agreed with her."

I shook my head decisively. "It's time for all of us to start living. Including Lilah."

"When you speak in that tone of voice, I almost believe you can make it happen." She looked actually hopeful now.

A smile twitched across my face. "Before you get too excited, you should probably be warned that living involves more chores than you've gotten away with doing so far."

Tallie rolled her eyes. "Convince Mother to stop keeping me chained to her side, and I'll do all the chores you like."

"*All* of them?"

She laughed. "Well, some of them, then. But honestly, I'd rather spend some of the day doing chores and the rest living than sitting around here doing nothing at all."

"I'll take that as progress." I shook my head. "And I'll remind you of those words when it comes time to do the chores."

A determined look transformed her face. "You won't have to. I know you're right, Dee. I let you do too much. I probably don't seem like I appreciate it, but I do. Everything has been so much better in our little family since you joined it. Mother was always stressed and sad before—like she's been since Damon's attacks. For a long time after you came, she didn't have to work so hard, but she was still able to make more jewelry." She paused, looking a little embarrassed, as if unsure about whether to say more. But after a brief moment, she blurted out one more thought.

"But it's not just the practical things. You're always so kind, Dee—there's just something about your presence that's pleasant. You're easy to love, I guess. I think having you with us helped bring Mother peace after—"

She cut herself off, biting her lip as if she'd said too much.

I stared at her in surprise, unsure what to say. What had happened in the past to cut up Lilah's peace?

Tallie dropped her eyes, discomfort crossing her features as she misunderstood my confusion. "Ouch. Your surprise hurts. But I suppose I deserve it. I haven't exactly been showing any appreciation for you in my actions. I do mean it, though. And I will help more in the future."

I smiled, touched. "Thank you, Tallie." I pulled the younger girl into a hug before pulling back with a mischievous grin. "Although it's too bad we didn't realize before now how to convince you to do more chores. All we needed was to lock you in an inn for two weeks with threats of crazed rebels to keep you in place. I could have had help with the chores for two years."

Tallie laughed. "You can do a lot, Dee, but not even you can produce crazed rebels on command." She looked doubtful. "I don't think."

I laughed. "No, I don't think I could."

"It's so nice to see you two smiling and laughing." Lilah looked down at us with a smile of her own. "It's been too quiet around here lately."

I glanced at Tallie before looking up at her mother.

"Actually, we were hoping to talk to you."

Lilah quirked an eyebrow.

"But not here," Tallie said quickly. "Up in our room."

Lilah gestured for us to precede her. "Lead the way. I just hope this isn't more nonsense about that ball."

I ignored her words, climbing the stairs at a quick pace, eager to get to the conversation now I had decided it was necessary. I wished I could start by being open about my own situation, but I still wasn't permitted to tell them the truth. Even if I hadn't been forbidden from telling anyone, it wouldn't be fair to them to place that burden on their shoulders so unnecessarily. By the end of the night, all of my secrets would finally be exposed. I just had to convince Lilah to let me go to the ball first.

When we reached the room, Lilah closed the door and turned to face us. She looked at her daughter, clearly expecting her to burst into impassioned speech, but Tallie just looked at me. Surprised, Lilah followed her gaze.

"I need to go to the ball tonight," I said.

"Absolutely not." Lilah looked disappointed at the topic of conversation.

"I am going to the ball," I rephrased. "And I won't let you stop me. I'm an adult, and you're not my mother." I paused as Lilah fell back a step, hurt filling her face. "But I'd like to have your permission, all the same. And I think you should let Tallie go as well. And you should come too, of course."

"After what happened last time?" Her hurt transformed into anger.

"What did happen last time?" I stepped forward, willing her toward some of the transformation that had been happening in me over the last few days. "No one was hurt. As I understand it, the worst that happened was you had your feet examined."

"Our shoes," Tallie clarified, but neither of us paid her any heed.

Lilah was shaking her head, but I pressed on, meeting her eyes.

"I'm not suggesting you take foolish risks. Isambard is a careful caravan leader. He makes considered decisions. You can trust in the caravan as a whole to be sufficiently cautious. At the moment, you're letting your fears rule you so much that they're affecting your ability to function. Soon you'll lose your position in the caravan and end up right at the back." I glanced sideways at Tallie. "And then you'll lose everything else."

Lilah's expression showed she understood my point, her eyes lingering on her daughter with fear in them. Tallie would be grown soon, and if Lilah wasn't careful, when that day came, Tallie would leave and not come back.

"Tallie has promised to help out more if you'll stop supervising her so closely and stop keeping her sequestered at the inn."

Tallie nodded eagerly, her eyes pinned to her mother's face.

Lilah shook her head again, although she looked torn now.

I took a deep breath. "I recently realized I was letting myself be controlled by my fear. Someday soon I'll tell you the full story. But for now, I just want to ask you what it is you're so afraid of? What do you fear happening if we go to this ball?"

"You might die!" she cried, her voice shaken. "You might be killed."

"It doesn't seem likely at a ball." I kept my voice level and calm. "Of course, death is always waiting for us, but what's the point of preserving life if it means giving up any chance of living it?"

Lilah sank down to sit on one of the beds.

"Children aren't supposed to die," she said in a rough voice. "But sometimes they do. Sometimes they never get to live life at all."

Sudden clarity filled me, and I sat gently down beside her, placing a hand on her arm.

"Lilah, what happened to your first daughter? The one I'm impersonating?"

Tallie looked between us before sitting on her mother's other side and putting an arm around her.

"She died." The words were wrenched from Lilah. "She died before she ever had a chance to live."

"She was born without breath," Tallie said softly.

I looked across at her. "You knew?"

Tallie nodded. "I've always known, but Mother doesn't like me to talk about it. She keeps her memory alive by talking as if I still have a sister."

"You do!" Lilah mopped at her streaming eyes. "She's with your grandparents, where we'll join her one day."

With family. Everything made sense now. The convenient persona for me to adopt...the way no one questioned it...even Lilah's tendency to forget I wasn't her true daughter. I had stepped into a place waiting empty for years. And Tallie said my presence had helped—but it hadn't been enough to keep the fears from resurfacing when a new threat emerged.

"I'm not your daughter, but I'm honored to have stood in her place for the last two years," I said. "And I'm saying this because I don't want you to lose either of your remaining daughters—either your blood one, or your adopted stepdaughter. You have to let go of your fear."

"I don't know how," she said.

"I'm still learning about that myself. But the first step is to let love into your heart to take its place."

Lilah stood, striding over to stand facing the window. "You say it just like that, but it's not so easy to actually do."

"No." I sighed. "It's not easy. But you can start by taking the first step. Recognize that I'm an adult and can make my own decision about the ball. Don't stand in my way."

"And please let me go, too," Tallie said all in a rush, her voice small in the face of her mother's emotion.

"Very well." Lilah didn't turn away from the window. "We can all go to the ball. And I'll think about what you've said, Dee."

"I can't ask for anything more."

Tallie's glee looked about to explode, so I opened the door and whisked her out into the corridor, before her enthusiasm convinced her mother to change her mind. All I could hope was that the seed I had planted would eventually bear full fruit.

"Eeee!" Tallie bounced up and down as we descended the stairs. "We're going to the ball!" She gripped my arm with both hands. "Which means we need to go shopping!"

CHAPTER 23

I didn't want to disturb Lilah, so I left a message with Anthea about where we were going. It was a risk to take Tallie shopping without getting Lilah's permission first, but I suspected she had known the outcome of remaining alone in our room. She had barely taken her eyes off Tallie in days. She had tested me often enough, and now it was my turn to test if she truly did mean to try to change.

When we returned to the inn, there was still no sign of her in the common rooms. Instead we found her sitting quietly where we had left her by the window of our room, gazing out at the inn yard. She must have seen us leave, then, but she offered no recriminations.

Tallie, at least, took this as an excellent sign, throwing her arms affectionately around her mother and beginning to recite a list of all the purchases she had made. Lilah smiled, responding as if Tallie frequently went on unaccompanied shopping outings in the city. I accepted this change without comment, showing her the dress I had insisted we purchase for her.

Some things transcended age, and Lilah showed a spark of real interest as she examined the fabric, demanding to know how much we had paid and declaring she could have bargained the seller down even further. Neither of us were in the mood to gainsay her, so we finished the conversation in perfect amity.

I had found a gown for myself, although it looked simple compared to the gorgeous dress I had worn to the previous ball. But I reminded myself that garment had come from Damon. No compliments could weigh in the balance against that one fact.

Still, feelings of wistfulness lingered when a knock sounded on the door. Lilah answered it, murmuring to someone outside before turning back into the room with two parcels in her arms.

"They're for you, Dee," she said. "Did a city merchant keep some of your purchases behind to make adjustments?" She looked mildly offended, as if I should have instead brought the items home to her so she could perform the task.

I frowned, shaking my head as presentiment crept over me.

"No, we didn't leave anything behind." Tallie came over to examine the brown paper in her mother's arms. "Open them, Dee! I want to see what they are."

I took the packages—one large and one small—with heavy arms, laying them on the bed and slowly unwrapping the layers of the larger one as Tallie peered over my shoulder. As I pulled the last of the paper away, she gave a sharp gasp.

When I didn't move, she pushed me out of the way to lift the gown up and hold it at full length, leaving the matching dancing slippers on the bed.

"Oooh," she breathed reverently.

Even Lilah looked astonished, her eyes round. "It's stunning, Dee! And it must have cost a fortune."

"But where did it come from?" Tallie asked. "We were at the markets together, and I definitely would have remembered you buying this."

"We couldn't afford a dress like this," Lilah said with certainty. "Look at that beading work across the bodice. And feel the material."

"There's so many layers." Tallie swished it gently through the air. "You're going to look like a princess!"

The eyes of mother and daughter met, and both of them stilled. I stopped breathing as I remembered the rumors about me at the last ball.

Lilah turned to me, eyes narrowing. "Where did this dress come from? Is there a note?"

I shook my head, keeping my eyes on the brown paper, as if examining it closely for the missing message I knew wouldn't be there. I could feel their suspicion as they remembered the mystery princess in the expensive dress—the one who had turned out to be nothing more than one of Damon's traitors.

"What about the second package?" Lilah asked. "Maybe the note is in there?"

The shock of the dress had made me forget the smaller parcel. I fished it out of the mess of brown paper on the bed. It felt heavy despite its small size, and I couldn't guess what it might be.

"Come on," Tallie said. "Hurry up!"

I ripped off the paper with trembling fingers, revealing a long hair pin that appeared to be made of steel.

"Is that a diamond?" Tallie gasped. She dropped the gown on the bed and pushed closer for a better look.

Lilah bent over and pulled a white slip from the brown paper I had let float to the floor.

"Look, here's the note." She handed it to me to read, watching me with an expectant expression. "Well?" she prompted when I didn't say anything straight away.

I looked back up, not quite able to meet her eyes.

"It's…it's from Percy."

"The prince!" Tallie squealed and snatched the paper from my hands.

But a moment later she wrinkled her nose. "It just says, *For the ball.* That's not very romantic."

Lilah, whose earlier tension had drained away, laughed. "It's a *diamond*, Tallie. That's a love note all its own."

I put my hands to my warm cheeks. "There's nothing...I mean, we aren't..." I stumbled over the words, unsure what I was trying to say. There was nothing official between us right now, but I couldn't deny I had hopes that might change.

I focused on Lilah. "You don't mind?" Ever since I decided to tell Percy how I felt, I had been worried about abandoning my merchant family.

Lilah looked at me with a sad smile. "You falling into our family was the best thing that's happened to us in years. I wish I could keep you forever. But you said it yourself just now. You're not really my daughter, and you have to live your own life."

"Even though it would mean I have to leave the Four Kingdoms?" I asked. "Even though it would mean a journey far away across the seas?" I could only imagine how that would set off Lilah's fears, quite apart from the blow my absence would cause her business efforts.

She gave me a slightly puzzled look. "If he truly loves you, then of course we have to let you go. I could never stand in the way of your happiness." She gave an amazed chuckle. "You have the chance to be a princess, Dee!"

As she examined me, the bemusement still lingering on her face, her expression softened. "I know I'm not always a good mother, but I do love you, Dee, as if you were a true daughter. And wherever you go, you'll always be part of our family."

Tears leaped into my eyes and spilled unheeded down my cheeks as I wrapped my arms around her and buried my face in her shoulder. I had decided to believe Clarisse and Percy, and to take a chance in accepting his love. But looking into Lilah's face as she called me her daughter brought the truth crashing from my mind into my heart.

I had worked so hard to earn a place in Lilah and Tallie's family, and yet earlier Tallie had said what she appreciated most was my presence. And now Lilah was embracing the idea of returning to their previous life of bare subsistence because she believed it was best for me. Neither of them required anything from me at all, and yet they still saw me as family.

I tried to get control of my emotions. "I can never thank you enough for everything you've done for me. And I don't know if there even is anything with Percy—"

"Oh, pish! Look at that dress!"

I pulled back, chuckling weakly, not knowing how else to respond. The gown didn't come from Percy, and it wasn't a token of love. The two packages might have been delivered to our room at the same time, but they hadn't come from the same source. But I couldn't tell Lilah or Tallie that. I had to let them assume the gown also came from Percy.

Looking at the folds of the midnight blue skirt, soft tulle over full satin, and the fitted bodice, covered with small beads that shone like diamonds, I couldn't help reacting to its beauty despite its source. I would wear this dress and tell my prince I loved him. And after that, I would face Damon. It was the kind of gown that gave you confidence just from wearing it.

Several hours later, as I stood at the ballroom doors, I wondered where that confidence had flown. I had let Tallie arrange my hair into a myriad of tiny braids which she had swept up into an elegant arrangement on top of my head, warning me to be careful after she nearly pricked herself on the sharp point of my new hair pin. But I could no longer grasp the graceful feeling that had gripped me when I looked in the mirror.

"You can do this," I whispered to myself, but I wasn't sure if my heart was beating so hard from the thought of facing Percy or Damon. Now that I stood in a ballroom full of brightly dressed courtiers, my earlier sense of certainty had evaporated, and I nearly wobbled on the unfamiliar heels of the dancing slippers Damon had sent.

But as I hesitated there, my eyes picked out Clarisse from the crowd. The princess looked resplendent in deep purple, easily standing out among the throng due to both her beauty and poise. At sight of me, a broad smile lit her face, and I felt some of her goodwill buoy me up. She was proof of Percy's assurance that kindness had a place at court.

I stepped forward into the room, my skirts swishing in a satisfying way. The murmuring sound spread out from me, transforming, as heads turned and whispers followed me. It had been the same at the first ball, but then I had worn a mask. Now it was me they looked at and whispered about.

I lifted my chin. I might just be an orphan girl, adopted into a merchant caravan, but tonight I was dressed like a princess. I was through letting fear control me—not with Damon, not with my family, and not in a ballroom either. No matter how many people looked, I knew I belonged here, and that was all that mattered.

The rustle of murmurs intensified, and the people in front of me parted as someone pushed their way toward the front of the room. A familiar face appeared, eyes locked on me, and everything else disappeared.

If the music was still playing, I no longer heard it, and the dancers became hazy and indistinct.

Somehow my feet carried me forward, despite the unfamiliar heels. No thought of fetching Damon or of hostile watchers entered my mind, as Percy pushed his way through the last of the crowd to reach me before I had taken more than a few steps. He reached out his arms, and I stepped into them as easily as taking a breath.

For a moment we simply looked at each other, and then he pulled me into the dance with a shaky laugh.

"We'll attract attention if we just stand there." He swept me in a circle, guiding me expertly through the unfamiliar movements.

"I think we already did." I bit my lip, memories of my other purpose tonight surfacing. "Hopefully it's too late for any stories to be carried to Damon."

Percy's arms tightened around me. "I'm not sure I can bear to let you go off alone to face him."

I gave him a stern look. "I'm not backing out now. The whole plan depends on me, remember."

"I don't like you taking the risk." He sighed. "But I know I can't stop you. I just wish we could go together."

I took a deep breath. "When this is over, and Damon's safely locked away, we can be together."

His steps faltered slightly before he caught himself and maneuvered me around for another circle of the room.

"You mean…"

I smiled up at him, my nerves gone at the sight of his beloved eyes shining back down at me.

"You were right before. I thought I had overcome my fears, but I had only tackled one layer of them. There were deeper fears underneath, holding me back. But I don't want anything to hold me back from you. You've showed me what it means to have true courage. You're thoughtful, persistent, and true. I only have to look at the way your men follow you—despite not being from your own kingdom." I hesitated. "I'm ready to accept your love and face your court, as long as you're sure you want to take me back to them. Aren't they expecting you to make an alliance with someone from the Four Kingdoms? Your family will be disappointed…"

A fierce look sprang into his face. "I dare anyone to tell me so after meeting you. They'll just have to be satisfied with an alliance with Eliam." His look melted into a laugh. "That's assuming Snow will accept me as an alliance partner for you."

I chuckled. "She might deem you just suitable."

Percy looked around with a rueful grimace. "There are far too many people in this room. How shocked do you think they would be if I kissed you mid-dance?"

I shook my head. "Don't you dare!"

His eyes laughed down at me. "What, having second thoughts already?"

"About you?" I gripped him tighter. "Never. About wanting to be a spectacle in front of such a crowd? That's not second thoughts. I've always felt that way."

"Then you definitely shouldn't have worn that dress." The admiration in his voice and eyes made me flush. "I can assure you that everyone is looking at you."

I buried my head in his shoulder. "Don't say that! I'll trip over myself now or something."

I could feel the vibration of his chuckle. "I wouldn't be such a clumsy partner as to let you. But it's no use trying to hide your beauty."

I straightened, giving him a stern look. "You can't hoodwink me with such talk. I remember you spouting words about my beauty the last time we danced—only I was wearing a mask then!"

"I remember explaining it to you at the time, but I could see you didn't believe me. You carry yourself with elegance, Daria. I think it might be your inner beauty, seeping out of you no matter what you wear. Your face is beautiful, of course, but it's only one part of your whole. If the two balls had been reversed, I would have recognized you in a second, even with the mask." He paused for a moment. "But I see this time you're wearing my gift."

His voice sounded pleased, and warmth washed over me. Once again the sensation of safety filled me as I stood in the circle of his arms.

"Thank you for sending it to me, despite..."

His arms tightened around me. "I just want you to be safe. I just want tonight to be over."

Somewhere a clock chimed, and I stiffened.

Percy exclaimed under his breath. "It can't possibly be time for you to go already."

I let my arms drop, and he reluctantly did the same, taking my hand and tucking it into his arm as he led me off the dance floor.

"You remember what you need to do?"

I swallowed and nodded. The feeling of security had fallen away completely, replaced with a sharp awareness of my rapid pulse. Would Damon be able to sense my nerves?

The clock chimed again. I looked up at Percy, pierced by a horrible certainty that this one perfect moment was all we would ever get. Something would go wrong, and the vision of a future with him would be ripped away from me.

I shook myself, rejecting the thought. Such ideas only fed my fear, and I was finished feeding it. I would face this challenge for now and deal with the future when it came.

I disengaged my arm from Percy's.

"This is the part I have to do on my own."

He leaned in close, his face a breath away from mine.

"One small kiss?" he whispered.

For a second, I let the moment hang there before I swayed away from him.

"When this is behind us, you can have as many kisses as you like."

He pulled back, sighing. "So cruel."

"Focused, I think you mean."

The smile I loved so much transformed his face. "And beautiful and kind and deadly to villains. I could do this all night."

I grinned back, despite my anxiety. "See you soon, Percy."

CHAPTER 24

The smile fell from my face before I left the ballroom, the earlier sensation of approaching danger growing stronger with every step. In Percy's arms, it had been easy to forget the menace of Damon, but alone in the night, everything felt different. I wished I had a cloak to pull around me, my gown now feeling like flimsy protection against the darkness.

But Damon had sent me a second distinctive gown for a purpose. I had entered with the merchants, my right to be at the ball unquestioned. When I entered again shortly with Damon by my side, I needed to be sure the guards recognized me. We didn't want any questions.

"Going so soon?" one of the guards asked when I reached the gate.

"Only briefly," I replied, proud of my steady voice. "One of the others has gotten himself into trouble and needs rescuing." I forced a grin onto my face. "I tried to tell him his wagon wheel needed work, but do men ever listen?"

The guard guffawed. "We have to keep ourselves interesting somehow."

I rolled my eyes. "Women could do without the kind of interesting that drags them away in the middle of a ball."

"I only wish I had a beautiful damsel to come rescue me next time I find myself in trouble," the other guard said.

"Just as long as you don't do anything to ruin that dress," a woman chimed in, as a couple joined us. "It's worth a small fortune."

My smile faltered, and I only just pinned it back on in time. I didn't know the newcomers' names, but I recognized them from Caravan Hargrove. All the merchants were supposed to have arrived already. It could ruin everything if I crossed paths with someone on the way back and they recognized Damon wasn't a merchant.

"I'll be careful," I said to the concerned woman before nodding to the guards and hurrying out into the city.

Once alone, I stopped to draw in some shuddering breaths. I had achieved my first goal. The guards would surely recognize me on my return and ask no awkward questions about Damon's right to enter the palace.

I frowned. Or had the king and queen put trusted guards on duty who already knew not to question us? Had that all been a show for the merchant couple? My fear was making my thoughts swim.

I straightened, forcing myself to focus on the next step. It wouldn't be helpful to make Damon suspicious by keeping him waiting. I picked up my skirts and increased my pace.

My breath rasped sharply in and out of my mouth by the time I reached the eastern gate. I could see no sign of any guards and only hoped they had been removed in some non-violent way.

"There you are." Damon stepped out of the shadows, making me stifle a squeak.

He raised an eyebrow. "Jumpy, my dear?"

I ignored both the endearment and the mocking humor in his voice.

"We need to get back. I don't know when the guards at the palace gate change shift, and we want to enter while the ones who will recognize me are still there."

"Lead the way." He gestured for me to start walking, and it occurred to me he could have no familiarity with this city.

I shook my head at the audacity of his attempt to claim it as his own.

Little light shone from the partially obscured moon, but I could still make out the street beneath my feet. The man at my side didn't speak, his silence somehow more unnerving than any threatening words. Only the occasional sound of movement or call from inside a house broke the still of the night.

I glanced at him sideways, trying to read his face. Had anyone carried suspicious tales of me to him in the last two weeks? Did he guess something wasn't right?

His expression gave no sign of discomfort as he looked around the city with an assessing gaze. We passed no one else walking at such a late hour, a thought that only gradually seeped into my consciousness.

I stopped. A few steps ahead of me, Damon also stopped, spinning to give me a stern look.

"We're not inside the palace yet."

"I can hear something," I hissed. "Behind us."

I hadn't thought anything of the soft sounds of movement at first, but we were the only ones on the street.

I knew it couldn't be an ally of mine. We had agreed that the risk of exposing me or losing the element of surprise was too great for anyone else to shadow me. Whoever was out there in the dark, they weren't with me.

Sudden comprehension dawned, and I stared at Damon's impatient face.

"You have men following us." I didn't phrase it like a question, and he didn't agree, although he didn't bother to deny it either.

"That's not the plan!" I stepped forward, letting my fear show in my face. "I can't get more than one person through the palace gates. Just you. That was what we agreed. You're going to get us both captured."

"Relax." He sounded bored. "Do you see my men?" He spread his arms in an expansive gesture to both sides. "I'm not asking you to get anyone but me through the gates."

"Oh…" I regarded him suspiciously. "I told you once before that a title is no good to me if I'm dead—well, it's no good to me if I'm languishing in prison, either."

"If you know what's good for you, you'll get on with the role you agreed to play." The friendly tone he'd adopted at his camp had gone, the threat no longer even partially concealed.

I swallowed and nodded, starting to walk again. His attitude put me on edge, and the change to our plan rattled me further. My brain raced. Everything had been built around the idea he would come alone, as an assassin. The room they had chosen was small, and all the guards inside would be needed to wear down his protection.

How many people had he brought with him? And what were his intentions for them?

I had thought my heart beat loudly when I walked alone through the streets to meet Damon. It now beat a staccato rhythm so loud it reverberated through me like a drum.

The more I considered this new development, the more I saw potential problems. I couldn't see how our plan would work now, but at the same time, I was locked into following it. With no way to communicate with my conspirators, I had no choice but to lead him to the room where they waited.

I tried to listen and judge how many men followed us, but it was impossible to tell from the faint whispers of sound that reached us. I could only be certain that they numbered more than one or two.

As we neared the palace, I slowed. My mind was still half on the unknown force following us, but no solution had presented itself.

"We're nearly there." I reluctantly slipped my arm through his. "I told the guard there was a problem with your wagon wheel, but you wouldn't listen to me when I warned you."

"Very well, then." His rough voice sent shivers up my spine. "Let's get this over with."

We walked close together now, and it took all my willpower not to look over my shoulder as we approached in sight of the gate. Where had Damon's men gone? What havoc were they wreaking in the city?

"So you did make it back," one of the guards said in a friendly voice. "I see your rescue was successful."

"Don't worry, I'm suitably chastened." Damon chuckled, his grin natural and his manner relaxed. I had never seen such a thorough transformation, no sign now of his previous taut, predatory bearing and irritated expression. I had been warned of his superb acting abilities, but I still hadn't been prepared.

Without changing anything of his light, happy appearance, he managed to pinch my elbow, and I also produced a smile.

"He'll know better than to ignore me next time."

"That I will." Admiration glowed in his eyes as he looked down at me, and I instantly felt the urge to scrub myself clean. His falsity made me ill to my stomach.

Both guards chuckled as they waved us through without further comment. I could sense some of the pleasure on Damon's face becoming real, and I instinctively knew he was satisfied with the success of the scheme he had devised.

I didn't voice my own query as to whether it would have worked without the cooperation of the palace. We had been thoroughly checked on our way in that evening, our merchant tokens no longer enough after my performance at the first ball.

As soon as we were through the gate, Damon slipped an arm around my waist and whisked me into the shadows near the palace wall. He pulled me close, and it took all my willpower not to thrust him away.

"They won't question my wanting a quiet moment with you all to myself," he whispered into my ear, and I shivered. "Now I need you to lead me to the side gate."

"I don't know anything about a side gate," I whispered back. "I told you from the beginning I'm not familiar with the palace. The merchants aren't being housed here."

"Then we'll find it together." He hadn't let go of my arm, and I didn't dare try pulling it free.

Instead I let him drag me along the wall. We had to circle several outbuildings, but eventually we found a sturdy looking wooden gate, securely latched.

I peered around into the darkness. "Where's the guard?"

"There isn't one. This door is designed to be impossible to open from the outside."

I tried to tell myself it was a good thing there wasn't a guard for Damon to harm, but his intentions were now obvious, and it was all I could do to keep from panicking. What would I do once he had his men inside the palace? Should I try to stop him?

I could call for the guards at the front gate, but would they come? They might think it an attempt to lure them from their posts. And even if they did respond, by the time they reached us, Damon would have his own people inside to face them. We would have lost our advantage, and Damon would slip away, yet again.

Just as before, I had to accept there was no choice. I had to lead them to the green receiving room and hope the king and duchess could handle the increased numbers.

While I had been considering my options, Damon was already opening the door. His men poured in, and I gulped as the stream of people went on and on. I lost count in the darkness, but I estimated at least thirty of them.

They milled around in the dim corner of the palace yard, alert and watchful. They had dressed for a ball, but each of them had a deadly looking weapon strapped to his waist. When the last one had entered, Damon turned to me.

"Take me to the ballroom."

I licked my lips. "Follow me."

I led them through the back way Lady Anhalt had shown me and, as promised, it was empty of servants or guards. If Damon found this quiet suspicious, he said nothing.

My head felt light, the tension of the last hour reaching a crescendo that threatened to overwhelm me. I clung hard to my strength of purpose, however. I would see this through. Percy waited for me on the other side, and our happiness was so close.

Finally I saw the door of the receiving room in the corridor ahead. My eyes attached to it, clinging as to a lifeline.

But when I stopped in front of it, my hand on the knob, Damon's arm whipped out and blocked me.

"That doesn't look like the door to the ballroom."

"No." I glanced shakily over my shoulder at our entourage. "It's a receiving room off the ballroom. Queen Ava retires here several times during the evening for a private moment to refresh herself. All you need to do is wait here for the next time she appears."

Damon shook his head, his eyes glittering. "I think not. I asked you to take me to the ballroom, and that is where we will go."

CHAPTER 25

*H*is hand closed over my upper arm like a vise.

"I will kill the upstart queen in her ballroom for all to see. Let the whole kingdom know to fear me."

Frantically I shook my head. "I don't think that's a good idea. It would be much better if we—"

"This is not a discussion." He cut me off, his expression contemptuous.

I forced myself to speak more calmly.

"Do what you like. But I'm not interested in being part of any public spectacle." I pointed at the door with my free hand. "That receiving room opens into the ballroom. You can go through there."

Damon's lips curled in an unpleasant smile. "My men can go in there, but you and I are going to the main entrance."

I tried to read his face, sweat dripping in a line down the middle of my back. Did he suspect the trap waiting for him? Or was he truly motivated by a desire to make a dramatic entrance?

I shrugged, feigning nonchalance. "As I said, do what you like. But I'm not coming."

His grip didn't weaken. "Oh yes, you are, my dear. I can't enter the ballroom without a partner. And you look suitably magnificent, thanks to my gown."

I gritted my teeth, letting some of my irritation seep through.

His grip only tightened further. "The entrance?"

"The main entrance is this way." I spoke loudly, hoping my words would penetrate the solid wood door and be understood by someone inside. It was only a small hope, though.

I started down the corridor, and Damon easily kept pace, not letting me go. When I glanced over my shoulder, his men remained behind us, poised in the corridor outside the door to the receiving room. I bit my lip, my mind dwelling on the countess and the king inside before I thrust the thought away. I needed to focus on myself and Queen Ava now. The others would have to take care of themselves.

Damon's grip lightened before lifting completely, and I considered running. But before I could take action, he grabbed my hand and slipped it through the crook of his arm. I glanced up at him, startled, only to feel the prick of something sharp against my side as he pulled me close.

My eyes dropped from his urbane smile to where our arms entwined. The hand of his bent arm concealed the hilt of a stiletto dagger, its blade lying along the inside of his forearm, and its needle-sharp tip pressing against the bodice of my dress.

I swayed, cold washing over me, but Damon held me firm. Whether he knew I had betrayed him, or had always intended to betray me, I didn't know. But I now knew he didn't intend to let me go.

He propelled me forward, and I went with him, twice nearly tripping over my heels. Did he intend to use me as a hostage or a shield? Neither option sounded promising for me.

Worse still, he had his healing ability on his side. In the receiving room, he would have been outnumbered ten to one. In the ballroom, I knew from experience that the panicking crowd would hamper the efforts of the guards to reach us.

But there would be one person watching for my reappearance —someone who would hurry straight to my side.

My breathing came rough and shallow. In an equal match, I would put my trust in Percy's ability, but how could he fight someone who couldn't be hurt?

We reached the main entrance of the ballroom, and I glanced back a final time. Still none of Damon's men had followed us.

"They'll come through your receiving room," he said in a smooth voice that carried a threat for those waiting inside the room.

I bit my lip, looking down at the brief flash of steel showing between us. The tip pressed harder against me, and I pulled my gaze back up.

"Steady now," Damon said in a voice that carried a stronger threat.

I gave a small nod, my mind whirring. That brief sight of steel, and the prick of the dagger's tip, had triggered an earlier memory of steel and Tallie's laughing voice warning me to be careful of the sharp tip.

Tallie and Lilah had been so preoccupied with the significance of the diamond, I hadn't recognized the gift for what it truly was. But tonight Percy had said he just wanted to keep me safe. I realized now what he meant. Knowing I was going to face Damon alone, he had sent me a miniature stiletto—one I could easily conceal within my ball outfit.

I wasn't entirely defenseless, then. But how could I use the weapon against someone who could heal from any injury? How could I hope to replace the ten guards who should have stood at Percy's side when he faced Damon?

We stepped into the ballroom together, everything before me a riot of color and movement.

There had to be a way to wear down his power.

A guest jostled against Damon in his effort to skirt around the dancers. Damon turned on him, every muscle taut, as if he expected the movement to hide a hidden threat. The unsuspecting merchant apologized briefly and strode on.

Damon watched him go with a calculating gaze, his head briefly turned away from me. I seized the moment, my right hand flying to my hair and extracting the pin in one swift movement.

When Damon turned back to me, his eyes narrowed, I already had my hand hidden among my skirts, my fingers wrapped around the blunt length of the blade. His eyes caught on something over my shoulder, and he stiffened again.

"Her Royal Majesty." He spoke slowly, drawing out the words.

My hand spasmed around my hidden blade. He had seen Ava.

At the same moment, my eyes locked with Percy's on the far side of the ballroom. A light sprang into his eyes, followed immediately by a look of shock when his gaze saw the man beside me. His mouth opened, as if to shout, but I couldn't hear him over the loud music and the chattering of hundreds of voices.

Damon, oblivious to my distraction, still had his focus fixed on the queen.

"Let us dance, my dear." Before I could process his words, he had both his hands on my waist and was spinning us in among the dancers. I stumbled, feeling the unyielding length of steel lying openly along my back now. He must be trusting in our movement and speed to hide it from notice.

Instinctively I raised my left hand to his shoulder and swept out my right, my skirts clenched in my fist, along with my hidden weapon. All around us, other couples danced in the same position, but Damon skillfully maneuvered us through the whirling throng.

Each time we spun, I caught a glimpse of the queen, oblivious still to our approach. She barely looked at the dancers, her attention instead focused on a distant door—one which led into the green receiving room. The two guards on either side of her were less distracted, but I recognized neither of them, which meant they wouldn't recognize us either. We would be on them before they realized something was wrong.

As we spun the other way, my eyes searched for Percy. I couldn't always find his moving figure among the dancers, but each time I did, he was closer. He wasn't pretending to dance, instead darting between the couples with careful movements that possessed their own sort of elegance.

He would reach us before we approached close enough to the queen for Damon to attack. I knew I should be glad, but fear for Percy clogged my throat. I had to help him.

I lifted one foot, bringing it down at an awkward angle with enough force to snap off the heel.

"My shoe!" I cried, stumbling and lurching against Damon.

As I jostled him, I let go of my skirt and drove the sharp point of my miniature stiletto into his lower back. He cried out as I pulled back, limping now with only one heel.

I bent and snatched the damaged shoe off my foot, knowing I might need to be free to move quickly.

"What did you do?" His swift anger transformed into a laugh. "Foolish girl. Don't you know you can't hurt me?"

Around us, other dancers faltered, thrown from the rhythm of the dance by our sudden stop. One of them screamed.

"Sword!"

Damon, alerted by the cry, spun away from me, his hand reaching for the hilt at his waist.

Percy managed one sweeping slice, cutting a large gash across Damon's chest. The same woman screamed again, but the wound healed in front of us, leaving only a trickle of red to run down his torn clothes.

I grinned in savage satisfaction. That single trickle represented a chink in his impenetrable enchantment.

Damon's blade whipped up to meet Percy's before it could strike again. The screams and cries spread across the ballroom in ever increasing ripples. A circle of space grew around the two combatants as dancers faltered, stopping, and pressing back against each other.

The disruption hadn't reached all corners of the immense ballroom, however, and somewhere in the distance, the musicians still played. Closer in, I could hear the cries of guards, but as the crowd near us jostled back, those further away pushed forward, trying to see what was happening. The resultant crush prevented the shouting guards from moving with speed.

With one panicked glance, I saw the queen had been whisked away. My full attention returned to Percy, locked in battle with Damon. Both men showed considerable skill with the blade, their weapons flashing almost too fast to follow as they circled each other, lunging and parrying.

Percy appeared to have a small edge on the other man, and Damon gave little effort to his own defense, but the wounds Percy's blade made on Damon's arms and body barely slowed him.

A guard managed to break through the crowd, coming to a stop beside me. He started forward, falling back when the assailants spun away from us, turning so it was Percy's back which faced us.

"They're moving too fast." I didn't take my eyes from the fight. "If you try to intervene, you're just as likely to end up hurting Percy as Damon."

The man looked over his shoulder, likely hoping to spot further reinforcements, but I didn't take my eyes off the fight. Percy had expended an enormous amount of energy at the beginning, and he was starting to lag.

Damon made a lightning fast thrust that Percy barely managed to parry, a glancing blow ripping open his sleeve and sending red blood dripping onto the floor.

Unlike Damon, Percy's wound showed no sign of healing, and his movements slowed further. My breathing became ragged, my hands clenching so tightly they ached. I leaned forward, following each movement of the fight.

Percy hadn't managed to touch Damon for some time, and if something didn't change, Damon was going to gain the upper hand. Every time Percy lunged, the sight of his wound made my stomach roil, the red flashing before my eyes.

The combatants spun yet again, and I gasped. The red in front of me didn't come from Percy at all.

The guard beside me stirred again, but I was too focused to pay him any heed. My hands clenched even tighter, and I dimly registered what my right one held. My damaged shoe.

Damon lunged forward, and Percy fell back, barely managing to parry the thrust. I saw Damon's muscles shift, ready to drive home his attack, and I didn't stop to think.

Drawing back my arm, I threw my shoe with all the force I could manage at his head. My impromptu projectile hurtled through the air and glanced off his ear. He staggered, his arm dropping as he struggled to maintain his balance.

"Now, Percy!" I screamed. "He's vulnerable!"

Percy didn't hesitate, leaping forward and driving his blade deep into Damon's right thigh. He pulled it cleanly free and danced back out of reach.

But this time, Damon didn't instantly recover. He lurched, staggering and then dropping to his knees.

"I...don't understand." He looked blankly down at the freely bleeding wound before looking up again, his face deathly pale. "It's not healing."

Percy sprang forward, wresting the blade from Damon's now limp hand. Damon had grown too used to his protection, and his whole fighting style had been built around it. When it was stripped away, he crumbled.

The guard beside me hurried forward to assist Percy, pulling a length of cord from his belt and using it to bind the hands of the injured man. Damon looked from his bleeding wound up into Percy's face, black rage twisting his features.

"How did you do that? It's impossible."

I stepped forward. "Actually, it was me."

Damon's head whipped around as he transferred the full force of his anger to me. "What do you mean?"

I dropped to a knee behind him, ignoring his snarl as I gripped the diamond still protruding from his back and pulled my stiletto hair pin free. I held it up.

Percy's eyes lit up. "You left it in him? Genius!"

"Didn't you wonder why I stabbed your back of all places?" I asked Damon. "Of course I knew about your ability. If I'd been wanting to do you a great injury, I wouldn't have aimed for your back. I struck somewhere you couldn't easily see or touch. And thanks to Percy's distraction, I don't know if you even noticed I never pulled my blade free."

"The enchantment noticed, though." Percy mopped at his brow with his uninjured arm before gripping the sleeve in his teeth and ripping a length of material free. "The whole time we were fighting, it was trying to heal a wound which couldn't be healed. Its strength has weakened enough from all the hits you've taken in the last two years that the effort exhausted its power. I don't know if you're permanently vulnerable now, but it doesn't matter. Queen Ava and King Hans will ensure you're locked away where you can't threaten anyone again."

"I am the true king! She's the imposter!" Damon sounded slightly crazed, although whether from the destruction of his plans or the pain, I couldn't tell.

I hurried to take the strip of material Percy had torn free from him.

"Here, let me do that. It will be easier with two hands."

More guards piled into the circle of calm around us as I carefully tied the material around Percy's injured arm. They rushed to reinforce the one who currently stood over Damon's hunched form.

"It's the Traitor Prince!" one of the guests with a front row view cried, and the words were taken up by others behind him, spreading across the ballroom.

One or two cries of alarm were quickly silenced as another message spread from one clump of guests to another. Finally, after two years, the Traitor Prince had been captured.

More shouts, this time of joy, sounded throughout the ball, and the musicians struck up a jaunty tune that made Percy chuckle.

I knotted an extra tie in my temporary bandage, looking up at him.

"He didn't come alone, Percy. There must have been thirty men with him. He left them behind at the door to the green receiving room."

CHAPTER 26

*P*ercy jolted. His sword, which had been dangling at his side since the end of the battle, swung up into alert position again.

"The king!" he cried, spinning in the direction of the distant room.

"Not you!" I snapped. "You're injured." I turned to the closest guard. "Take as many guards as you can muster to the green receiving room to assist your king. He's holding off thirty enemies with a single squad."

When the guard looked like he wanted to question me, Percy shouted, "Don't waste time! Go!"

The furor around Damon's capture had now reached even the most distant corners of the room, and this time a path cleared in front of the guards as a number of them charged across the room. A warm, strong hand gripped mine as Percy and I stood shoulder to shoulder, both watching their progress with bated breath.

Before they could reach the receiving room, however, the door burst open. I gasped, and Percy's arm went around me. But the first person though the door was King Hans, the Countess of Anhalt at his heels.

"Oh!" I slumped in relief. I had failed to get Damon into that room, but it hadn't mattered. We had defeated him anyway. And the king had defeated the men who were supposed to swoop into the ballroom to defend Damon after his assassination was complete.

Percy whooped and, ignoring his injury, swung me into his arms. He pressed his lips against mine and, forgetting the ballroom of witnesses, I kissed him back. Lightness filled me until I thought I might float off the ground altogether.

I wrapped my own arms around him, tightening them as he deepened the kiss. He pulled back with a moan, however, and I instantly let go.

"Oh no! Your wound! I'm so sorry. Have I made it worse?" I tried to pull his arm around so I could get a better look.

"Daria." He stopped me with a flash of his brilliant smile. "You could never make things worse for me."

I grimaced. "You're injured, Percy."

He groaned. "You really make me work for every moment of romance, don't you?"

"Well I can't risk taking you back to Talinos with a mutilated arm, now can I? They'll think I'm not fit to take care of you."

His eyes lit up. "So you really do mean to come back with me?"

I put my hands on my hips. "That depends. Do you mean to let me take care of you until this wound heals, at least?"

He leaned in for a kiss, pulling back before I could react or chastise him. "You can take care of me for the rest of our lives. So long as you let me take care of you as well."

"Deal." I smiled up at him. "As long as we're together, I'm even willing to brave court."

He slipped his good arm around my waist. "You're too good for me, Daria of Eliam. Or do you prefer Dee of the merchants?"

I considered. "How about Daria for formal occasions, and Dee when it's just us?"

He smiled down at me. "Hmm...Princess Daria of Talinos and Dee of my heart. They both sound perfect to me."

"Ahem." A loud throat clearing broke through the background noise.

We fell apart. I turned, flustered and awkward, but Percy looked completely relaxed, his face shining despite the pain he must feel from his arm.

"Yes?" he asked.

"If you would come with me?" The guard gestured to one side of the ballroom. "We have a doctor ready to see to your wound."

"Good!" I took Percy's hand and tugged him forward, following the man who quickly cleared a path for us through the eager, curious crowd.

While we had been distracted, the guards must have led Damon away because I could see no sign of him. The musicians had subsided, but sound still swelled in the cavernous room as every person present discussed the battle and the defeat of Damon in excited tones. Many of them pushed forward, calling questions to us, but Percy merely smiled back at them all, not attempting to answer.

"Through here." The guard ushered us into another receiving room on the opposite side of the ballroom.

This one had been decorated in soft gold, but it was hard to see the furnishings due to all the people crowded inside. A cry went up at our appearance, and more questions bombarded us from several sides.

"Give them space." The commanding tones of the queen brought instant obedience, and everyone fell back.

Only one woman moved forward with a determined gait, the bag clutched in her hands explaining her focus.

"If you'll sit down here," she instructed Percy, and I pushed him into the seat the doctor indicated.

As she examined his wound, I turned to the waiting group. Clustered around the king and queen, stood Lord Adelmar, the captain of the guard, and Princess Clarisse. A few steps away, an unfamiliar man had his arm around the waist of Lady Anhalt. I could only assume he was the count, and the man on the countess's other side must be Lord Adelmar's son considering Sarah clung to him with wide, horrified eyes.

On the other side of the room, Ariana and Isambard stood with a number of Ariana's senior merchants and the Guardsmasters of both caravans. But it was Lilah who drew my attention. Her eyes looked shocked and worried as they dwelt on me, but she didn't speak or attempt to join me. A hint of sadness gripped me. My place was at Percy's side now. It was a future I had chosen, and Lilah had freely given her blessing, but that didn't stop the grief at leaving my merchant family behind.

"Well done, Dee," Caravan Bryant's Guardsmaster said. "I saw that throw. It was a neat bit of work."

"It was far from her only contribution," Percy said from the sofa where he was being bandaged. The pride in his voice gave me the strength to face such an exalted crowd. I nodded to each group in turn.

"I think we need the full story." Queen Ava stepped forward. "Clearly tonight did not go to plan."

I winced. "No, it didn't. Although I did my best, Your Majesty." I glanced at the merchants. "With your leave, I'd like to go all the way back to the beginning. After sheltering me for two years, I think the merchants deserve to hear the whole story from me. Especially you, Lilah." I looked her directly in the eyes, pausing until she nodded, a grave look on her face.

The queen glanced at the merchants and then back at me. "Certainly."

I took a deep breath and told the whole story of my dealings with Damon, starting with the attack on my delegation two years before. Lilah looked shocked at my confession of my true identity, but not as shocked as I had expected.

I was still in the early parts of the story when loud shouting outside the room made me break off. The captain of the guard strode over to the door and pulled it open, only to leap back out of the way.

Arvin stormed in, whinnying and shaking his mane.

I don't care if I'm a horse. I'll go anywhere I please, and I'll thank you to make sure those officious servants of yours know it.

The queen, who appeared to be attempting to suppress a laugh, assured him gravely that she would pass on the instruction. A harassed looking guard put his head through the door, apologies on his lips for allowing us to be disturbed. But the captain pushed him back out of the room before he could even finish, assuring him no one would hold him responsible for Arvin's actions.

The horse, meanwhile, had surveyed the room, taking in the various groups and the way they were all arranged with me as their focal point.

Daria. I knew it. I said you'd be at the center of it all.

I smiled at him affectionately. "And where have you been?"

Me? He looked at me in surprise. *Where do you think I've been? I'm a horse. I've been in the stables.*

Percy snorted. "I notice you switch between being a horse and being a superior being from the Palace of Light as it suits your convenience."

Arvin looked down his nose at him. *Well, naturally. Who else's convenience should I suit?*

"I for one would like to hear the rest of the story," the king said, giving the horse a stern look. "You're welcome to be here to hear it, but I would appreciate it if you would allow Daria to continue."

I am not preventing her, Arvin whuffed, but I noticed he looked slightly chastened.

I hurried back into speech and had soon told the rest of the tale.

"I did hear your comment about the main entrance through

the wall of the receiving room," the countess said. "I couldn't understand what was going on, but it was enough to have us all on the alert when Damon's men burst in. So thank you for the warning."

"I'm just glad you're unharmed," I said.

"It was a close fight." She looked across at Hans who nodded.

"Yes, they had superior numbers, but the size of the room hampered them. They couldn't all get in at once."

I nodded my relief as others chimed in, questioning, exclaiming, or clarifying certain parts of the events.

Finally Princess Clarisse cut across them. "I, for one, would like to offer the two of you my congratulations." She smiled. "I assume congratulations are in order?"

Percy, finally released by the doctor, sprang to his feet and slipped an arm around my waist. "They certainly are. I'm stealing Daria away to Talinos as soon as the dust has settled here."

Ha! True love! I told you so. Arvin sounded smug.

I opened my mouth to reply, but a flash of light ripped through the room, momentarily blinding me. When it faded, someone new stood in our midst.

The gray hair of the woman reflected the hint of gray in her wings, but both gave the impression of spun steel rather than grandmotherly comfort.

"Godmother." The queen's voice sounded welcoming although the woman looked far sharper than I had anticipated.

"It's good to see you again, my dear," the godmother replied. "Although I'm not really here to see you this time."

"I kept wondering when you were going to make an appearance in the story and was astonished when you didn't do so," Ava said. "Although they seem to have found true love anyway." She glanced at Clarisse. "At least if Clarisse is to be believed."

I cleared my throat awkwardly. "She's not my godmother, Your Majesty. I'm not a princess."

"Yet," said Percy promptly, from my side.

"Of course I'm your godmother," the woman said briskly. "It's not only princesses we serve, you know. We also work with all kinds of deserving folk." Her eyes twinkled as she looked at Percy. "Usually the kind likely to inspire princes with true love."

"Oh." I looked up at Percy before lowering my eyes again, overwhelmed at the emotion in his. "I never saw you."

"No indeed," the godmother said. "There was no need when the young princess was performing my role quite adequately without my assistance."

I blinked at her, my surprised brain taking a moment to realize that when she said young princess, she meant Princess Clarisse. We all looked young to a godmother, I supposed.

"So you're here to meet your charge, then?" the queen asked.

"Actually, I'm here for the horse." A long-suffering note crept into her voice.

Don't tell me you finally mean to let me return to the Palace of Light? Arvin sounded half-hopeful, half-resentful.

"You're to be allowed back in, yes."

Outrageous! I didn't even do anything to defeat that traitor. Two years ago, I saved the royal family, and you turned up your nose. This time I was munching oats in my stall when I heard a ruckus. By the time I trotted over here, the whole mess had been cleaned up—yet I'm to be rewarded.

She rolled her eyes. "It's a wonder to me you're to be permitted back," she muttered before saying in a louder voice, "Your lesson was never about saving people, Arvin. Haven't you worked that out by now? You're coming back because you chose to help Daria. You recognized the good in her even though she didn't compliment you or fawn over you. You learned to look beyond your nose. Your extremely long nose," she added in another mutter.

"Well, he is a horse," I said quietly, and she laughed.

I bit my lip, not having meant her to hear, but she beamed at me in a kindly way.

"You needn't look so nervous, dear. Unlike this graceless horse, I'm very fond of you."

"Of me?"

"Yes, I'm glad we don't have to keep you waiting any longer."

"And my friends?" I asked eagerly. "I'm told they're under your care as well. Will they have to wait much longer?"

"Cassandra is busy enough as we speak, but I'm afraid Daisy has a little longer to wait." She gave a wry smile. "Not a great strength of hers."

I grimaced. I hated the idea of just abandoning the others, but from the manner of the godmother, it was clear she had no desire for us to interfere.

I turned to Percy to see how he was reacting to the godmother's presence, but his look of surprise made me whip back around. The godmother had disappeared.

"Where did she go?"

They like their dramatic exits and entrances, Arvin sniffed.

"But I thought she was taking you with her?" Percy said.

I don't need her to transport me. Arvin looked offended. *Now that I'm permitted home, I can find my own way there easily enough.*

"I'll miss you," Percy said. "When I suggested you travel with me, I never expected we'd spend two years together."

Arvin looked at him with an unexpected softness in his eye. *For a human, you've been surprisingly bearable. Please also pass on my farewells to Giselle. I will visit you both from time to time.*

He turned around and trotted out the door before anyone else could say anything.

"I wouldn't count on seeing him anytime soon," Ava said into the surprised silence. "If he's anything like the godmothers, they don't have our sense of time."

Percy chuckled. "I can just imagine him turning up at our child's wedding and looking surprised when we comment on how long it's been."

The queen smiled, turning to me. "I would like to extend

Rangmere's sincere gratitude for your part in apprehending Damon. I can assure you we don't intend to let him escape. We've already sent forces to his camp, and I have no doubt we'll have his followers rounded up in no time now that he is no longer leading them."

"You're more than welcome, Your Majesty." I curtsied. "I hope you will extend any goodwill you might feel toward Percy or myself to Talinos. I know that Percy's people would greatly value an alliance with Rangmere."

Percy gave me a subtle squeeze of approval, jumping in to support my suggestion. "Yes, indeed, Your Majesties."

Ava glanced at Hans before nodding. "Rangmere would be honored to enter into an alliance with any kingdom of yours, Prince Percival."

I smiled. "Thank you, Your Majesty."

I turned to the merchants. "And I hope you'll accept my apologies and gratitude. I brought danger into your midst without warning you, while you offered me only kindness and safety. I owe an apology to you all, but especially toward you, Lilah."

She stepped forward before either of the caravan leaders could respond. Putting her arms around me, she pulled me close. After a wordless moment, she drew back, turning to face Ariana and Isambard.

"I was the one to claim Dee as family, and I claim her still. She has every right to the protection of the caravans."

For a brief moment there was silence. Then Ariana nodded.

"Certainly it is your right to claim what family you choose, and none of us would gainsay you."

Isambard nodded his agreement, and Lilah beamed. Seized by a sudden impulse, I turned to Percy with a question in my eyes. He nodded, and I swung back around to face Lilah.

"I know it's a lot to ask, but would you consider coming with us to Talinos? It would mean so much to have family beside me as I meet my new family."

"To visit, you mean?" Lilah sounded cautious.

I bit my lip. "Actually, I was thinking to live. Don't you think Tallie would enjoy a more settled life in a city? And with a new alliance with Rangmere, I'm sure there will be many opportunities in Talinos for a merchant with familiarity with the Four Kingdoms."

Percy leaned forward. "Please do consider it. Any family of Daria's will always be welcome in Talinos."

Lilah nodded slowly. "Thank you. I will certainly consider it." She looked at me. "And discuss it with Tallie."

"Thank you."

While we were talking, the rest of the room had dissolved into small groupings, discussing the happenings in hushed voices. Lilah crossed back over to the merchants, her face thoughtful, and I turned to Percy.

"Thank you." I looked up at him, hoping the overflowing love in my heart showed on my face.

"What for? I'm the fortunate one—stealing you away. I couldn't begrudge anyone who wanted to follow you. And I think Lilah will find a comfortable home in Talinos. After the darkness that gripped our whole kingdom, there are plenty of people who have had to find their way through debilitating fear and out the other side. There will be people there who can help her learn to manage her anxieties."

I beamed at him. "I hope so. My place is with you now, but that doesn't mean I have to leave my other families entirely behind. I'll want to visit Eliam as soon as possible as well. And I want that letter from Snow now that I'm not keeping secrets anymore." I bit my lip. "But are you sure you're all right? The doctor said your arm will heal?"

"She had only good things to say," he assured me. "But I don't want to talk about arms right now."

"No?" I grinned up at him. "What would you prefer to talk about?"

"Hmmm..." He pretended to think. "Why don't we start with lips?"

I only had time for a tiny gurgle of laughter before he captured my lips with his and we did no more talking at all.

EPILOGUE

J watched eagerly as the passengers began to unload from the ship, smiling at their unsteady gait. Memories of my first ocean voyage resurfaced, along with more recent ones from my trip to Percy's kingdom of Talinos. It had only been weeks since our arrival, but already it felt like home.

Of course, this ship hadn't traveled from as far as the Four Kingdoms. It had only come from Eldon, carrying Princess Giselle to Talinos for our wedding. I was delighted to see Giselle again, and curious to meet the Lanoverian husband she had brought back from her own adventure in the Four Kingdoms two years ago. What I didn't expect was to see other familiar faces.

"Daria! Daria! Daria!" A blond blur threw herself into my arms, nearly knocking me backward.

"Poppy?" I hugged her back, trying to understand how she could be here on the docks of the Talinosian capital.

"We came to surprise you!" she announced, beaming up at me. "Are you surprised?"

"Very!" I laughed, looking over her head at the small crowd pressing up behind her.

My eyes widened as a lanky fifteen-year-old wrapped her arms around both of us.

"It's amazing to see you again, Daria," Danni said, "but I do *not* like sea voyages."

I pulled back, chuckling. "You do look a little green, Danni. I'm sorry it was a rough journey." I shook my head. "But I still don't understand what you're all doing here. I was planning to come visit you as soon as I could get away..."

I glanced back at Percy who stood with his parents, although his attention was on me and my surrounding crowd. King Clarence and Queen Sapphira wouldn't be coming down to the docks to greet all the arrivals for our wedding, but they had come with their daughters, Pearl and Opal, to meet Princess Giselle's ship. Both girls were looking forward to seeing their friend but, more importantly, were eager to see the two cousins she had brought with her.

As I glanced toward Percy, two handsome young men bowed over the princesses' hands. From the looks on the twins' faces, there was no doubting they were the brothers Pearl and Opal had fallen in love with.

The four of them had met when the twins visited Eldon for Giselle's wedding, and the Eldonians had now received the king and queen's permission to become officially betrothed to the princesses. Given Pearl and Opal's status, their betrotheds had agreed to leave their own kingdom behind and relocate to Talinos, a concession that had greatly influenced the queen toward the matches since she didn't want to lose her daughters.

Pearl said something, and both men chuckled, Opal's laugh ringing over the top. I smiled.

"They've certainly changed since the days of the Princess Tourney," a familiar voice said. "It's good to see them freed from their kingdom's curse. Although I hear they're still inseparable. I'm glad they found brothers to marry."

"Snow!" I disentangled myself from Poppy and Danni and curtsied to Queen Blanche.

She laughed and shook her head.

"You're a princess now, Daria. You can get away with a dignified head nod." She reached out and pulled me into a hug. "I'm so glad you're safe," she whispered in my ear.

I squeezed her back. "I'm so sorry for worrying you all. But you got my letter, at least."

"That letter!" Snow pulled back, a wry note in her vote.

"I know," I said quickly. "I realize now you all weren't going to let me just disappear off into the Four Kingdoms."

"No! We sent a team to search for you, you know. But you were well hidden."

I grimaced. "The traveling merchants helped with that. And I think my godmother had a hand as well." I shook my head. "It's still strange to say that. I never dreamed I would have a godmother of my own."

"Or be a princess? I can't believe you're a princess!" Poppy bounced up and down.

"Well, I'm not a princess yet," I said.

"But she will be soon." Percy's arms slid around my waist. "And she would be already if I'd had my way."

Danni sighed. "So romantic," she murmured.

Apparently while I was away, Danni had reached the age to think about romance—unlike Poppy who was looking slightly revolted. I met Snow's eyes, the side of my lips twitching at the eleven-year-old's disgust.

"Royal weddings take a great deal of arranging," Snow told Percy sternly. "And poor Daria is adjusting to a new kingdom as well." She sighed. "I'm most put out that you're not coming back to Eliam, Daria."

A tall, familiar man strolled up to stand beside Snow. "What my wife means to say is that Eliam is honored to have a formal alliance with Talinos."

Snow returned his humorous look. "Yes, of course," she said, all innocence.

I grinned. Even back in the days of our cottage in the woods, I had liked seeing Snow and Alexander together. They made a good pair.

"It's good to see you again, Daria," he said, more seriously. "And we're both delighted for you. I know you wrote you would come visit us after the wedding, but as soon as Snow heard there was to be a wedding..."

"Well, of course I wasn't going to stay in Eliam and miss your wedding, Daria!" Her eyes twinkled at me. "Even if I wasn't invited."

"Of course you're invited! But you have a kingdom to run, and I didn't want to assume..."

"It was an easy enough matter for Giselle's ship to pick us up on the way past," Snow said. "And I knew you would want the children here."

"Thank you." I put as much meaning into the words as I could before turning to Anthony with an apologetic look.

The tall young man looked disgusted at being called a child, but when I met his eyes, he surprised me by stepping forward and giving me just as big a hug as the girls had done.

Over his shoulder I met the eyes of Willow, their foster mother. Under her love, and the security of their life in Lestern, Anthony had softened and deepened. The hardened, scoffing boy I had known in the woods was truly gone.

"Are you a guard now?" I asked him.

He smiled proudly. "At the end of the summer I will be."

"And an excellent guard he's going to be, too." Captain Tarver stepped forward to greet me, his wife on his arm.

"I've heard a lot of stories about you all," Percy said when the general introductions and greetings were completed. "It's nice to finally meet you. I'm sorry for stealing Daria away." He paused, smiling down at me. "Well, no, I'm not really sorry at all."

I leaned back into him, enjoying the warmth that filled my heart as much as my body at his nearness. "But you'll all always be welcome in Talinos. And I hope you'll visit often."

"Is your stepsister here?" Danni looked from side to side at the milling crowd.

I shook my head. "They've only recently arrived from the Four Kingdoms, so they're still settling in. I'll introduce you as soon as we get back to the palace, though. In fact, I hope you'll be able to help Tallie get used to the way we do things here in these lands. You're almost the same age."

"Danni has been looking forward to meeting her," Willow said in her gentle way. "As I've been looking forward to meeting Lilah. I'm so glad they decided to come and join you here."

"Me too. I hated the idea of abandoning them back there while I came here to live a life of luxury."

Willow smiled. "It's easy to understand why Prince Percival fell in love with you, Daria. You're always thinking of others."

"Percy, please," he said with his charming smile. "We're basically family now."

Willow chuckled. "In a somewhat convoluted way. But thank you, Your Highness." He gave her a mock glare, and she corrected herself. "Percy."

She began to gather the children together, bringing order to the group with the assistance of Ben who had grown even more broad-shouldered in my absence but who greeted me with the same gentleness that had always characterized him.

As we began to move off the docks, Snow took the place beside me, shooing Percy back to walk with Alexander.

"How are you finding your new home?" Her eyes dwelt on the king and queen ahead of us.

"It's lovely. Everyone has been friendly and welcoming." I looked sideways at her. "I understand I have you partially to thank for that. By the time we actually arrived, Percy's parents already had your initial letter—the one that left them with the impression we were as good as sisters."

Snow laughed. "I may have exaggerated the situation the slightest bit." Her voice warmed. "But you're the sister I wish I'd had, Daria. So it basically counts. And in all honesty, Eliam is delighted by the alliance with Talinos, so it wasn't purely selfless of me. And from what I hear, the alliance proposal you brought with you from Rangmere also helped generate goodwill with your new family."

She glanced behind us. "And it's easy to see Percy is utterly smitten with you, anyway. He would never have let his family reject the marriage."

I bit my lip, unable to help the smile that any thought of Percy brought.

"I'm just glad I had him at my side when I met them for the first time. I was terrified." I shook my head at the memory. "But they were kind and gracious, and Pearl and Opal soon put me at my ease."

"Can you tell them apart yet?" Snow asked in a whisper.

I chuckled. "I think so? But only in the last few days. Thankfully they're not inclined toward playing tricks on people, or I would definitely have been made to look foolish by now."

"And they're not resentful that your wedding is to happen before their own?"

I shook my head. "Not that they've shown. It's not exactly fair, since they're both older, but their fiancés couldn't leave Eldon until now. They had business to wrap up and personal affairs to organize, apparently. And the queen wants sufficient time to plan a double wedding now that the grooms are actually in the kingdom."

"Is Adelaide here?" Snow looked around for the wife of Percy's older brother. "I'm sure she's been welcoming. She was always lovely."

I shook my head. "They came up to meet me, and she couldn't have been kinder, but they're not living here at the moment."

"Oh yes, of course. I heard they've taken up residence in one of the other royal castles for the time being," Snow said. "But I suppose they'll be up for the wedding?"

I nodded. "And they've invited Percy and me to join them after we're married if we want some time away from the capital to settle into married life. We're considering it."

"I think it sounds like a lovely idea." Snow slipped her arm through mine. "And it sounds like we should all have a wonderful time on this visit. It's a real reunion."

I looked across the grass at my new husband, my heart over-flowing with love as I remembered our vows, uttered only hours before. The moment he caught my eyes, he cut off his conversation and strode over to join me, taking both of my hands in his and lifting them to his lips.

"If you keep looking at me like that, I'm never going to finish the obligatory round of all our guests, you know," he murmured quietly.

I chuckled. "You're the one who suggested we split up."

"Only so we could get through all the well-wishers more quickly. I'm delighted my family and my kingdom has embraced you so completely, but I'm ready to sweep you away for a couple of weeks all to ourselves."

I reached up onto my toes and brushed a kiss across his lips. "It has been a little chaotic recently, hasn't it?"

He immediately wrapped his arms around me and gave me a deeper kiss. Before I could pull away and remind him we were still at our wedding banquet, loud cries and startled exclamations made us break apart.

I looked up just in time to see something large approaching

quickly through the sky, enormous wings spread wide as it glided in for a smooth landing. It took a moment for my mind to register that I beheld a magnificent golden horse and not a bird.

"Arvin!" Giselle cried, wonder in her voice.

"I knew it!" Percy shouted. He rounded on me. "I told you!"

I couldn't help laughing at his boyish excitement, even while my own mind whirled with astonishment. Arvin tossed his head, whinnying loudly as he folded his wings and trotted toward us. I could tell from his preening manner that he was well aware of the attention he was receiving, but he kept his focus on us.

Congratulations, Princeling, Dee.

"Arvin, you have wings." The words spluttered out between giggles. "You told us you weren't a flying horse."

He gave me a condescending look. *I don't remember saying anything of the kind. And I'm not sure why everyone sounds so surprised to see me. You didn't think I'd miss your wedding, did you?*

"Of course we thought you would," Percy said promptly. "You're a *flying horse* from the Palace of Light. We figured you'd turn up in a few decades, oblivious to how much time had passed."

Arvin swung his head around to bore into Percy with one eye, clearly trying to assess if he was serious. Since I didn't want him to see the answer to that question, I threw my arms around his neck.

"Thank you for coming, Arvin. We're delighted to have you here. And I'm so glad we decided to have our wedding banquet outside. I wouldn't have wanted to miss such an impressive arrival."

Arvin whuffed and rested his soft nose against my head. He was careful not to cut himself on the diamonds of my elegant tiara, and I softened when I realized he was also avoiding disturbing the elaborate arrangement of braids that had taken two hairdressers most of the morning to perfect.

"You didn't have wings when you were with me," Giselle said, sounding put out, although her husband beside her looked as if he were trying not to laugh.

Greetings, Giselle, Arvin neighed, ignoring her complaint. *It's good to see you again.* He looked around suspiciously. *You didn't bring that sister-in-law of yours, did you?*

Philip chuckled. "You can relax. Celine isn't here. She would have loved to come, of course, but no one in their right mind would put those boys on a ship."

Boys? Arvin sounded wary.

"She had twins." Giselle's voice bordered on gleeful. "Twin eighteen-month-old boys named Oscar and Otto. Thankfully they weren't crawling yet when she made the voyage home from Lanover, so they both survived the journey. No one will be risking letting them on a ship for another few years now, though."

Good, Arvin whuffed. *We don't need more children here. There seem to be enough already.*

I followed the direction of his gaze and saw Louis and Jack, the two youngest boys who had once lived with me in a cottage in the woods.

"Daria," Jack said with awe, "you didn't tell us he could fly!"

"I knew he could," Percy told them in a loud aside. "I always knew it."

"Do you think he'd give me a ride?" Tallie asked, coming up behind them with Danni shadowing close to her side. "I always wanted to fly."

Arvin narrowed his eyes. *I don't give rides to children.*

"But it's my wedding, Arvin!" I tried to give him my best pleading look.

Many apologies, I don't give rides to children, he corrected himself.

I shook my head, chuckling. "Sorry, everyone. I don't think he's going to be obliging."

The boys murmured disappointedly but remained in place,

transfixed by the horse. Tallie, on the other hand, rolled her eyes and dragged Danni away. I was glad to see the two girls getting along given how sad Tallie had been to leave her best friend Aida behind with Caravan Bryant.

I smiled at Lilah who stepped up beside me in Tallie's wake.

"She seems happy, don't you think?" I asked.

Lilah nodded, watching her daughter hurrying toward one of the refreshment tables. "She seems to like it here. Thank you for inviting us, Dee."

"Do *you* like it here?" I asked.

She paused, considering the question. "More than I expected, actually. And I'm already making valuable connections with some of the local merchants. I think after a few shipments between here and the Four Kingdoms, I should have enough coin to open a small store to sell my jewelry."

"That's wonderful!"

Percy had offered to buy Lilah a store, but she insisted she needed to establish her own business. According to her, housing her and Tallie at the palace and arranging for introductions with some of the merchants in the city more than repaid their hospitality to me when I was with the caravan. And apparently being known as family of the new princess already went a long way toward helping her establish herself.

Seeing her so industrious still filled me with joy. When she had first arrived off the ship, she had been physically ill from the anxiety of the journey. But Percy had introduced her to several women who had been hit especially hard by the curse on their kingdom but who had managed to work their way through the fear that continued to cling to them after the darkness lifted. Already Lilah had become close friends with one of them, and the two were often found drinking tea and talking together.

Lilah's face softened as she watched me.

"You look beautiful, Dee. That gown is even more incredible than the one you wore to the ball."

I brushed my hands softly against the layers of white satin and tulle, letting my fingers linger on the lace of the bodice.

"I couldn't quite believe it when I first saw it," I admitted.

She leaned forward and pressed a gentle finger against my collarbone. "But you are more beautiful than the dress. Inside and out."

"She certainly is." Percy slipped an arm around my waist and smiled down at me. "And I'm now going to steal her away so we can finish accepting everyone's congratulations."

Lilah laughed. "'It's your wedding day. Forget everyone else and go enjoy a dance with your bride." She grinned at me. "Only this time try to avoid snapping your shoe, Dee. Or stabbing anyone."

I grinned back. "Don't worry, I wore flats today. I want to spend all afternoon dancing on the grass, just like all those times we danced with other merchant caravans." I looked up at Percy. "Except this time I'll be dancing with the man I love."

If Lilah replied, I didn't hear her. Percy, his eyes lighting up at the emotion in mine, pulled me into his arms and started dancing, right there beside my stepmother and a talking horse with wings attended by two boys. But I didn't register any of them.

All I knew was the feel of Percy's arms, the love in his eyes, and the happiness of celebrating my wedding day surrounded by all the members of my various families.

NOTE FROM THE AUTHOR

Discover what happened to Cassie in The Desert Princess: A Retelling of Aladdin, coming in mid 2021.

Or if you missed reading about how Ava became queen, you can find out in The Princess Fugitive: A Reimagining of Little Red Riding Hood.

Or read about how Daria became friends with a queen in A Dream of Ebony and White: A Retelling of Snow White.

To be kept informed of my new releases, please sign up to my mailing list at www.melaniecellier.com. At my website, you'll also find an array of free extra content.

Thank you for taking the time to read my book. I hope you enjoyed it. If you did, please spread the word! You could start by leaving a review on Amazon (or Goodreads or Facebook or any other social media site). Your review would be very much appreciated and would make a big difference!

ACKNOWLEDGMENTS

I've touched on the Cinderella story more than once in my Four Kingdoms world, but it's such a quintessential fairy tale that I wanted to come back and give it a full novel. I deviated from the traditional background for the character (which was used for one of the characters in my very first retelling), but I still enjoyed working in other elements of the original. I hope you enjoyed discovering them all.

Before writing The Mystery Princess, I had a short break from fairy tales, and I have enjoyed diving back into my retelling world again. From here, that world will be expanding even further, and I'm reinvigorated and inspired to continue to explore the possibilities.

I am grateful, as always, to my editors and beta readers for helping to shape and hone the story. Rachel, Greg, Priya, Katie, Mary, Deborah, and my parents—I couldn't imagine writing a book without you all.

Thank you, Karri, for another beautiful cover. I never get tired of ordering new covers from you and seeing the works of art you create.

And to my wonderful family who continue to put up with my haphazard writing ways even as life gets more chaotic, thanks to our adorable new baby—I love you all, and I appreciate the joy you bring to my life. I am so thankful to God for giving you to me, as I am thankful to Him in all the joys and challenges of life.

ABOUT THE AUTHOR

 Melanie Cellier grew up on a staple diet of books, books and more books. And although she got older, she never stopped loving children's and young adult novels.

She always wanted to write one herself, but it took three careers and three different continents before she actually managed it.

She now feels incredibly fortunate to spend her time writing from her home in Adelaide, Australia where she keeps an eye out for koalas in her backyard. Her staple diet hasn't changed much, although she's added choc mint Rooibos tea and Chicken Crimpies to the list.

She writes young adult fantasy including books in her *Spoken Mage* world, and her three *Four Kingdoms and Beyond* series which are made up of linked stand-alone stories that retell classic fairy tales.

CPSIA information can be obtained
at www.ICGtesting.com
Printed in the USA
LVHW030226210522
719225LV00004B/48

9 781925 898323